Under the Blood Moon

By
Patricia Santos Marcantonio

www.DarkInkBooks.com

www.AMInkPublishing.com

To Mom and Dad
who shared all their good stories

Under the Blood Moon

If my blood asks, I give myself blood
Old song of the Mexican Revolution

Joey's Bar served cheap pork *carnitas* and even cheaper beer. In Guadalupe, New Mexico, that made the place very popular.

As usual on Wednesday night, people crowded in for the hump day specials. Two chicken tacos for a buck-fifty. A Corona with lime for the same price. For five bucks, a huge plate of nachos dripping with cheese and the owner's green chili. They stood elbow to elbow, gripping cold bottles or frosted mugs of Bud or Coors that weren't a special. No light versions there. They were for wimps. Those who didn't have to work the next morning added short snorts of Jack or tequila. Others chowed down on the tacos that were greatly improved by the salsa. The bar owner had stolen the recipe from a vendor in Ensenada but claimed his mother had invented it.

Many of the patrons relaxed after toiling at jobs they hated, most at the March Copper Mine and Refinery west of town. Others celebrated the few days left before the weekend where they could do what they wanted, within reason and without committing too many sins they'd have to confess to their parish priest later in the week.

Framed photos of famous Hispanics ranging from Cesar Romero to Cesar Chávez to Jennifer López covered the walls of Joey's Bar. The Mexican flag hung on an even keel with the American flag, although owner Joey Méndez was a fourth-generation American and couldn't remember where in Mexico his ancestors had moved away from. He knew just enough Spanish to take the customers' orders and to make sure no one was talking smack about him. A man of round proportions, Joey did know the names of his customers and greeted them all in a boisterous voice custom-made for a raucous bar.

In one corner, a three-piece band played traditional Mexican favorites and covers of newer songs. Dancers hugged each other because the dance floor was the size of a modest living room, but they enjoyed hips touching hips. Although a majority of the people there had known each other all their lives, they still had lots to say, especially after the beers and shots loosened them up. Because of the music, they spoke in loud voices to hear each other. The bar regulars talked equal amounts of English and Spanish, which were the official languages of Guadalupe.

Sitting at the scuffed bar, Juan Gallegos and Mo Luna attempted to catch a boxing match on one of the large flat screens in the place, but the two men became more and more annoyed with the racket and having to yell their conversations. With age, both were losing their hearing, though Mo's had progressed enough that he had to wear a hearing aid. They gave up watching TV and reminisced about their years at the March Mine from where they had retired ten years before. They loved to talk about how they had earned a good living there, as well as detested every minute they had to clock in. And everything reminded them of the mine, including the fight on TV.

"Hey, remember that fat bastard George Tone? How he got in a fist fight with Sam Díaz?" said Juan, who was thinner and taller than his *amigo*.

"Yeah, ole George claimed Sam was poking his wife when he had to work swing." Mo was a year younger and never let his friend forget that. He had more hair on his head, which he also lorded over him.

"Don't know how anyone would want to be with that woman. She looked like a pig with pin curls."

"She did have a juicy behind."

"Sam probably just closed his eyes." Mo's laugh sounded like an engine in bad need of a tune-up.

Juan checked out the clock embedded in cactus-shaped green plastic.

Twenty after midnight.

"Damn." Clicking his fingers, Juan swigged the beer left in the mug because he believed leaving a brew unfinished amounted to a criminal offense. He motioned to his friend. "Let's go, man."

Mo had to lean to hear him. "The night's young, *compadre*."

"But we're not. *Vamos*."

They both laughed as they slid off the high barstools. Struggling past the crowd, the old guys shared the profound laughter of men who shared fifty years of friendship, who stood up in each other's weddings, and baptized each other's children. Juan had been at Mo's side when his wife died of a stroke two years ago and had helped him move in with his son but that tragedy was a minority event in a lifetime of camaraderie and mostly good times.

Straggling outside, they swayed from one beer too *mas*, which was why they never drove to Joey's Bar on Wednesdays. Fortunately, Guadalupe happened to be the right size town to walk home. Besides that, they lived on the same block.

"*Ay, yi, yi*. My wife's going to kill me," Juan said.

"What'd you say?" Mo shouted.

"Turn up your hearing aid."

Mo did. "You don't have to shout, *compadre*."

"I said my wife's going to kill me."

"No, your wife's going to kill *me*. She already thinks I'm a bad influence."

"You are a bad influence, old man, but that's why we're *amigos*. Let's cut through the park. It's faster," Juan said as they stood outside.

The song "La Bamba" filtered out from the bar band and the men started singing along loudly and badly. The music faded as they headed deeper into the park located across the street.

Locals called the City Park the town's *corazón*. The heart of everything. Within the ten-block square lay ballfields, playgrounds, and a swimming pool. In the middle of the park was a sizeable plaza right out of a Mexican village complete with red paver stones. A cedar gazebo with a blue tiled roof was large enough to seat the Guadalupe City Band that performed there every Thursday evening during the summer. Rows of aging wooden benches surrounded the gazebo for concert audiences. The site was popular with brides and grooms posing for wedding photos, as well as for vandals to chip their names into the gazebo wood.

To the north of the gazebo stood a ten-foot tall white stone fountain revealing cracks of age and overuse. Cracks or not, the townspeople believed the park one of the prettiest in New Mexico. Kids splashed in the fountain on hot days, and people danced on the red stones during any festival that happened to offer music. Many such events were held in a town whose residents loved to party in the name of anything. Be it Cinco de Mayo, Independence Day, or El Día de los Muertos, not to mention many festivals in-between. Way past midnight on a weeknight, however, the park was lonesome and dark when Juan and Mo made their way home.

The men walked through shadows thrown onto the grass by healthy stands of aspen, maple, and fir trees. The full moon didn't help guide them because it was concealed by clouds. Juan and Mo took small steps of oldness and caution because they both shared a fear of breaking their hips. That would amount to a one-way ticket to a nursing home and the grave. They had seen this happen to more than one of their senior friends.

A circle of lights illuminated the plaza ahead of them. As Juan and Mo approached, the lights sparked brightly and then flicked out with a whiff of ozone.

"What the hell?" Mo said. "Damn city can't even keep on the lights."

"They always shut them down at one in the morning."

"How do you know?"

"Read it the paper," Juan said.

"Well, they should keep them lit so the vandals won't run wild. And besides that, I can't see a damn thing." Mo took even smaller steps. In the darkness, he ran into a park bench, banged his knee, and cursed. Juan laughed and Mo cursed again.

"Shhh. Do you hear that?" Juan stopped so suddenly that Mo ran into his back.

"Son of a bitch. Watch where you're going."

"Listen."

"I don't hear nothing, *compadre*."

"Turn up your hearing aid, Mo."

Mo moved the dial up on his device. "Is that crying?"

"Yeah, and it's coming from there." Juan pointed toward the gazebo.

They jumped when the lights sparked back on.

"I thought you said they turned them off at one," Mo said.

"Never mind that. Look."

"A girl."

"A really pregnant girl."

The young woman sat on one of the benches and sobbed as if her heart had been crushed into dust. Her long hair reached to her waist and created a dark curtain around her. She wore a long red skirt and Mexican peasant blouse that exposed lovely shoulders.

"What kind of asshole would leave a pregnant woman all alone and crying?" Juan said.

"A big fat asshole, that's who," Mo answered.

"Let's go see if she needs help."

"Don't walk so fast. My arthritis is acting up."

They reached the woman whose hands shrouded her face. Her crying intensified until her whole body trembled from the sadness.

"You all right, *señora?*" Juan said.

No response from the woman.

"Did someone hurt you?" Mo said.

"Can we call your family?"

The old men looked at each other when she didn't answer.

"We'll help you," Mo said.

"Come on. No need to cry." Juan held out his hand.

The woman placed her hand in his, but kept her head down. Her hand felt like a piece of meat left out in the snow, which surprised him since the night was muggy. In fact, the chill made Juan's own arthritic knees twinge. "You're cold as winter, lady. You need some hot coffee in you."

She said nothing but kept crying. Her weeping sounded of a secret river flowing underground. Liquid despair that grumbled and echoed.

"Maybe she don't speak English," Mo said.

Juan repeated his assurances in Spanish. She didn't respond but kept crying.

Mo whispered into Juan's ear. "What the hell do we do with her? We can't leave the lady here." He took his cell phone out of his pocket. "Let's call the law."

Juan and Mo disliked using their cell phones because they considered them a bother and believed they caused brain cancer with too much use.

"I got a better idea. We walk her to the police station. We'll get there faster than the time it'll take them to round up officers and get them out here," Juan said. "And you know the cops in this town."

"Do I ever."

The men jumped again as the lights in the plaza blinked off.

"What's going on with those things?" Juan said. "I'm going to call Mike at Parks and Rec and complain."

"For now, let's help this girl."

With gentility, the men each took one of her arms to help her stand. She continued crying as they made their way through moonlight as gray as a dead man left out in the sun. At last, they reached the edge of the park that faced Main Avenue. The woman stopped abruptly on the sidewalk before they stepped into the street. She pulled away from them and placed her hands at her sides. Her crying ended. She raised her head.

Under the streetlight, the men got their first really good look at the woman.

"Ay, what a beauty." Juan didn't mean to say that out loud. His cheeks warmed.

Mo shook his head hard in agreement. Both of them drew in ample guts over their belted jeans.

Hers was a face made for love. Her skin, amber silk. Sensual lips parted with a sigh. Although she had been crying, no redness dusted her nose or appeared in her eyes, which were dark and wide. Juan and Mo, who each had been married for almost fifty years, both fell in love with the woman at that moment. She reminded them how it felt to be young men bursting with expectation and lovemaking.

The woman stood still and stared at the men. Her perfect face displayed no emotion.

"What's wrong, *señora*? The police station is just a little ways down the street," Juan said.

In a flow of movement, she squatted, slid up her skirt, and grunted. Her breathing droned like a wasp hive.

"My God, she's having the baby right now."

"Holy hell," Mo said.

The woman's grunts increased in quantity and force.

"Hold on, lady. We'll get help. Maybe, I'll just run over to the police station."

"You can't run, Mo. Your legs are bad. Use your phone, *pendejo*. Besides, you ain't leaving me alone with a pregnant woman!" Juan scanned the street. No one else was out at that time of night.

Mo took the phone out of his pocket but the battery was dead. "Mine's no good. Try yours."

Juan's was in the same condition. He shook the phone. "Damn thing. I charged it before we left."

The young woman panted faster. Her voice lowered to guttural as she held her legs and pushed. With the grating of stone upon stone, her mouth stretched wide until each side reached her ears. She opened pale lips, revealing two rows of straight box-like teeth. She slammed them together again and again with a horrible crunch at each push of her body. Her eyes became perfect circles and then hardened into a shiny gray.

Juan and Mo knew they should get the hell out of there, but confusion and fright held them fast, along with a twinge of curiosity about what would happen next. Besides, they both believed there was nothing they couldn't handle.

The woman's round gray eyes stared at the two petrified men, and she chomped her teeth together. With a terrifying yell, she gave a final push. From between her legs, glutinous black liquid oozed out onto the sidewalk. Juan and Mo backed up. The stink teared up their eyes and they became nauseous from the smell of sulphur.

The devil's ass, thought Juan.

The woman moved her arms under her squatting and caught a fat shape. She held it out to Juan and Mo as if seeking a blessing. Against their wishes, they were drawn near. The creature resembled a baby reptile with lumps down its back tapering off into a stubby tail. Its head twisted toward them. A thing without eyes. From a slit of a mouth whipped out a round and dark red tongue that flicked at the men. It snarled.

Forgetting bad legs, arthritis, and the fear of breaking a hip, Juan and Mo yelled and ran down the street. No way were they looking back.

The young woman rose, hugged her child, and shuffled back into the darkness of the park.

Chapter 2

Matthew Francisco Riley summed up for a jury and wished he was dead. All the air in the courtroom seemed to have been sucked out elsewhere. The Mesquite County judicial building was icy from the cranked up air conditioning, but under his new suit coat, Matthew sweated into his shirt. Wet tissue paper might have been tucked under his arms.

He lost his pacing almost as soon as he had started the summation and wondered where his timing went. He glanced at the jurors. Their eyes glazed over like holiday hams. Throughout the trial, two attractive young women on the panel had pursed their lips and flitted eyelashes at him in obvious flirtation. Now, they had lost total interest. White-haired Judge Howard Aaron rested his head on one hand, his eyes barely open.

Matthew cleared his throat and continued, hoping a surge of confidence would conceal his absolute lack of it.

"Ladies and gentlemen of the jury, you heard it yourself. Two Bar Zee Ranch hands testified they saw the defendant load four cows onto his truck and drive away." Matthew pointed to the most pitiful suspect he ever prosecuted at the defense table.

Defendant Curtis Mondragon was only seventy-one but could have easily passed for one hundred. His skin was cracked as the planet before the Great Flood. Wearing a tan suit one size too large, Mondragon held his hands on his lap while his eyes fixed on a distant place, perhaps another courthouse. The public defender, who looked like a teenager who just happened to pass the bar, doodled rows of circles on a yellow pad.

Trying his best not to exhale frustration, Matthew held up the evidence numbered 4B. "This invoice from Mac's Butcher Service shows the defendant had the cows slaughtered there. And those cows had displayed the Bar Zee brand, according to the butcher. This all amounts to a case of cattle rustling. As a result, Curtis Mondragon must be found guilty of grand theft." Matthew took his seat.

"Finished, Mr. Riley?" The judge finally lifted his head.

"Yes, your honor."

The judge drew back a yawn.

****

Matthew drank a weak cup of coffee in the court clerk's office, but he really wanted a bounce of whiskey straight up. Even though he won the case, he hoped the trial against an ancient and pathetic cattle rustler would not become his legacy as the Mesquite County Prosecutor.

The coffee tasted worse with that possibility.

A hand on his back whipped him out of his self-pity. When he veered around, he faced clerk Margaret Haymire. Margaret sniggered. She loved to snigger.

"Way to go, Matthew. I feel so much safer now that you put that old fart away." She snorted. "The streets of Guadalupe are more secure thanks to you."

"Give me a break, Margaret."

"Yup, a regular Perry Mason." The clerk walked off, sniggering some more.

"Perry was a defense lawyer, you know," Matthew called after her.

Hauling files from the trial, he headed to his office. He passed Art Alvarez, a bailiff so puny that Matthew was amazed he didn't topple over from the large gun on his belt.

"Hell of a job, counselor. It'll go down in the annals of Mesquite County prudence as the quickest conviction ever."

"Shut up, Art. And that's *jurisprudence*."

"Whatever. You may be joining the State AG's staff, but tell the truth. Aren't you going to miss these exciting cases?"

"No."

"Don't hold back, Matthew. Tell me how you really feel."

Matthew wanted a double whiskey now.

In thirty minutes, the jury had found Curtis Mondragon guilty of felony theft, but no one considered it much of a ruling, not even Matthew. Up to that point, he'd been proud of his ninety-two percent conviction record. That included many more important criminal trials during his tenure as prosecutor, not to mention boasting a balanced budget in his office and his work eliminating arcane laws from the county books.

But all that would be for shit.

He was going to end his job with a cattle rustling because his four deputy prosecutors were all busy and he had to take the case before a jury. He cursed Mondragon for refusing his really generous plea offer so they could all skip the trial. But the old man had stuck to his claim of innocence and "wanted his day in court" to tell everyone that the Bar Zee owed him those cows for his unpaid work on the ranch's septic system. The ranch owner's response: Mondragon did such a crappy job he didn't deserve to be paid.

To lessen the career humiliation of the rustling case, Matthew would ask one of the deputies to handle the sentencing. The *viejito* had no criminal record and would probably be placed on probation because no way could he survive one hour at the state penitentiary south of Santa Fe.

Matthew shrugged. What did he care? He'd be gone soon, and then Mondragon could start up another crime spree.

He could rustle goats.

Exiting the judicial building, he entered the courthouse next door. Always taking that route, he passed the combined office of the county sheriff and Guadalupe Police, which was haughtily called the Mesquite County Law Enforcement Agency. County and city officials believed they could save money by sharing dispatchers and other expenses. And they were right. It helped that the sheriff and police worked well together.

Siren wailing, a patrol car whizzed out of the garage around the back of the building. Matthew couldn't help himself. He was curious about where the hell the officers were going and why, and then chided himself. He hated his nosy personality. He always had to know what was going on, a trait he attributed to his mother, who would have made a great police detective.

The receptionist saw him, opened up an enthusiastic smile, and waved him over to her desk. Joanie Gideon wore too much lipstick. Her mascara was dense as street tar, which gave her the look of perpetual surprise. She brazenly flirted with Matthew whenever she saw him, which whipped up his heart into palpitations. Joanie's trucker husband had a quick temper and fists like a sledgehammer. The weird thing was that after he and Isabel had separated three months ago, women began to flirt with him. That included Joanie, as well as several court clerks, secretaries, and a female police officer, no matter if they were married or not. He considered himself attractive and a reasonable catch. He was a lawyer, after all, and there was nothing sweeter other than a doctor or millionaire. That was a real joke because he knew lawyers in town still paying off college debts and would be until the next millennium.

When he and Isabel were together, no women dared flirt with him because they were afraid of her. Isa had a jealous streak expansive as the desert. Not that she would beat up another woman who tried to entice him, but she would insult them into submission. He had to smile at that, but unfortunately the receptionist thought it was for her.

"Matthew, you have the nicest smile." Her long eyelashes batted like crazed butterflies. "And such a beautiful suit. It brings out your dreamy blue eyes."

God, he hoped her trucker husband was out on the road.

"I'm going to miss seeing those eyes when you leave." Seductively, she pulled down on her blouse to reveal more than ample breasts.

Man, he was glad her husband wasn't there. "What's up with the sirens?"

"A car accident over on Ninth Street."

"Anyone hurt?"

"No ambulance was called so probably not." Her tongue traced her lips. "And congratulations on winning your case. The deputies and officers were all laughing about it but I told them to shut up."

Matthew gave a limp nod and hurried on saying he had lots of work. To avoid any more ribbing from county personnel, he took the back stairs to his office, which was located on the second floor of the courthouse. He liked the eighty-year-old building and its rich character. Cream-colored walls complimented the dark wood of the stairs, doors, and moldings. An abundance of stained-glass windows gave it a diffused ambience, even in the summer's glaring light. Months before, the county commissioners had voted a significant expenditure to remodel and he hoped the building wouldn't end up as sterile as a dentist's office. After spending four years as a deputy prosecutor and another five as prosecutor, the courthouse had become his second home though it sometimes smacked of body odor, ammonia cleaners, and wood polish.

He waved at his secretary Kitty Cardenas and headed straight into his office, closing the door behind him. Moving aside a high pile of case files, he loosened his tie. Kitty knocked and entered with pad and pen. Her upper body was normal but her thighs and behind were quite enormous. She had the shiniest jet black hair and claimed to use lard on it once a week to keep it that way. Kitty was superefficient and bossed him around, which he didn't mind. Her only fault—a horse laugh at the off-color jokes she repeated from the clerks downstairs.

She laughed now and he knew why.

"Don't say one word, Kitty, not if you want to keep your job."

"Then how can I tell you that Mr. Watson from the Attorney General's office called?" She handed him a stack of phone messages. "It's the top one. You're a popular guy this morning, Matthew."

"I'm amazed the AG's office still wants me after my stellar win over a senior-citizen cattle rustler."

"Well, they do. I was hoping they'd change their minds."

"Kitty."

"Okay. Want me to order you a steak sandwich for lunch? I'll bet Curtis Mondragon has a few to spare." She gave her horse laugh.

"Very funny. Now get back to work."

She winked as she shut the door.

"*Madre mía.* I got to get out of this town." He rocked his head in his hands.

****

After returning calls and clearing the next day's cases, Matthew took a break. Admittedly, it was a challenge to concentrate on a job that was terminal. And really, since he was elected to the job, no one was going to fire him. He ducked out of the back exit and heard more sirens but tried not to give in to calling his best friend to see what was going on. If it was bad, it would eventually show up on his desk. If he was still around.

Main Avenue was hectic with cars and pedestrians. While Guadalupe's population was 46,000 and change, it ballooned daily with business and visitors from the rest of the county. People waved or called "hello" as Matthew sat on a bench outside of The Bitter Bean Shop and sipped an iced coffee. He was not surprised about how many people he knew by name. Those he met either through church, work, his bowling league, or when he prosecuted them for a crime. The latter mostly threw him a fish eye or as his mom called it, *el ojo.* The evil eye. A scraggy guy across the street was giving him *el ojo* at the moment. Matthew had prosecuted him into jail for DUI. Twice.

Matthew had always thought of himself as a walking demographic for the town in which he was born and raised. That being a mix of Mexican and Anglo blood, each one rising to the top depending on the circumstance. No matter their ancestry, the locals loved the town. A majority of the kids he'd gone to high school with still lived in Guadalupe or close by. They'd complain about the smallness, about the provincial politics, or lack of this or that, but they didn't leave. He was finally breaking out, but also felt like a prisoner hesitant about escaping in the first place.

In eight weeks, he would be a new deputy attorney general working in the criminal division in Albuquerque. A member of a team representing the state when felons sought appeals or criminals fought extraditions. He might even end up appearing in front of the state supreme court and in federal courts. The work would not be as exciting as the boots-on-the-ground criminal law he had practiced in the prosecutor's office, cattle rustling aside. Yet, he had handled enough drug dealing, thievery, and assaults that the excitement had worn off at times. Since the county's homicide rate was one of the lowest in the state, he had prosecuted only four murders. He regarded that as most fortunate. A majority of the homicides involved manslaughter or second-degree murder. Crimes of passion and fights that ended badly. He had taken one first-degree murder case to court and that was against a meth head who had beaten his girlfriend to death with a shovel. The guy sat on death row.

He was actually looking forward to taking refuge in paperwork. He wanted a sanctuary from the human weaknesses he'd seen in the courtroom. Victims who'd never be truly comforted. The misery of the damaged. The cruelty of those who did the damage. The criminals whose faces appeared time and again until he helped direct them to prison as three-time offenders. Reward came from bringing the bad people to justice, but sometimes that blurred with plea bargains. He understood that he could never escape sad and mean behavior altogether, but when written in briefs it would be less egregious. Still, his eyes itched at what he would be leaving behind and the betrayal his departure carried.

Tossing the plastic cup into the trash, Matthew walked back towards the courthouse in not much of a hurry. Parked farther down on Main was one of the town's fire engines. Accompanied by the hum of hydraulics, Fire Chief Ben Smith rode the ladder upward. He and his second-in-command were attaching a banner to the streetlights as they did the same time each year. Guadalupe had as many large fires as murders. As a result, the firemen counted the hanging of the banner as one of their primary duties along with the annual fire inspections of businesses, clamping down on illegal fireworks during July Fourth, and organizing the fireman's ball and barbecue in City Park every September.

"Get your ass up here and help, Matthew," Smith called down to him.

"I'm afraid of heights, Ben. Besides, I don't want to wrinkle my lawyer suit."

The hunky fire chief laughed and tugged at the banner, which hung over the busy street. It read:

WELCOME VISITORS
FEAST OF THE NIÑO DE LUZ AUGUST 27-30

Shown on each side of the banner was a picture of the baby Jesus statue for which the town was famous. Over the years, the feast had become as much of a commercial event as a spiritual one to honor the statue's discovery in the 1880s by two Apache Indians out in the desert. They brought it to Guadalupe's priest and the miracles began for those who believed. Miracles of the lame walking. Of droughts ended. Soldiers returning safe from wars after their parents made pilgrimages. Healing physically and mentally. So many miracles the community raised money to erect a church to house the statue right on Main Avenue. Similar to other New Mexican churches, theirs was an adobe structure with twin bell towers, tile roof, and a courtyard. Although no miracle had been reported for the last thirty years, stories about the earlier ones were told again and again.

Matthew didn't believe the miracles. He believed in evidence and the only thing he knew with certainty was that the Feast of the Niño de Luz caused traffic jams and a rise in crime.

The firemen climbed down from the ladders and checked out their work. They gave each other high fives and left.

"*Hola*, Matthew."

"*¿Qué pasa*, Guillermo?"

The young owner of a pizza joint stopped sweeping his sidewalk long enough to admire the banner. "I'm on the festival planning committee this year."

"Good for you."

"Bet your ass. We added a dance and car show to the schedule."

"How exciting." Matthew didn't mean it.

"Guadalupe is growing up. According to the census, we're going to hit 50,000 people in the next five years."

"I should live so long." He adjusted his tie.

"You're such a pessimist." His braid whipped around as he swept up.

"I'm an attorney. It's the same damn thing."

Guillermo boomed out a laugh and shook dust off of his pant leg. "We're expecting more than two-thousand people this year for the festival. That's good business."

"What is?"

"Faith, Mateo, faith." The pizza man picked up the pace with the broom.

Chapter 3

"*Ay.*" Matthew slapped his leg at the sight of his mother buzzing over the lawn with the power mower. He walked into her path.

"Stop." He stepped around the mower and hit the off button.

"*¿Qué?*" Consuela Riley asked ever so innocently. "What'd I do, Mateo?"

"Mama, I told you this morning I'd mow after work."

"You're a busy man, *mijo*. I can do it." She hit the on button.

He turned off the mower. "It's too hot."

"You're telling me."

"You're making me crazy, Mama."

"I have to get used to doing this when you leave."

The statement clouted him right on the jaw. His mother could sling guilt like an Olympian throwing a disc but she excelled more at honesty, which hurt just as bad. "I've already talked with the Jiménez brothers. They're going to take care of the yard."

Crossing defiant arms, Consuela blew air through her lips. A familiar gesture whenever Matthew made a point that she'd usually ignore.

"Let's get out of this heat, Mama. It'll fry our brains like *frijoles.*"

Consuela removed her worn straw hat and whipped it back and forth to dry the sweat on her forehead. "You can finish mowing later, son."

"What a good idea. Why didn't I think of that?"

She laughed and sat on the cement porch of the house. He sat next to her, though she told him he'd ruin his suit. She placed her hand on his. Such a soft cool touch. He wanted to remember that touch all his life. Although her short curly hair was totally white, her skin belied her age of sixty-seven. Her only wrinkles appeared when she laughed. Matthew also kidded his mother that she would outlive him because her heart stamped on like a machine at the copper mill.

"It will be hard when I leave, Mama, but I'll visit every chance I get."

She slipped into Spanish, a language with which Matthew had grown up. "You've wanted to leave Guadalupe for a long time. I've accepted it, Mateo."

More honesty. He couldn't argue with the truth.

"How can you pass up such a good job? You might even end up attorney general of this state one of these days. I'm so proud of you. After your no-good father abandoned us, you stepped up, *mijo*. You may look like him but you got my guts."

Consuela Salazar had met Ken Riley at an elementary school where she worked as a secretary in the front office. The bricklayer was helping to build a new annex, plummeted off a ladder, and sprained his ankle. Consuela aided him and he tumbled for her beauty as he had tumbled off the ladder.

Matthew had few memories of his father. His mass of blond hair and crystal blue eyes. How he hooted at dumb TV shows. His endless patience when teaching him to fish Brazo Creek a few miles from Guadalupe. Those were the good things.

The bad ones—Ken Riley turned out to be a drunk who frequently chased whiskey with a six-pack. During drinking fevers, he insulted Hispanics as untrustworthy and un-American, including his wife. During one rant against his mother, Matthew kicked his dad in the shins as hard as he could. Ken laughed so much he shut up and went to bed.

One day, Ken went to work and kept on going. Matthew was five. Ever since then, his mother always referred to Ken as the "no-good father" and divorced him for abandonment but she had a beautiful son and that made things all right, or so she always told Matthew. She didn't remarry, saying that she didn't get it right once and didn't want to try it again. Still, she held onto a photo of her wedding day hidden in a drawer in her room. Matthew had found it while searching for change to buy an ice cream.

Growing up, he had been ashamed of his blond hair and eyes the color of warm ice because his was the face of his father. He was happy when his olive skin tanned in the summer. Then he would hold his arm next to his mom's and pronounced with pride, "See, we're the same color." That had caused her to laugh.

Sitting on the porch, he smiled at his mom. A dimpled smile that hinted of smart-ass, which definitely belonged to his father. "I've heard that no-good-father-Matthew-stepping-up speech before, little mother." She hated when he called her that.

"But I never get tired of saying it." She gave her own smart-ass grin.

He squeezed her hand. "Besides, I couldn't have done anything without you."

"No, Mateo, it was you."

After his father's disappearance, his mother worked tirelessly to support him, including cleaning houses on the weekends for extra money. He prayed he had inherited her guts, especially the closer he got to pulling his own disappearing act and leaving Guadalupe and his family for extended periods between holidays and visits.

"No, it was all *you*." He kissed her cheek.

"Look at the time. It's after one. Come and eat lunch, Mateo." She put her small hand on his shoulder to help herself up. Her knees creaked like a gnarled door. "My God, it's hot. Maybe after lunch, I'll finish the lawn." She surveyed the yard.

"Forget about it."

She laughed.

In the kitchen, Consuela placed a plate of food in front of Matthew. Two beef enchiladas, rice and beans, and the special mix of onions, cabbage, and carrots in vinegar. "Your favorite, son. Now eat everything."

Before he started, Matthew rolled up his shirt sleeves and tossed his tie over one shoulder. "Mama, this looks great, but if I do eat everything, I'll fall asleep in court this afternoon, and Judge Herrera already hates me."

Consuela brought him a glass of iced tea. "If John Herrera gives you any trouble, just remind him how he had *mocos* running from his nose in grade school."

"I'll be held in contempt if I say that."

"Then *I'll* tell him the next time I see him at church."

"Great. Then he'll throw you in jail."

"You'll bail me out, son." She winked.

A car pulled up. Matthew looked at his watch. His friend was punctual when it came to lunchtime. "Come on in, Benny," he called.

The screen door squeaked open. Sheriff Benjamin Ortega lumbered into the kitchen.

"Hey, *compadre*. Take a seat." Matthew motioned at him.

At six feet and two hundred and thirty pounds, Benny did nothing but lumber these days because of a bad back from chasing and catching an uncooperative druggie. In high school though, Benny bolted down the football field crushing opposing players like rabbits under the wheels of a semi-truck. Matthew was content earning his letter in basketball.

Sometimes, when Matthew squinted, he saw a younger version of his friend, sleek and muscled, hair black and wavy. Despite the added pounds, Benny was still formidable enough to subdue barroom fighters in town and filled out his dark blue sheriff's uniform with equal parts of muscle and grit. His knees, however, were bone on bone.

Benny set down his immaculate tan cowboy hat on the coffee table, took a seat across from him, and tucked a napkin under his chin. They shook hands and knocked knuckles, their routine greeting. His mother gave Benny an equally hefty serving of lunch. Before digging in, he took a cinnamon toothpick from his mouth and placed it on the side of the plate. He loved cinnamon toothpicks, which he called his trademark.

"Looks good, Consuela." Benny's voice matched his demeanor. Grumbly, as if it had come directly out of the earth's core.

"What's the news?" she said.

Benny laughed. "Something really weird, at least that's what Juan Gallegos and Mo Luna reported to us."

Consuela sat down because she loved gossip almost as much as cooking for her son. "Well, what happened to those two old fools now?"

"They were going home from Joey's about one this morning and cut through the park. They said they found a beautiful pregnant girl crying near the gazebo and decided to take her to the law enforcement office."

"That's nothing." Consuela waved her hand.

"Yeah, but get this. When they walked her out of the park, they claimed the beautiful girl changed into a monster.

That black goo came out of her body and she gave birth to a baby snake demon right there on the sidewalk."

Consuela floated a raspberry.

"What?" Matthew said.

"I already heard their story."

"Where the heck did you hear that?"

"From Gloria Smith. Her husband's a dispatcher."

"Of course, you know everyone in town, Mama."

"It's great isn't it?" She smiled.

"Were Juan and Mo drunk?" he asked Benny.

Benny shook salt on his food. "Not really. The whole story's going to be in the newspaper tomorrow. Isabel interviewed them."

"Can you imagine if it's true?" Consuela crossed herself. "Demons in Guadalupe. God help us."

"Mama, you need to get out more. There're demons all over town on Saturday nights," Matthew said.

"Those old guys swore that baby demon flashed a snaky tongue at them." Benny dug into the enchiladas.

"I didn't think Mo and Juan had any imagination," Matthew said.

"Sure, they do. Last summer they claimed an alien spaceship landed behind the Supermart. They said the aliens probably wanted to probe their anus but turns out it was just a fancy silver sports car."

"Those two are so full of shit, particularly after they've spent time at Joey's Bar."

"Mateo, watch your *caca* mouth," Consuela said

"It's the summer. Everybody goes a little unhinged in the summer."

"An officer went with them to the park, but they couldn't find anything," Benny said. "No pretty lady. No demon. No black stuff on the sidewalk."

"A damn waste of time," Matthew said.

"Never mind the demon, eat, you two." His mother poured them both more iced tea.

"Yeah, Matthew, you need strength for more cattle rustlers." Benny smiled, his teeth pasted with food.

"Shit, has everyone in town heard about that?"

Consuela gave a supportive look and tried to serve him another helping of food, but he held up a hand against it. "Mrs. González was on the jury and I ran into her at the grocery store today."

"Great," he said unenthusiastically.

His mother spooned out more rice just the same. "Don't worry, son. She did say you did a good job of putting that old man away."

Chapter 4

After early morning mass, Alma Chacon emerged from the church, put her hand above her eyes, and frowned. A reddish tint surrounded the shadowy moon in the blue sky, as if the moon bled slowly from a cut that refused to heal. The tint around the moon meant something but she couldn't remember the significance, which deepened her frown. At eighty-one, she admitted she'd reached the age where she forgot more than she remembered. That frustrated her worse than trying to figure out all the buttons on the TV remote.

The heat burned her eyes, and she looked away and back at the church.

During that morning's homily, Father Henry Cantu, who was the younger of the two priests, had talked about the end of days. As he did, he strode up and down in front of the parishioners, waving arms and talking loudly. Young priests tended to be more enthusiastic until they learned they didn't have to yell. He described the signs leading up to the Rapture and the coming of a New Jerusalem as written in the Scriptures but a red tint around the moon wasn't among the warnings. The priest probably skipped that part.

She glanced up at the reddish moon again. Probably nothing or maybe it was something she'd seen on TV. Yet, her lower gut seized up with an ache. Whatever the red tint meant, it was no *bueno*. In fact, for the last month she had experienced similar pain in her stomach as if a lizard devoured her insides. She'd also been dreaming of a red mist stealing upon the town in the night. People screamed and blood trickled down the walls of the buildings, even the church. Hooded men emerged from the mist as if they had been born from it. They seemed to be made of blood.

She'd wake up choking on her own spit.

Her daughter was skeptical of the dreams and their prophetic meaning and suggested she stop eating crackers and butter before she went to bed, but Alma knew it wasn't the crackers.

She clutched the rosary in her hand. If the end was coming, she was ready. She'd made a good confession and had taken the communion host. That should get her through any final turbulent days ahead.

With the simple, pleasant resolution, a smile passed over her face as she waited in the shade of a business awning for her daughter to pick her up. Besides faulty memory, Alma suffered from waning hearing and didn't hear two boys laughing, tearing down the sidewalk, and heading straight at her. As they grazed by both sides of her, she stomped down her cane so she wouldn't fall.

"*Bandidos*," she twisted around and shouted after the boys.

"Sorry," one of them called back as they sprinted on.

She sighed at the lawlessness of young people. They careened around the streets in colorful cars, blasting music with swear words, or they rode those skateboards with abandon down the sidewalks. The girls wore too much makeup and too tight clothes. The boys had on those baggie pants that looked as if they would collapse to their ankles any minute. Their parents weren't much better. Too much running around with cell phones pasted to their ears. The town used to be so tranquil. Now it was all busy busy busy, and it might get even busier from what she read in the newspaper about a new resort development outside of Guadalupe.

All *that* should have been another sign in Scriptures that the end of days was near.

Alma waved at her daughter, who drove around the corner. Soon she'd get out of the heat and out from under the red moon that meant something she had long forgotten.

****

Ronnie Calderón and Tim Mitchell spent the morning not only swerving around the tiny elderly woman but anyone else blocking their direct path to the city pool. The twelve-year-old best friends raced toward swim team practice and no one was going to get in their way. The townspeople swore at the boys in English and Spanish as they buzzed past and bumped them. Ronnie and Tim thought the curses were hilarious and laughed, which only stirred up more curses.

After being late to practice twice, their coach warned them that one more time meant they'd be kicked off of the summer team, but the boys liked swimming more than the baseball league because it was a whole lot cooler.

Ronnie and Tim kicked up speed. The pool was located at the eastern end of the city park.

Already wearing their swimming trunks under their shorts, they arrived a good forty minutes before the rest of the guys on the team to ensure they'd be on time. As a bonus, they'd be able to play in the water before the rigors of practice set down by Coach Bill Henderson, who was as friendly as a cold plate of pasta. The boys pulled out their yellow pool passes to show the teenage girl manning the desk.

"Don't run," she yelled at the blur of boys and yellow.

Ronnie, the fastest and heftiest of the two, threw down his backpack under a bench and tore off his shirt, shorts, socks, and tennis shoes. He took a run back from the water and cannonballed into the deepest end of the pool. At that early hour, there were no other swimmers. His buddy Tim, decidedly slower at getting undressed, hollered in protest when Ronnie splashed him.

"Hey kid, no running," shouted one of the two teen boys who worked as lifeguards. They were heading to the other end of the large pool, rubbing sunblock over their bronze skin as they walked. They didn't so much sport a six-pack as a four-pack.

"And no cannonballs," shouted the other lifeguard at Ronnie.

The boy just laughed and squirted a mouthful of water at his friend who sat down on the bench struggling with his shoes.

"Quit it." Tim removed his glasses.

"Come on in." Ronnie jetted more water at his friend.

"I got to put my glasses away in a safe place so they don't get smashed. My mom yelled at me because she already had to buy me a new pair."

Ronnie splashed Tim again and laughed.

"Stop messing around, kid," shouted one of the lifeguards.

"Yeah," added the other guard.

They turned and started bringing out gear for the swim league from the storeroom in the back.

Ronnie ignored the warnings and kept flapping his arms at the water.

Finding a good spot for his glasses, Tim shot up. "Okay, move over, dude. I'm coming in next." He ran back to get a good start but stopped one foot from the edge.

Ronnie had stopped laughing. His face scrunched in pain and his arms beat about frantically like needles in a hurricane. "Something's got me! It hurts! Help me! Help me!" He started crying. "It won't let me go."

"Give me your hand, Ronnie." Tim kneeled down and reached out. He saw nothing in the water but his friend.

Ronnie just sputtered and slapped at the surface, as if the insubstantial water would keep him away from what was hurting him below.

"It's got me."

"What's got you?"

Mouth open, Tim watched helplessly as Ronnie was pulled and pushed roughly from one side of the pool to the other and back again. Ronnie whacked into the edges with a terrible fleshy thud. The jerking stopped, leaving Ronnie five feet from where Tim held out his hands for his friend. The boy gulped water and disappeared under as if yanked down with tremendous force.

The water rippled and stilled.

"Oh shit," said one of the lifeguards who'd seen Ronnie go under. He dropped what he was carrying. Running to the pool, he leapt in and swam twenty-five yards to the spot where Ronnie had gone down. The other lifeguard sprinted to the front of the pool and dived in. Tim stood at the edge watching them swim around.

After what seemed like forever to Tim, both lifeguards came up for air, breathing hard. They went down again. They covered the length and depth of the pool five times before they rose to take more deep breaths and cough out the water they had swallowed. After more searching, the lifeguards heaved themselves out. When they emerged, their hair glistened with water and their faces distorted with fear and confusion. Desperation weighed on their chests as they lay back on the concrete. Tim looked down into the pool. The water had settled.

Ronnie was just gone.

Chapter 5

Matthew heard the sirens from upstairs. He didn't fight the urge to quit working on a brief and walked downstairs to the law enforcement office. Benny stood in the middle of the activity. The ends of his mouth looked like they'd gone through the floor and straight into the basement. Matthew knew that face. His friend wore it anytime there was death.

"Oh, hell," Matthew said.

****

Matthew and Benny stared down into the drained pool. At the bottom stood Fire Chief Ben Smith and Guadalupe Police Sergeant Bill Rathburn. They both looked up at Matthew and Benny and shook their heads with bewilderment.

They climbed up. Their pant legs were wet because six inches of water still sat at the bottom of the pool.

"There is no way in heaven or hell that boy could have been sucked into the main drain. It's bolted down. The other drains are too small for anything larger than a baseball to go through," the fire chief said.

"So where is he?" Benny said.

"I have no idea."

Benny thanked him for helping out.

"If you don't need me anymore I'm going to go home early, hug my grandkid, and have a drink." Smith left.

Matthew heard chatter at the pool entrance. A police officer kept out the curious. Among them his soon-to-be ex-wife Isabel Sánchez Riley, the reporter. She bobbed up and down for a better look and then held her camera over her head and snapped photos.

On a bench near the front building sat Tim Mitchell with a towel around his shoulders. His father had his arm around the boy, whose face was vacant. From crying, his eyes were as red as his tennis shoes.

He and Benny were joined by Rathburn, a brick of a guy. Since Benny outranked him, Rathburn nodded as to who would lead the interview.

"Tell us what happened, Tim," Benny asked in a kind voice.

The boy could have been wearing his nerves on the outside.

"Go on, son," his dad said.

"Ronnie dived in. A cannonball. I was about to jump in, but then he started calling for help. Like he was hurting."

"Maybe he had a cramp," Tim's dad said.

"So he was in pain, Tim?" Matthew said.

The boy nodded. "Lots and lots. His face was all twisted like. He was even crying. I've never seen him cry before. He was calling and calling for help."

Rathburn jotted down notes as the kid talked.

"What happened then?" Benny said.

"He was yelling that something had a hold of him underneath." Tim began to cry again.

"Who had hold of him?" the police officer said.

"I didn't see nobody in the water, sir, but Ronnie was pulled around the pool like he was a doll. Then he was jerked down and he didn't come back up. He didn't come up." Tim cried harder. His dad hugged him and dried his son's face with the towel. "He's my best friend."

"You can take the boy home," Benny said.

Tim's dad picked him up.

Matthew, Benny, and Rathburn walked over to the lifeguards now pale under their tans. They sat on another bench, their heads lowered. They gripped the sides of the bench.

"You heard Tim. Was that how it happened?" Matthew didn't wait for the officers to ask. He was troubled and confused and bet he wasn't the only one at that point.

"We told the kid not to cannonball and not to run. At first, he was laughing in the water," said one of the teens.

"Where were you?" Benny said.

"At the other end of the pool setting up for the swim practice. Then all of a sudden, we heard him shouting for help. The next thing we knew, he was going under," said the other teenager.

"Man, it was more like he was sucked under. We went in and searched but couldn't find him anywhere. It was no more than a few seconds."

"He just disappeared, man." The other lifeguard opened and closed his hands.

Matthew glanced up. There was only one entrance to the pool, which was surrounded by an eight-foot-tall wire fence.

"You see anybody else hanging around the pool before the boys arrived?" Benny said.

The lifeguards shook their heads.

"The only people here were the two boys and the girl up front and us. That's it. I'm totally freaked out." One of the teenagers swayed a bit.

"Put your head between your legs," Matthew said and the teenager bent down.

"It wasn't our fault." The other teen's eyes were as shiny as water. He wiped at them.

"No, it wasn't. You did your best."

"You guys can go," Benny said. After they left, he turned to Matthew and Rathburn. "What the hell is this?"

A tall black man, Rathburn's bushy eyebrows pushed together with bewilderment. "Damned if I know."

Matthew glanced down into the empty pool. "I'll second that."

A police officer rushed to them. "Sheriff, Sergeant, the kid's mom and dad are here."

"Shit. Well, show them in," Benny said.

The Calderóns were well-built people. The mom had a wet face and red eyes from weeping. The father's face had solidified like a metal that would soon melt and never be solid again.

"Where's our son?" Mr. Calderón shouted. "Benny, tell us."

"We can't find him."

"How could he just vanish?" Mrs. Calderón whispered as she clutched a red-beaded rosary.

Benny sweated and drew out his handkerchief. Matthew touched his back. His friend, bulky as he was, disliked confrontations with victims. Benny could handle criminals. The miserable were another thing entirely. His friend wasn't much of talker—except about cars, fishing, football, and classic westerns on TV. In their relationship, Matthew was the one who usually did the talking and would do so now.

"Mr. and Mrs. Calderón, here are the facts so far. Ronnie dived in and appeared to be in some kind of distress soon after he hit the water. He went under and the lifeguards dived in but they couldn't find him in the pool." He felt dumb saying something so unbelievable.

"That don't make no sense." Mr. Calderón walked to the edge of the drained pool. His right hand swept at the emptiness.

"I agree, but that's what happened."

"Did someone take him?"

"No one else was around the pool area except for Ronnie's friend and the two lifeguards," the police sergeant said.

"A person can't just disappear." Mr. Calderón's face appeared as if it might crack wide open with equal amounts of grief and anger.

Mrs. Calderón wept anew.

"We're going to do everything we can to find your boy," Benny said at last. "My deputies, the police, and the county search crew are going to look for Ronnie."

"Why don't you take your wife home?" Matthew told the husband. "The sheriff will call when he has more information."

"People don't just disappear," Mr. Calderón uttered again and again as he and his wife stumbled back home.

Benny sat on the bench and Matthew joined him. Rathburn's wide shoulders sagged.

"Mr. Calderón is right, Mateo. It don't make no sense for a kid to vanish like that. If he had died in the pool, we'd have found his body. The lifeguards didn't see anybody else, so how could he have been abducted?"

"I don't have an answer." Matthew perspired from the inexplicability and removed his jacket. "Just have your people keep on searching. And Benny, you're right on every count. This doesn't make any fucking sense."

They both looked at the empty pool.

Deputy Jackson Rogers came running up to them. With a white blondish crew cut and the physique of stacked barbells, he had a gruffness built from his belief he could manhandle anyone, anywhere, anytime. Before he put on the badge, he had frequently demonstrated that in bars.

"Sheriff, Cal Napier heard what happened and brought his search dog."

"Bring him on in," Benny said. "Okay, Bill?"

"I think that's a great idea," Rathburn said.

Napier had a big gut and bigger heart. As head of the county search and rescue volunteers, he was always the first one out to find a missing person and stayed the longest in the search. On a leash was his dog, Major, a magnificent golden Labrador Retriever. Major had shown his worth time and again locating missing hunters in the Sangre Mountains or the desert. The animal was intelligent, cooperative, and friendly.

"Thanks for coming, Cal," Matthew said.

"I hope Major and I can help."

Matthew wasn't much of a dog person, but Major always made him change his mind.

"Do you have anything belonging to the boy?"

Rathburn handed him the shirt and shorts left by the missing Ronnie. Napier let Major smell the clothing and then unhooked the dog's leash. Nose to the cement, Major followed the path that the boy took before jumping into the water. The dog began to circle and circle the pool, and finally returned to the edge where Ronnie dove in. The retriever sat down and started to whine as if someone was pinching him. He kept it up for ten minutes until Cal Napier took him home.

Chapter 6

As a county official, Matthew was often obligated to make an appearance at city and county events outside of the courtroom. This happened to be another of those. A check passing in front of the fountain in the middle of the park.

Matthew coerced Benny into joining him so he wouldn't feel so silly standing there like an elected bump on a log. Mostly, he wanted to get Benny out of the office. It had been four days and there was no sign of young Ronnie Calderón after he disappeared from the middle of the city pool. Deputies, city officers, county search and rescue members, and many volunteers from the family's church had fanned out for ten miles in any direction they could think of but they didn't find Ronnie. Not even a trace of Ronnie. Finally, Benny called off the search and passed the information onto the FBI. He'd been depressed ever since. During the last six years, Benny had already diminished somewhat from worry about the failing health of his wife, Camilla. That showed in the packed luggage underneath his eyes and increasing white dusting his black hair.

After the kid went missing, Benny appeared even more haggard. Although the disappearance took place inside city limits, he viewed the whole county as his jurisdiction and responsibility. This ceremony probably wouldn't help Benny, but Matthew hoped it would get his mind off of the kid for a bit.

His friend wasn't alone in the anxiety department.

Matthew couldn't stop thinking about what had happened, either, and was grateful down to his soul for each day his son was safe. He did forbid him from swimming at the pool for the next month.

Standing at the back of the crowd with Benny, Matthew pretended to pay attention to what was going on at the presentation. Mostly, he enjoyed the fresh air and looking at Isabel. Taking notes, she displayed a natural enthusiasm that was her calling in life. She exhibited passion in everything she did—from reporting to being a mom, wife, and human being. From her face, she maintained an actual interest in the boring ceremony taking place in front of the fountain at the park's plaza.

They had separated exactly three months and six days ago. He looked at his watch. And ten hours. She was still so beautiful, as if he expected she would wither away after he moved out. Wavy black hair hinting of red. Eyes green as a morning sun edging over a pasture. A voice that deepened when she was angry or when they made love.

Staring at her, he felt like a goddamn fool.

"Ahhhmmm." Benny lifted his boot toward the presentation. "Remember why we're here, bro."

"Oh, yeah." Matthew smiled and waved when Mayor John Stuart introduced him and Benny for the presentation of one of those ridiculously large checks. This one was from Chamber of Commerce President Chic Montez to the city as represented by Stuart and other council members who took time off from their work.

Since his election five years ago, John Stuart had proved to be a good mayor. He helped entice a store warehouse and meat-packing plant that created jobs for three-hundred people, as well as leading a project to upgrade the sewer system. He was a personable outgoing man who didn't look like a guy who pushed cattle around for a living. Instead, he could have been a male model of a cowboy. Rumor had it that half of the single female employees at city hall had asked him out on a date, but Matthew thought that Stuart's eyes resembled steel washers. Polished, chill, and lifeless.

Chamber President Chic Montez, on the other hand, seemed to wear the same black suit to every official event. Older and shorter, Montez ran a tortilla factory, which distributed to stores in five surrounding counties. His tortillas came in clear wrappers with his picture on the label. He had told Matthew he was researching how to make the gluten-free kind not taste like wallpaper. Montez truly believed Guadalupe the best community in New Mexico and said so at any opportunity. Of course, he had never lived anyplace else, but then again, neither had Matthew—other than the time he was away at college and law school at the University of New Mexico.

Since taking over the chamber presidency, Montez had promised to raise funds for the repair of the one-hundred-year-old fountain that had stopped working late last summer. Age cracks marked the white stone and more than a few town teenagers had scratched their initials into its ceramic and tiled side. The pipes were rusted red-green.

"The Guadalupe Chamber is happy to present this check to complete the repair of our historic fountain. Chamber members, donations from the community, and money from fundraisers made this possible." His voice carried even without a microphone. "We look forward to our fountain again flowing and brought back to its former glory." Montez's grin couldn't be contained because his promise was so close to being fulfilled.

The small crowd applauded politely.

"Thank you, Chic and the business community." Stuart's smile pandered to his constituency. "The people of Guadalupe are proud of this park. And I'm proud to announce the restoration of the fountain should be complete in time for the Feast of the Niño de Luz." He pointed to a crew standing off to the side taking a break under the trees, a few enjoying smokes and sports drinks. He waved at the workers. Only one waved back.

"This contribution from the chamber marks the end of a yearlong effort," Stuart said. "So, let's get to work."

The crowd clapped louder. Most of those in attendance were staunch members of the chamber and the county historical society who headed the restoration project. The society members were aged but feisty when it came to the past.

The presentation ended as nondescript as it began. The crew started up work on the fountain.

"Please, Mayor Stuart, Mr. Montez, another photo for the paper," Isabel asked the men.

They posed with the check and she took a few shots from different angles.

"Just look at Isabel. She loves this small-town shit," Matthew told Benny.

"When you'd get so damn cynical, Mateo?" Benny moved his toothpick from one side of his mouth to another.

"I don't see it as cynicism, Benny. I call it realism."

Benny spit out the toothpick and put in a fresh one. "You're so full of crap, *compadre*."

"Now, that's friggin' cynical. Okay, we did our duty as elected officials. Let's get the hell out of here. Come to my office before she sees us," Matthew joked but sneaked a last look at Isabel. Benny noticed and gave his usual snort of a laugh as they headed to the courthouse through the park.

"She *is* the most enthusiastic person I've ever met," Benny said.

"You got that." Matthew particularly missed that enthusiasm in bed, though not necessarily when they fought.

The people they passed waved, nodded, or smiled at them as if he and Benny were one entity. Matthew grinned because that was partly true. To the longtime residents, he and Benny hanging out together was a common site. That's because everybody knew everybody else's story in Guadalupe, as far as Matthew was concerned.

As boys, he and Benny dashed through the streets looking for trouble or running from it. When they got older, they roared around in Benny's gloriously baby blue Chevy truck. He had rebuilt it from a junker they discovered at his dad's salvage yard. They were a contrast as kids. His hair a light blond and his eyes bright blue. Benny's dark hair and intense brown eyes. He was slender. Benny filled out. People called them "salt and pepper" in front and behind their backs but that only made them laugh.

Matthew had helped Benny with his homework and occasionally wrote essays or reports for him so his friend could keep up his grades to stay on the football team. Kids who ridiculed his half-and-half heritage didn't dare touch him otherwise, they'd run into Benny's fists. As the kids said today, they had each other's backs and had ever since Matthew could remember. He was damn fortunate to have such a friend, though he never admitted that to Benny. Maybe he didn't have to because his friend surely knew.

They were still contrasts. Matthew in a suit and tie. Benny in his uniform but Matthew was glad his blond hair had darkened.

Back in his office, they talked legal business. Benny reviewed the weekend's criminal activities so he could prepare for what kind of caseload his office could expect. It was a regular activity, although the topics of the latest football or basketball games and planned fishing trips often crept into the conversations.

"You have much better coffee in your office than mine." Benny drained his cup. "Hmm, French vanilla."

"You're right. The stuff in your office tastes like motor oil." As Matthew poured him a refill, Isabel walked in.

Benny put his hand up in mock fright. "Oh, no. The press."

"Don't you knock, Isabel?" Matthew said.

"I'm still Mrs. Riley to your secretary." Isabel's face was as determined as her stride. "Come to think of it, I *am* still Mrs. Riley."

"We're doing important work here," Matthew said and then blew on his hot cup of coffee.

"Oh, I can see that. What's brewing today? French vanilla?"

Isabel helped herself to a cup because she agreed that Matthew's coffee was also better than the inky brew in the newspaper office.

"So how'd you like the presentation, Isabel? It going to be the front page story tomorrow? A great big banner headline?" Matthew's hands measured the supposed size of the font. "News flash: gas passing at the park."

"Maybe it was you who passed the gas, Matthew," she said.

"Good one, Isabel," Benny said.

"Don't encourage her, bro," Matthew said.

Setting down her coffee cup, she took out a pen and notebook from her large purse. "Benny, anything more about the disappearance of Ronnie Calderón from the pool?"

Benny gave his head a shake. "I wish there were. I've sent his photo over the wire to other surrounding law enforcement agencies, but just like it was reported. He vanished."

"That is so incredibly sad." She looked at Matthew, who saw that she too was grateful for their son's safety.

"Benny, any follow-up to what happened to Juan and Mo at the park Wednesday night?"

"What kind of follow-up would there be? Those guys must have been hallucinating," Matthew said.

"I wasn't talking to you."

"Isabel, it was all there in your article. Good descriptions on the she-devil, by the way. You're a good writer." Benny stirred sugar into his cup.

"Thanks. That demon stuff was a good story. A lot of people said they read it." She held up her coffee mug in a salute.

Isabel loved compliments on her writing and was wary of those on her loveliness. And she was lovely, which made him still hurt because of their separation. But the best way to shake off his nostalgic feeling was kidding her, though he felt bad about it later. "She-devil, huh? So where were you on the night in question, Isa? Do you have an alibi?"

She glanced at him with a crumpled mouth that made Matthew both insane and excited. "Don't call me Isa."

She then winked at Benny. "So what wasn't in the report?"

"*Nada*, Isabel. It's the festival. People always go nuts the closer it gets, you know that."

"If people aren't seeing images of Jesus and the Virgin Mary in burnt tortillas, they're seeing the devil tramping around Main at midnight." Matthew opened a file. "Now don't you have some corruption to uncover?"

"Don't you have old shoplifters to torment?" Her mouth went up in a wonderfully teasing smile.

Benny put up his hands. "Can't you guys give it a rest? You got separated so you wouldn't fight anymore."

"It's more fun this way, isn't it, Isa?" Matthew said.

"You're still taking Angel this weekend, right?"

"Absolutely."

"And please don't fill him with junk food like the last time. He woke up with nightmares for two days afterward."

"I plead the fifth on that, your honor."

Isabel batted her eyes and licked her lips. Her face became soft and sexy. Her voice matched. "Matthew?"

"What?"

"Oh, Matthew."

"Isabel." He sat up.

"Go suck a *huevo*."

Benny laughed. She left as quickly as she entered but whipped her pretty head around. "Bye, Benny."

Benny leaned against one corner of Matthew's desk. "I still think you're the biggest *pendejo* in the state for letting her go."

Matthew wasn't joking anymore. "I didn't have that good of a grip in the first place."

Chapter 7

At La Sol Bakery on Flor Street, Phil Nunez tapped his fingers on the glass counter he had just cleaned. After another long day of ovens and dough, he wanted to get home for dinner and watch the Golf Channel. He loved his family, baking, and golf. The order depended on the day and how he felt.

"María, *vamos*. Please." He scowled at this wife who said she'd only take a minute to finish up, but that minute stretched to fifteen every time. María wiped down shelves in preparation of closing the bakery for the evening. Hips made wide from too much sampling of their pastries, she shook them with each swipe of her rag. Still, on some days, the jiggling reminded him of their young days in the back of his Ford station wagon at the drive-in.

"How long, María? I'm starving, woman."

"You ain't starving, *hombre*."

He laughed and rubbed a circle on his plump belly. A tribute to his own fondness for the variety of fresh Mexican bread they made daily.

"Oh, remember the birthday cake, Phil. The Worth family's going to pick it up in five minutes."

"Dammit, I completely forgot about them. I got it in the cooler. I hope they hurry up."

"Well, go get it. The sooner they come, the sooner we go home. My corns ache like the devil."

Phil headed to the walk-in cooler in the back where he often took refuge to cool off during the scorching summer months in Guadalupe. He brushed his hands among the boxed cakes on the shelves and found the one he wanted. "Worth" was written in his wife's neat handwriting on a pink note taped on the side. He set the box out on the counter, where his wife popped gum and complained more about her sore feet.

"Just got to write 'Happy Birthday, Susan' on it," said Phil, who was more talented with the icing tube than his wife.

He lifted the paper sheet from the top. His face emptied of color.

"What is it?" María said. "My feet are swelling."

He took a step back, grabbed the trash can, and vomited.

"Phil, what's wrong for God's sake?"

His shaky hand motioned toward the cake. She looked down at it and screamed.

Pink and gray maggots covered the entire top and sides of the cake. They squirmed like a realized bad dream. From out of the middle of the cake arose more of the hideous insects, as if they were newly forming amid the flour, sugar, and eggs. The cake heaved with the maggots like an animal taking a final breath.

Then the cake burst, throwing the insects, icing, and crumbs against the walls as well as on the faces of Phil and María Nunez. She fainted and he again threw up in the wastebasket as the maggots continued to wriggle across the floor.

Chapter 8

At dusk, a crimson hue painted the town the color of a cactus flower. A delicate orange of the desert. Then the moon rose, silvery and magnificent. Matthew stood outside of the high school auditorium and admired the scene.

So lovely.

Miraculously, the moon appeared larger in Guadalupe. As if the godforsaken town was closer to the heavens than any other spot on the planet. While attending law school in Albuquerque, he'd climb up to the roof of his apartment and question whether it was the same one he'd seen at home. Back for breaks and holidays, he saw a round brilliance that bared no resemblance to the puny satellite over the city. Chalk it up to pollution and more lights, he reasoned, but his heart told him the moon above his hometown was special and always would be.

Moving back to Albuquerque for his new job, he'd not only miss his son, mother, and Benny, but that moon and the town itself. The people had so much personality he could forgive them for making him more than a little nuts.

He would also miss Isabel.

How she used to wake him with the lightest of kisses in the morning. The feel of her skin. Her face illuminated like the Guadalupe moon. At that moment, he wanted a cigarette bad, although he'd given them up as a sophomore in college. He always desired nicotine whenever he doubted himself, and he doubted himself now. Should he really go to Albuquerque? He had a good career in Guadalupe and could probably keep the job of county prosecutor until he was so gray and crooked that they'd have to wheel him down to the courtroom.

And the hardest question. Was the AG job worth the cost of leaving behind his family and friends?

Matthew grazed a hand over his face to brush off the misgivings. He could deal with the law in such a precise manner, but his own life would sometimes waver worse than a sheet left out on a clothesline in a windstorm.

No. He had to take the AG job. Staying in town would mean he hadn't reached his potential, what he was capable of. Everyone he knew considered him the wonder boy for getting a scholarship to law school and working his way up to county prosecutor. No matter his accomplishments though, he still believed he hadn't been challenged and if that continued, he'd become as fallow as an unplanted farm field. He had to move up, go to the city, or else he'd be stuck and empty in Guadalupe all his life. Hell, maybe he had just inherited too much DNA from his bum of a dad.

He stomped dust off of his newly polished shoes.

All that thinking about the moon and what he'd miss every day would do him no good and in the end make him lonelier when he did move away.

"No good at all," he muttered out loud.

Looking up, Matthew spotted a gray desert cottontail down the street. It hopped around and stopped in the lit circle under the streetlight. Not an unusual sight in Guadalupe. The desert rabbits raided gardens and dug holes in the park's grass to the chagrin of the city crews. As he headed to the auditorium, the light flashed and went out. He swiveled back. The rabbit stood up on hind legs as if smelling danger, shook violently, stiffened, and dropped to the ground, its tongue out.

"Son of a bitch."

He walked over to the little body and pushed at it with his shoe. Stiff as new wood. The streetlight burst on overhead, causing him to jolt.

He got out a handkerchief, picked up the animal by its ears, and dropped it into a trash can in front of the auditorium. In his peripheral vision, a shadow of a man zipped about in the gloomy alley off of where he was standing. The shadow was distorted like he was out of focus.

"Hey, you. What you doing over there?" Matthew called.

The shadow stopped. Though it was dark, the figure seemed to turn toward him. At once, it whooshed into the dark.

Either the whole town was going wacky or he was, he surmised. Shaking his head, he walked into the auditorium already full with other loony townspeople.

****

Standing against a back wall, Benny had his arms crossed, a sign he was on duty. He glanced around the auditorium. "Haven't seen so many people gathered in one spot since the time Guadalupe beat Gallop for the state basketball finals. You were forward on that team, bro."

"Nah, more people came out for the zoning hearing about the new strip joint on Cactus Street." Matthew nudged Benny in the rib.

"Forgot about that." Benny gave his large smile, the one that took in everything. "They were the ugliest strippers I'd ever seen. Even uglier than the ones we saw in Tijuana that summer."

They both laughed at that memory, which they kept between them for good reason.

The auditorium was crowded and loud. Matthew spotted Isabel sitting up front with her camera strap around her neck and holding a notebook and pen. Her face was excited and glowing. Then she saw him and the glow faded. He swore it was replaced with regret. She whipped around in her seat toward the front.

Dammit, Isabel. Dammit.

County Commission Chairman Nick Vargas climbed the steps to the stage. The commission post was only part-time so Vargas's real job was his construction company and business was excellent from what Matthew read in the newspaper about the bids it won. That included the building of the new hospital in the north part of Guadalupe. Although short, Vargas was as compact as the rock and concrete he used in his construction. Matthew had discovered his toughness in middle grade when they fought over a girl named Lolly. He only escaped Vargas because he was a faster runner.

Vargas was still tough and had no patience for people who didn't agree with him. He steamrolled over the other two commissioners but did so with considerable charm. As the county's attorney, Matthew had to work with him and they often clunked heads. Vargas's attempts to cut corners probably made him excel in the private sector, but Matthew reminded him that such maneuvers didn't work in the public one.

The result. They tolerated each other.

Standing beside Vargas was Mayor John Stuart and Richard Wright, who ran the largest real estate office in the county. Matthew knew Wright only by reputation. The man apparently owned a long list of properties in town, the county, and state. At over six feet, he was stoutly well fed, as if he ate all the money he made. His eyes shifted all over the place like he was looking for the next deal.

Up on the stage, Vargas, Stuart, and Wright laughed and touched forearms and backs as if in a secret fraternity.

"God, look at them up there," Matthew told Benny. "Ambition personified in their expensive suits and pricey watches."

"Come on, Mateo. Nick Vargas isn't a bad guy."

Benny knew about his distaste for the commissioner because he had told him about it—many times.

"Only if you like the kind of men who'd eat their own young."

Benny clicked his tongue.

"We've known Nick all our lives, Benny. When did he ever do anything that didn't benefit himself?"

Benny let his cinnamon toothpick droop, a sign that Matthew was right. "Well, Stuart's done a lot of good for the town."

"Yeah, he has. I'll give you that but he lives awfully high for a cattle rancher. His spread is north of town, but he had a gigantic house built within the city limits to run for mayor. And did you check out the car he drives? It must cost more than my house."

"The cattle business is probably really good."

"Either that or the mayor is in debt up to his ever-loving, nicely groomed hair." He placed a hand on his friend's shoulder. "Benny, you always see the good side of people."

"Not always."

"My curse is that I always see the bad side. Comes from being a prosecutor, I guess."

A sturdy man entered the auditorium from a side door. Wearing a suit shiny with affluence, he took a seat in the front row. Licking two full fingers, he ran them down the razor-sharp crease of his pants. He had an abundance of white hair and not one blade was out of place. His face was strong with arrogance and a pronounced belief that his was the only opinion that mattered in the world. The crowd buzzed louder as if a Satanic Elvis had entered the building. To Matthew, it was almost the truth.

"Samuel Uhlig. What the hell is he doing here?" he asked Benny.

"He's Wright's new attorney, I heard."

"Now this guy *is* bad news."

"Why?"

"The AG's office investigated him two years ago for representing a company that promised to build a new milk processing plant in Hidalgo. The town put up lots of incentives and other honey to sweeten the recruitment pot, but the company flew and so did most of the money, and the AG couldn't prove a thing."

"That means he didn't do anything wrong."

"God, Benny, he also represented Mark Haggerty, remember?"

"The guy who bought up all the water rights for a subdivision?"

"And then it never happened."

"So that's him."

"Lots of farmers suffered because of Uhlig."

"I can see why he's not so popular."

"Well, Richard Wright, Stuart, and Vargas like him. They're almost kissing his ass."

The county commissioner, mayor, and real estate czar waved graciously to the attorney as if Uhlig was their private financial hero.

"They're just businessmen, *compadre*. All businessmen do is want to make money. It's in their genes," Benny said with weariness. He let go of a massive yawn.

"You okay?"

"Camilla had a tough night last night so I didn't get much sleep, but it's all good."

"Anything you need, I'll be there."

His friend smiled at him. "I have no doubt about that, Mateo."

This wasn't the first time he offered help, but Benny never took him up on it. Nor did Benny complain or even talk about his worries at home. This hurt Matthew because his friend had shut him out of his personal life. Growing up, Benny had confided in him plenty about his mean old man and timid mom. About his shame at not doing well in school. About everything in their lives. But in the last few years with Camilla's illness, his friend kept that part of his heart hidden away. He wished Benny would unburden himself about his wife and how he was dealing with her medical problems. A shiver climbed up Matthew's spine as if a veil had dropped between them, a veil made of the sheerest and strongest material.

The clamoring in the auditorium hushed when Vargas and Wright walked over to a podium on the left side of the stage. Stuart took a seat in the audience next to attorney Samuel Uhlig. The microphone hummed to life.

"Thanks to everyone for attending tonight. I'm excited to see all of you. It shows how much you care for our town and county. We have very exciting news for you this evening. I'll let Richard Wright explain."

With a confident step, Wright took to the podium. The lights dimmed and a giant screen descended in back. The screen lit up with an artist's rendition of a luxurious resort influenced by the southwest and lots of money. All tile, terra cotta, and carved wood—as if the plan had passed through Las Vegas on its way to New Mexico.

"This is your destiny: the Desert Rose Resort development." Wright paused to let the words sink in. "This venture will offer a first-class hotel for visitors, not to mention townhouses and condos for people who want to call this home. From a pro-designed golf course to a gracious day spa to an Olympic-sized pool, the resort will have it all. With a scenic backdrop of the Sangre Mountains, Guadalupe will become a destination not only in the state, but the nation."

Projected on the screen were drawings of a resort plan boasting shops, tennis courts, swimming pools, and a movie theater. The works. The audience collectively leaned in.

As he watched, Matthew kept thinking of that old saying about all that glitters.

"This project will also open up hundreds of new jobs to the people of Guadalupe," Wright said.

"All at minimum wage," Matthew said to Benny.

A mature woman sitting in front of them shifted around in her chair and told Matthew to "keep still."

"This will also mean a boom to your own businesses," Wright said.

"And an increase in your property taxes."

"Desert Rose will become a place where everyone will want to live."

"But of course, none of you will be able to afford to live there."

Benny didn't laugh.

The same woman threw Matthew another dirty look. He returned a winning beam.

"With county zoning approval and your support, we can start moving earth in three months," Wright said. Excitement and chatter from the audience rushed the stage. He held up hands for quiet. "Guadalupe's future is bright and even brighter with this development. While other communities are struggling with a dismal economy, this project means good jobs, more business, and a foothold in prosperity."

Wright's hand motioned to a table along the right wall of the auditorium. Smiling pretty young women sat in front of piles of pamphlets. "Please take more information from our lovely volunteers, and of course, I'll be here to answer your questions afterwards."

The lights went up and most of the people clapped, all except Josh Vale, a flinty young man wearing a camouflage cap and scruffy goatee. Vale stood up with defiance. He was a Duck Dynasty devotee who ran a garage at the edge of town. A conservative's conservative but with the best mechanic skills for two-hundred miles in any direction.

"Don't you people realize what this so-called resort will do to us?" Vale thrust a finger at the drawings.

"Josh, we're not taking questions at this time." Vargas stood up. "This is merely an informational meeting. When the project comes up at the zoning and county meetings, you'll have plenty of opportunity to comment."

"Ain't got no questions. I just got something to say. All of this is nothing but trouble from strangers. I want no part of it, and neither should you all." Vale had a roughened-by-cigarettes voice.

Wright came to the front of the stage. "Josh, I grew up in Guadalupe, and so did my parents. I'd never do anything to hurt this town. This project will only benefit all of us."

"I'm talking about him." Vale's finger swung over to Uhlig. "He's a crook and he'll steal from us. He did that to another town. I read it on the Internet."

Uhlig stood. "That is slander, sir."

"I don't do slander."

"I'm merely attending this meeting as a legal advisor to Mr. Wright. This is his project, and of course, yours." Uhlig's voice harkened of detachment.

"You build that resort or whatever you call it and this town will become messy as hell. We'll turn into a big city and that's not why I live here. We'll have to deal with more traffic and more people and more crime. The air will get smoggy and bad. Our taxes will go through the roof and we won't be able to live in this town anymore. Yeah, there might be lots of jobs come out of this thing, but they won't pay shit."

"Clearly, a smart man," Matthew said to Benny, who gave a feeble smile.

"Stop this plan and leave our town alone or you'll be sorry." Vale spoke steady with a touch of eccentric in each breath. "It'll be the end of Guadalupe. So start packing." He gave a large wave goodbye.

"You're exaggerating, Josh." Vargas stepped to the microphone. "As one of your county elected officials, I'll personally be watching out for our community interests."

Vale smirked. "And why the hell should we trust you? I didn't vote for you."

A few chuckles shot up from the crowd until Vargas threw down a mighty stare, and then the place went silent. Vale didn't even look down at his wife, who was almost double her husband's width. "Come on, Louise. Let's go home while we still got one."

They walked out. But Matthew and everyone else noticed that Josh Vale unloaded a hateful stare at the men on the stage. Vargas and Wright locked eyes as if they had swapped an unspoken communication. Then, as Matthew had often witnessed, Vargas slapped on his practiced and patronizing smile reserved for the public. The commissioner asked for calm.

"Folks, there always will be people who can't see beyond their nose," the commissioner said. "But I hope you will at least want to learn more about Richard's proposition."

Immediately forgetting Josh Vale's warnings, the crowd clapped. Vargas and Wright shook hands. Isabel snapped a picture of the moment. But Matthew cringed at Vargas's borderline endorsement of a project before it came up for a county vote. He planned to talk with him about that tomorrow.

After the meeting ended, people milled around chatting with Wright and Vargas, collecting information about the proposed resort, or checking out the resort drawings displayed on easels set up in front of the stage.

Matthew studied a five-by-five-foot map. The proposed resort property had been outlined in red. He searched for Benny, who hung back near a wall. His friend was the most gregarious man in Guadalupe at parties, weddings, quinceañeras, and any other informal gatherings, but he hated official meetings because he said they made him feel like he was back in school—lost and waiting for the school bell.

Matthew waved him over. When Benny joined him, he brushed his fingers over the map. "Isn't that old Mecho Hernández's land?"

Benny briefly looked at the map and gave a sharp nod.

"Remember when we were kids and tried to sneak a look at the old pueblo? He damn near took off our heads with a shotgun."

"Yeah, that was him. He was *loco* as the day is long."

"What'd old Mecho finally die of?"

Benny stared toward the exits as if wanting to escape. "A heart attack. Poor bastard, no family or nothing. Just that no-account piece of land."

"Not so no-account anymore."

"Sheriff. Matthew." Vargas had come up behind them with Uhlig at his side.

Uhlig extended his hand to Matthew. "I've heard good things about you, Mr. Riley."

"And I've heard about you." Matthew shook the hand without enthusiasm and immediately wanted to check to see if his wallet was still in his pants pocket.

Nonplused, Uhlig pulled out a card and handed it to him. "I could always use a talented lawyer in my firm. Come and see me if you get tired of public service."

"I've got a job, thanks."

"I understand you're going to Albuquerque and the AG's office. Doesn't that amount to hiding out from the real world?"

"No, just protecting the great state of New Mexico from those who will take advantage of her. In fact, didn't you and the Attorney General have dealings before?"

"Ah, that trumped up business."

"The Attorney General doesn't trump up investigations." Matthew had sunk one into Uhlig and it felt good.

"Good night, Nick." Uhlig spun away, ignoring Matthew and Benny. He walked off without a crinkle in his suit.

Matthew tossed the man's business card into the nearest trash can.

"That's pretty dumb, Matthew. He's a powerful man," Vargas said.

"With one of the worst reps in the state, Nick. Why the hell are you even talking with that guy?"

"He and Richard Wright can help this town. I don't want to see it dry up and blow away. After the copper mill cutbacks, we need more growth. The Desert Rose development will not only help Guadalupe, but put us on the map."

"Nick, if you vote for the project when it comes before the commission board, your construction company can't build the damn thing. That's a conflict of interest. Or do you want me to quote the statute?" Matthew loved being a lawyer.

Vargas looked ready to spit cactus. His eyebrows crashed with irritation. "What are you accusing me of, Matthew? You should know better."

"So should you, Nick. Of course, you can always resign from the commission and then build away." He smiled.

"I will serve this county the best I can."

Benny stepped in between them and slapped Vargas on the back. "I'm no real estate expert, but this resort thing could be a good deal for the county."

"It is, Benny. It'll show people what we've known all along."

"And what's that?" Matthew asked.

"That this is God's country." Vargas pulled down his jacket and walked off.

"Benny, let's get a beer. Too much of a good thing is making me thirsty," Matthew said.

As soon as they left the auditorium, Benny slicked back his hair, put on his cowboy hat, and placed a new toothpick in his mouth. "I'm going to give you a raincheck, bro. I don't want to leave Camilla alone too long."

"No problemo. I have paperwork to do anyway. Give her my love."

Returning to his office, Matthew completed motions for two pending cases. He didn't want to leave a mess for his successor, namely whoever the commissioners appointed to serve the two years left in his four-year term. When first elected, he *had* inherited a disorganized office from predecessor Mort Wilson, a likeable fellow who spent more time at his ranch with thoroughbred appaloosas than minding the legal business of the county. When the time came, Matthew didn't want to hand over a similar catastrophe to his replacement. He had decided he would throw support to his chief deputy, Myra Santiago, a class act and great lawyer.

After three hours at his desk, Matthew was ready to go home and walked to his car parked in back of the courthouse. Light from the third floor splashed onto the dark lot. He looked up. It came from Nick Vargas's commissioner office. In front of the large window, Vargas paced like an expectant father, animated and grinning. He then shook hands with a person out of Matthew's vision.

Matthew checked his watch. Twenty to midnight. He spit. Vargas better not be with another county commissioner, which would have constituted a quorum and an illegal meeting. He had already warned the three elected officials about such a violation when they used to gather for coffee in the back room of the Mesa Café before their regular and officially notified meetings.

He should have gone up there and checked, but he was exhausted. Instead, he got in his car and drove home, certain that something had gone down on the third floor.

Chapter 9

At a little past midnight, Nick Vargas walked spryly to his car parked a block from the courthouse at Victor's Garage. He paid fifty bucks a month for a protected site there because he disliked the county lot. His new Lexus had been scratched the first day he left it there, even though it was parked in the Reserved for Commissioner spot.

He loved that new red car, which was as sleek as a woman's thigh. In Albuquerque, he put so much money down he got a spectacular deal. Running his hand along the hood, he smiled. He fucking deserved that car. Walking along, he whistled at the mostly positive reception to the resort. He'd drag the town and county into prosperity with his hands and teeth if he had to. He'd make money and the naysayers could kiss his flat butt. That included Matthew Riley.

As Vargas unlocked the door, a gust of hot wind slapped his face.

"Whew, stinks."

Worse than a thousand dead bloated cows. The commissioner made a note on his phone to complain to the city about an open sewer line. They couldn't have such a bad smell on Main Avenue and not so near the festival.

The wind disappeared just as quickly as it arose, but the smell lingered. A new odor took its place.

Smoke.

Vargas glanced up the street. A line of fire raced toward him. The yellow and orange flames wavered like wings. He clicked his keys but the door wouldn't open. He pulled forcefully at the handle and heard only the inhalation of breath between his gritted teeth.

"To hell with this." He started to run away.

The licks of fire were on him so fast Nick Vargas didn't even have time to scream.

Chapter 10

Max Castro was too old and tired to hurry. Fact was, he hadn't hurried since 1985 and saw no reason to do so at this time in his life.

"No need to rush, Lupita," he told his best mule as they rode along the top of a cragged arroyo seven miles northwest of Guadalupe.

With brownish teeth, he grinned. What a figure he must cut, one right out of southwestern lore. Grizzled, long white mustache, poncho over his white shirt and jeans, and huge straw hat. He probably resembled Emiliano Zapata's granddaddy or maybe even a way older version of Andy García, his favorite actor.

His cell phone buzzed in his front pocket. So much for his visions of the old Southwest.

On the phone was his daughter asking his whereabouts. She always worried about him as if he were as ancient as the land over which Lupita walked. His daughter's concerns had increased ten-fold after his wife died five years before, which left him alone at their little ranch. So she had moved in without even asking him if she could. Still, she was a good cook and kept the house cleaner than he would. That helped when his bones felt dried out as the bottom of the arroyo.

"Okay, okay, I'm heading home," he told his daughter in Spanish. "Be there in twenty minutes. Just taking Lupita out for a spin. Don't worry about me, *hija*. Bye."

Putting the phone away in his pocket, he grabbed the bottle of water hanging from a string on his saddle and took a swig. "Lupita, she must think I'm a baby the way she checks up on me. She's a bigger nag than her mother, God rest her soul." He took another drink of the lukewarm water. "It *is* hot as hades out here. Even hotter, I bet, but I don't want to find out until it's my turn to go." He gave a crackled laugh and rode on. During the summer, he always rode out at six before the desert heated to unbearable conditions.

Removing his hat, he drew out his handkerchief and wiped at the salty perspiration stinging his eyes. When he could see again, he focused on a human form spread over a rock in the arroyo some thirty feet below the ledge. The man's legs and arms shot straight out as if he were trying to fly off the rock.

"Somebody must be hurt, Lupita. This land can be cruel." Cursing his aging eyesight, Max Castro got down from the mule. Standing right on the edge, his old face turned stony with disbelief and alarm.

The man on the rock had no skin.

Chapter 11

As Matthew drove up, a deputy puked on the side of the gravel road. The lawman bent over like a muscular jackknife tossing his breakfast into a spray of barrel cactus.

"This is not good," Matthew said out loud.

Sheriff's jeeps and patrol cars, and an ambulance lined up on one side of the dirt road. Matthew parked and walked slowly. He was in no rush to see what had made a deputy vomit like a queasy kid. Several other deputies gazed down into the arroyo, several shaking their heads. An old man sat in a patrol car visibly shaking with fright, while an equally old mule was tied to the bumper.

Benny met him. His friend's usual smile was long gone and he was as green as a young toad. "Thanks for coming, Matthew."

"What the hell? Your dispatcher didn't tell me anything but to get my ass over here."

"You've got to see this for yourself, Matthew."

Benny led him down a jagged path into the arroyo. On top of a sizable flat bolder, a gray blanket covered a body. Benny signaled another deputy, who pulled it off and turned his head away from what he had revealed.

"Jesus Christ." Matthew's own stomach undulated. He was glad he'd skipped eggs that morning.

The body of a man lay on its back. Every piece of flesh had been peeled off, leaving only purplish-red sinew and muscle. Its white eyes stared up at the sky. The effect was that of the melancholy essence of man. A creature rendered unfinished. Either that or punished.

Matthew had never seen a body so ravaged.

Along with the awful sight, a reality thumped him right between the eyes. Namely, how frail was the human body. He had seen dead people before. His Grandpa Paul and Grandma Juana. A fatality on the highway as he drove home from college on spring break. As for the murder cases he had prosecuted, he only examined the crime and autopsy photos of the victims and that was bad enough.

Until he walked down into the arroyo.

The body on the rock had been stripped to the essentials of humanity and it made his mouth dry with uneasiness.

Even without the flesh, Matthew recognized the victim.

"Nick Vargas."

"Skinned like a deer. Face to toe. We found his clothes nearby. His money and credit cards still in his wallet, but Matthew . . ." Benny dug his hands into pockets.

"What?"

"We can't find his skin."

"You've got to be fucking kidding."

"I don't think I could kid like that. I got deputies searching for it."

He asked Benny for a pair of latex gloves and got down on his knees. He moved the head of the late county commissioner to one side. "You've skinned deer, Benny."

"Yeah, I get one every fall. You never want to go with me."

"What can I say? I'm a wimp but is it ever easy to remove the skin off an animal?"

"No, it ain't easy."

"Well, this killer did a bang-up job." Matthew stood up and brushed dirt from this clothing.

"This is what I noticed." Wearing gloves also, Benny pushed the body onto its side.

A deep rough cut started at the middle of the body's head and ended at the lower back.

"You telling me whoever did this sliced Nick down the back and pulled off the skin?"

"That's the only explanation—to me, anyway."

Matthew touched the dry rock. "And there's no blood anywhere. There should be gallons of it. So he wasn't killed here."

"There's no weapon neither, least that we could find. And we didn't spot any footprints or tire tracks within a hundred feet of the body, except for the old man and his mule. My boys are still looking though."

"You make it sound like Nick Vargas was dropped out of the sky onto that rock."

"Matthew, you always did have a good way with words." Benny signaled for an ambulance crew at the top of the arroyo to come retrieve the body.

They stepped out of the way.

"The police reported that Nick's Lexus is still parked downtown." Benny pushed his hat back.

"I saw him at the courthouse near midnight, so he must have been snatched from there."

"What the hell was he doing there so late?"

"Talking with somebody in his office. I didn't see who, but Vargas looked like he had just won the lottery."

"Well, he didn't." Benny pulled his hat lower on his forehead. "That's all we need is a maniac running around and right before the festival."

"I'd say this goes way beyond your average psycho. We're talking about the kind of killer who deserves his own movie of the week."

"We should go talk with the guy who found the body."

"We?"

Benny smiled a bit. "Come on. Aren't you a little curious? Don't you want to uncover the truth?"

"Quit playing to my nosy streak, bro."

Matthew loosened his tie. Glancing back as the crew loaded the body into black plastic, he was cold even though it was ninety degrees in the shade.

****

Every bit of Max Castro trembled, from his lower lip to the hand he held out for Matthew to shake when he introduced himself.

"You see anybody around here before you spotted the body?" Benny asked in Spanish.

"No one."

"No passing cars or trucks? No one on foot or motorbike?"

"I swear to God, Sheriff. I didn't see anybody for the last hour. Nobody comes out here much anyway. The road's too tough. I was alone when I saw that thing."

"Max, were you acquainted with Nick Vargas?" Matthew said. His Spanish fluency was thanks to his mother and useful in a town where half of the population was Spanish surname.

"He's the county commissioner, no?"

"Yes. Ever meet him?"

"Once when he came to our house looking for a vote. You mean that's him down there?"

"Could be."

Castro's quivering ramped up even more. "If celebrities like him are killed, what chance do the rest of us have?"

Good question, Mr. Castro, Matthew thought.

One of Benny's deputies ran up to them. "A lady is at the roadblock and wants to see her father. She's screaming and carrying on."

"That's my daughter, all right." Castro hung his head in embarrassment.

Benny looked up at Matthew for guidance. They didn't have to speak. Matthew nodded.

"You can go, Max, but please don't mention what you saw out here to anyone else," Matthew said. "The sheriff will probably have more questions later."

"That means don't leave the county without checking in with me," Benny said.

They helped the old man to his feet. "Where am I going to go? One thing I can tell you, I'll probably have nightmares for the rest of my life, at least what's left of it."

As soon as the back doors of the ambulance shut, Isabel sped up in her small red Toyota truck, raising dust behind her. Camera hanging from her neck, hands full with a notebook and pen, she dashed out and toward Matthew and Benny, but Deputy Jackson Rogers stood in her way at the barriers set up across the dirt road.

"Isabel, stop here. Benny's orders. No reporters at the scene." Rogers held out his brute arms.

"Why?"

"We haven't completed our investigation. We'll have a statement for you later." Benny came up behind Rogers followed by Matthew.

Isabel tapped her pen against the notebook. One side of her mouth tipped up in a smile. "The last time you said that, Benny, there was a murder. And when was that, four or five years ago?" She glanced at the ambulance. "My God, it is a murder."

With his eyes, Benny pled to Matthew for help dealing with such a strident reporter. Both of them knew her to be as tenacious as a medieval tax collector short of his quota.

"We're busy here. Can't you just cooperate for damn once, Isabel?" Matthew said.

"No, I can't." Her lips curled up and she inched forward.

"This will take a little time. We don't have all the information." Benny took steps forward so she would back up. He towered a head and a half taller, but she didn't move.

"The public deserves the information. Haven't you guys ever heard of freedom of the press?"

The sun felt as if it burned a hole in the top of Matthew's head, and she wasn't helping. "Isabel, you work for the *Guadalupe News Journal*, not the damn *Washington Post*. Give us a break, will you? Let Benny do his job and he'll give you a statement later. He's got work to do."

He and Benny walked back toward the ambulance.

Isabel tried to follow, but Rogers cut her off and ordered her to retreat across the road and well away from the action.

She did so grudgingly and called after. "I'm going to write an editorial about this." She took up her camera and started taking photos.

"Well, just spell my name right," Matthew called back to her.

Chapter 12

Isabel decided that she'd wait out Matthew and Benny and hit them with more questions when the opportunity arose. She put her hair into a ponytail and walked over to a healthy stand of pinon pine trees on the other side of the road. This place was familiar. She smiled when she remembered. She and Matthew had picked pinon nuts from those trees the first year they were married. They roasted the nuts at home and ate them with beer in front of their fireplace.

The vantage spot was a good one. She could see what was going on *and* get out from under the sun. To her camera, she attached a telephoto lens she had to buy herself from Amazon since the newspaper wouldn't give her money for it. Through the lens, she watched Matthew and Benny talking. Their faces were as severe as she'd ever seen them. They both glanced in her direction every so often.

Something was definitely up.

There was an ambulance, so someone was either dead or seriously injured. And she bet it meant a homicide if Matthew the Prosecutor was there. She tapped her foot with excitement and then stopped.

God, someone probably was killed.

But that damn Matthew and damn Benny weren't telling her anything.

It would do no good to argue with a lawyer, anyway. She'd already experienced that while married to Matthew. When they had a disagreement, he'd try his legalese on her and she just told him to shove it. Although she had to admit that when she observed him in court, it rang her bell. He was so confident and intelligent. And he looked tremendous in his three-piece suits. He'd come home after a trial and she'd pull him into the bedroom if Angel was at his friend's house.

Lighting up a cigarette, Isabel blew out the smoke in exasperation that he could still drive her so crazy. When they were married, they'd often make up in bed after arguing. The sex was remarkable. Toward the end, they had a lot of sex.

Damn Matthew.

She took a drink of water from the bottle she always carried in her backpack. No time to think about him now. She did plenty of that at night. Before going to sleep, she considered calling him and working harder to solve their problems. Through their separation, she refused to change the byline on her news stories from Isabel Riley back to Isabel Sánchez. She prayed that he would call her. She didn't want him to go to Albuquerque. Often, she fell asleep with her hand on her cell phone.

"Shit," she said out loud. "Get your head in the game, girl."

Her editor at the *Guadalupe News Journal* preached to the staff that there was no such thing as a dull story, only dull reporters. She didn't want to be one of those, so she persistently asked loads of questions, conducted thorough research, took copious notes, and shot several photos in a town where breaking news predominately consisted of car accidents, drug busts, and bar fights. As a result, the proposed resort development outside of town had become a major story, along with the city's ban of skateboards on Main Avenue sidewalks. Then again, that's what she liked about Guadalupe. Not a lot of crime. She felt safe there and grateful that their son was safe there. Angel Patrick Riley may not always live a life without turmoil or aggression, but she was going to do everything she could so that he enjoyed the peace and quiet for as long as possible.

Sadly, the peace and quiet *had* gone to hell that day, and she just had to find out why.

The sparse dark green branches offered shade but not much escape from the summer heat and she was angry at herself because she'd forgotten to rub on sunscreen. She called her editor Brian Stoop.

"Yeah, I think somebody's been murdered, but Matthew and Benny aren't giving me any details—yet."

"Stay there until they do," said Stoop, who took gruffness to a whole new level.

"Exactly what I was planning." Isabel knew how to handle him, which consisted of not taking his shit.

"I have every confidence you'll get us a good story. You better." The editor hung up.

Isabel puffed away on her cigarette, again promising herself to quit. The ambulance drove off, probably to the morgue at the Mesa Hills Hospital. Then an old man and a middle-aged woman left with a mule in tow. Isabel snapped a shot of them just in case they were important to the case. They had to be eyewitnesses or related to the victim. She couldn't identify them, which was unusual, since she'd come to recognize a lot of people through her newspaper work. Still, somebody at the paper might. That way she could track them down for an interview to find out what they saw, what they knew. She just hoped the old man and woman would be talkative because Benny and Matthew weren't.

Isabel didn't notice that above her a flattened hand and arm wriggled down from the branch of the pinon tree. Pulled forward by its own weight, the flesh slithered like a deflated snake. From the hand fell a drop of blood, which hit Isabel's right cheek. Expecting sap from the tree, she brushed it off with her fingers and saw the red. She looked up at Nick Vargas's compressed face, very rubbery and lifeless. There were no eyes, just black holes. Before she could move out of the way, the entire skin that used to cover the body of the county commissioner dropped over her face and shoulders.

Isabel never screamed, but did so now with all her existence. She threw off the skin, sped by the deputies, and ran right into Matthew's arms.

Chapter 13

Matthew examined the skin crumpled on the ground. When faced with such dreadfulness, a person's first reaction should be yelling and crying like Isabel, but this abomination wrenched his gut because it wracked the normalcy he had both hated and in which he took comfort. He picked up one of the flattened arms. It flopped about.

"Holy fucking shit." Though inarticulate, his words were so damn appropriate.

"You got that right," said Benny standing near.

On Benny's orders, Isabel had been led away from the tree and told to sit in his sheriff's cruiser, which was kept running to provide her air conditioning in all the heat. The sheriff's forensic deputy took photos of the thing on the ground. The click and flash of his camera transformed the scene into a surreal tableau.

Benny glanced up at the branches. "How and why was it even in that tree?"

"That, my dear sheriff, is just one of the many thousand questions in this case," he said.

First stopping at his car, Matthew joined Isabel inside Benny's rig. He held out a can of beer to her. "I always carry a six-pack in the trunk of my car. No telling when you need a drink."

"I'd say this more than qualifies."

He opened the can and handed it to her, which she sipped with quaking hands.

She puckered her lips. "Never did like beer much, remember?"

"Yeah, I remember, but you need a slug. I'm sorry it's warm."

Isabel still shivered. He put his arm around her as though she was formed out of the finest glass and might break. She nestled into him and he experienced the same rush he felt when he had held her through bad times and mostly through the good. The shock of her warmth caused his heartbeat to rev up like a new car.

"I guess you finally got your exclusive, Isabel."

A tear glided down her face.

"Sorry." He squeezed her arm and pulled out a shredded tissue from his pocket. With great care, he took her chin and moved it up so he could dry her face. A lovely face. Even lovelier with her eyes luminous with tears.

"The most important story of my life and I blow it, Mateo. I scream and cry like a kid who saw the boogeyman. I should have been more professional. I should have had more guts. I *should* have taken a photograph of the skin."

"Even if you did, Benny would've taken away your camera."

"That photo would probably have been picked up by a national wire service, but no. I folded like a wet tortilla." Another tear spilled and she harshly wiped at it. "Worse, I became part of the story."

"You did great under the circumstances. Not everyone could hold up so well after a human skin fell over their shoulders."

"Oh my God, it really did. What is going on?"

Benny opened the door. "She okay?"

"She's tough," Matthew said. He and Isabel got out of the vehicle.

The three of them watched another crew as it loaded what was left of Nick Vargas in the ambulance. Isabel's sad face changed to irritation. A yellow van belonging to the local

TV station drove up to the wooden barriers, which had been moved farther down the road after the latest discovery.

"Damn those TV people," she said. "Benny, please give me back my camera."

"Sorry, you'll get it later."

Isabel snapped out of her grief. "This isn't a police state, Benny."

"No, but it is a crime scene."

"She didn't get any photos of the skin. It's okay," Matthew said.

Benny handed her the camera.

"Get out your notebook and pen," Matthew told her and she did. "The sheriff's office is investigating a suspected murder. The body was discovered a little after seven this morning at an arroyo seven miles northwest of town. The cause of death is still to be determined. The family of the deceased will first be notified before the release of the victim's identity. There's your statement. You can write about the skinned part but we won't confirm it."

Isabel threw down her pen. "Go to hell, both of you."

Matthew grinned to Benny. "Didn't I tell you she's okay?"

****

Matthew was impressed. "Just look at this place."

He and Benny drove under a wrought iron sign that proclaimed CASA DE VARGAS in the fanciest of metal lettering. Set down in a new subdivision just outside of Guadalupe, the Vargas house looked more at home in Italy than in the desert. Peach stucco walls, red tiled roof, fountain in a courtyard. Arched doorways made of stone.

"I had no idea he was so fat," Benny said.

"You saw how the guy dressed. He had *dinero*, man. And it all goes to his widow, Mrs. Vargas."

"Don't tell me you suspect the wife?" Benny gave a smile.

"Why are you grinning like a cat?"

"Have you seen her?"

"At a county Christmas party."

"Then that's why I'm smiling."

Patty Vargas opened the door. She stood five feet though her blonde curls made her appear taller. She probably weighed one hundred and six pounds soaking wet with cement. A woman all pretty porcelain and puff. Standing behind her was another woman, who looked like an older version of Patty, though a tad taller. She was introduced as her mother, Carolyn.

Patty Vargas had called the law enforcement office about her missing husband when he didn't return home the night before.

"Mrs. Vargas, I'm so sorry," Benny said as he and Matthew stood in the foyer.

"Where's Nick? Is he okay? When's he coming home?"

"We found your husband's body this morning." Benny used the voice he saved for delivering bad news.

The tiny woman seemed to shrink even more. Her large blue eyes exploded with tears. Her mother held her daughter's arm and led Matthew and Benny into the living room.

The women sat on a blue silk couch. He and Benny sat on matching chairs facing them.

"How? How did he die?" Patty Vargas choked out through copious tears.

Benny said nothing, so Matthew swallowed air and continued. "Nick was skinned."

"Pardon?" her mother said.

"Someone cut the skin off every inch of his body." Benny wrapped his fingers together as he spoke.

The new widow cried out. "Who would do that? Was he robbed?"

"No, ma'am." Benny shuffled his feet, obviously uncomfortable with not only having to convey sad tidings, but bizarre ones.

"Dear God," her mother said. "Who did this?"

"It had to be a psycho person, Mom," Patty Vargas muttered through her crying.

"I agree," Benny said. "Have you seen any strangers around your house?"

"No, no." She dotted her face with tissue.

"It's kind of an exclusive area so we would have noticed any unsavory types," said her mother with a touch of pride in her voice.

"Mrs. Vargas, did Nick tell you that he had ever been threatened?" Matthew said.

A shaken head. "He didn't seem afraid of anything or anyone. He didn't even own a gun."

"I knew him in school. Nick *was* tough."

"Sounds like a psycho did this," her mother interjected.

"Did he say where he was going last night?"

Mrs. Vargas drew more tissues out of the box. "He was going to that presentation about the development. That's all he said."

"When was the last time you heard from him?"

"He called me about eleven last night and said he was going to be late. He was meeting with some people and would come home straight after that."

"Did he say who he was meeting?" Benny said.

She shook her head again, this time while blowing her nose.

"What was his mood when you talked with him?" Matthew said.

"He was excited. He said the presentation about that development went well." She began crying again. "He also told me our future was set. That's exactly how he put it: 'Baby, our future is set.'"

Mrs. Vargas broke down again and stood up. "If you're done with your questions, I'm going to lie down for a while." Her mother started to follow, but she put out her hand. "I'll be okay, Mom." She headed up a designer staircase, but then, the whole house could have starred in its own TV show.

After she had left, her mother Carolyn mixed a large whiskey and water from the bar. She held up a glass, but Matthew and Benny declined. The older woman sat back on the silk couch. Wearing a white blouse and black skirt, she had the legs of a senior Rockette.

"I knew Nick would either end up governor of this state or dead." She sipped the drink.

"Why do you say that?" Matthew said.

"He didn't talk about his business."

"A lot of men don't."

"Once I asked him straight out about his financial status. He laughed and said Patty would always be taken care of, and then told me to mind my business. He was too damn ambitious for his own good. Always talking the big deal."

"Any specific ones?" Benny said.

"He wouldn't shut up about that Desert Thorn place."

"Desert Rose?" Matthew said.

"That's the one." The woman polished off the drink, got up, and poured another. "I guess that's what ambition gets you."

"What?"

"Sticking your nose where it doesn't belong. You can let yourself out."

She followed her daughter upstairs.

Chapter 14

In the basement morgue of the Mesa Hills Hospital, Dr. Rosemary Whitney slipped a white sheet off of the skinned body of Nick Vargas. Matthew wore a mask but that didn't cut down on the smell of death. The odor of conclusiveness burrowed into his nostrils and probably wouldn't fade for days. He'd definitely have to have his suit cleaned.

This was the first time he had attended an autopsy and never wanted to see another. The contrast between the silver metal, white tile of the room, and the marred remains of a human was disquieting and tragic. He didn't have to attend this one, but couldn't escape it because of the inexplicable way Vargas had died. A mix of the curious and professional drew him there.

Standing at the back of the room with Benny, he couldn't help but bite the tip of his tongue with a question. How could anyone explain what lay on the metal table? Nick Vargas wasn't a tall man, but his body looked even smaller on the stainless steel. Death never left a human in a grand state, but this was obscene.

Weariness slid up Matthew's bones. He had always believed in black on white, words on paper. Passages in law books. This murder had opened up a wormhole into that belief and he hated it.

Doc Whitney, as she was called by anyone she liked, stood over the body and exhibited intense concentration. Known for her efficient and empathic medical skills, her focus was like a Ginsu knife. It could slice through anything. She had taken the coroner's job out of what Matthew called a perverted sense of public service and because no one else wanted the post. In other counties, the coroner didn't have to be a doctor. He or she just had to run for office and perform administrative duties, while a medical examiner conducted the review of dead bodies. Mesquite County was fortunate to have Whitney as both coroner and medical examiner. The county agreed to up her salary to reflect both duties, but she was worth it. Whitney had extensive experience in forensic pathology from working at a New Orleans hospital before moving out to the desert. As for the administration side, she knew how to delegate.

Socially, he also liked her very much. Once a month, he and Isabel used to have dinner with Doc Whitney and her girlfriend, a slender dentist named Selma Teague. They were the only open lesbians in Guadalupe, although he guessed there were probably many more who just didn't come out as Whitney had. Most of the town residents accepted them because they were so likable, except for the few members of an ultra-conservative church on the outskirts of town who didn't like most people anyway. Those same church members would probably have called Vargas's murder the work of the devil, and he couldn't disagree with them in this instance. The exception: he wanted the devil caught and prosecuted.

Under Doc Whitney's rubber gloves, turquois and silver rings covered several fingers on both hands as she inspected the body with a magnifying glass. Long earrings of the same gem and metal hung from her ears. Her red hair was cut short and stylish. She had commanded Matthew and Benny to hold their questions until she finished her preliminary examination. So, they just watched her and lifted the masks they wore to drink lukewarm coffee that tasted slightly of alcohol.

Methodically, she scraped under the fingernails of the body. Whatever was there went into a glass dish that she handed to her forensic tech, a spindly young man with spindly black hair. Even though the tech wore protective gear, Matthew could tell he was pallid from the sight of this corpse.

"Jim, you okay?" Whitney asked.

"Yeah."

"Well, just don't throw up."

"I'll try not to."

"Good." With long tweezers she removed something from the cut at the back of the body and placed the specimen on a glass slide that she looked at under a microscope.

"Hmmm," she said.

Matthew wanted to ask what was so damn interesting, but knew better while she was so occupied.

"I'm going to make the chest incisions," the doctor said and switched on a digital recorder to note her findings.

"Time to go have a real cup of coffee," Matthew told Benny.

At the hospital cafeteria on the first floor, they bought fresher brew and doughnuts, which they didn't touch.

Matthew studied his friend. Benny hadn't said much since the arroyo.

"What's up?" he asked him in Spanish as they sat at a table. "You look like you were the one who got skinned. Come on, tell me, bro."

"I just hate to see this shit happening in my county. Big-city, serial-killer, wacko shit."

"I understand."

Benny held onto his coffee cup with both hands. "I feel like a failure." His eyes dimmed.

Matthew grinned, put a stick of gum in his mouth, and held one out to Benny. "You're not a failure if you find the killer. Then, *compadre*, you'll be a fucking hero."

"Asshole." Benny grinned back and took the gum. "You're not going to let me feel bad, are you?"

"Nope." He blew a bubble.

After an hour, Whitney called Benny on his cell phone to say she was examining the skin and asked if they wanted to join her.

"Shall we?" Benny said.

"It's not as if we see a crime like this every day," Matthew answered.

"Our first psycho killing in the county."

"We've escaped insane murderers this long. We were probably long overdue."

"I hope it's the last."

"Me, too."

Before entering the room, he and Benny again donned masks, as well as clothing protection, safety glasses, and gloves, as the doctor had asked. As they went in, the tech exited, appearing even pastier.

Matthew gulped at the site of Vargas's chest slit open from the autopsy, but then again, the body had already been so ravaged. As if reading his mind, the doctor replaced the white sheet over the body and turned to the skin laid out on another metal table. When it had fallen on Isabel's head, the skin was rumpled, but the doctor had spread it out so that it came off as a dejected flat puppet. She sliced off one of the arms and flipped it inside out. The sheer craziness of watching the doctor work with human skin held Matthew in place as if his feet were stuck in quicksand.

With a magnifying glass, she carefully inspected the skin and then stopped to extract something with tweezers. Whatever she extracted went onto a slide, which again went under the microscope. She worked delicately as if the skin would fall apart in her hands. At last, she covered the remains.

"That was certainly gross," she announced in her rough smoker's voice.

"How scientific, Doc," Matthew said. "What can you tell us really?"

"When I worked in New Orleans, I encountered a lot of bat shit stuff, but this beats that all to hell."

"What was the cause of death?" Benny said.

"Nick Vargas died of massive blood loss and shock, which is no surprise since his skin was peeled off."

"You'd think a person could live without it, at least without a lot of it," Benny said.

"No way. The skin is the body's largest organ. It weighs about six pounds for adults and covers twenty-two square feet."

Benny whistled.

"Your skin carries blood vessels, sweat glands, and nerves, and it regulates a body's temperature, among lots of other important functions. You can see that without it, you're dead."

"I can see that, Doc."

"What about that wound down the back? Benny thinks that's where the killer started," Matthew said.

"I think he's right about that. The incision cut through the epidermis and dermis, which is quite a feat."

"Doc, English please," Benny said.

"That's the two layers of the skin, from the thickest part on his heels to the thinnest on his eyelids. There were no other knife wounds. Except for the incisions down the back and around the eyelids, it's almost whole. The skin apparently came off in one piece from fingers to toes."

He and Benny exchanged WTF looks.

"It is extraordinary. I don't think I've even read about a death like this," she said.

"I saw him at midnight the night before at the courthouse and the old guy on the mule spotted the body at seven this morning. Can you determine the time of death?" Matthew said.

Her eyebrows raised above the mask in an obvious smile.

"What's funny, Doc?" Benny said with sharpness in his voice.

"The body's temperature is still ninety-seven degrees."

"That's strange, right?"

"Extremely, bodies will start losing heat at about one and a half degrees per hour after death. And it's been eight hours since the body was discovered. Body temperature is one way we can determine time of death."

"Can you explain it?"

"I can't even comprehend it. There's no sign of rigor mortis, which should start within one to two hours after a person dies. After thirty-six hours, the muscles lose rigor." She lifted the sheet off of Vargas's body and picked up the right hand, which was limp. "This should be as stiff as an ironing board."

"So you can't tell us the time of death?" Matthew said.

"Not under these conditions." She replaced the sheet over the body. "And don't you two give me the fish eye for saying this, but some kind of crude weapon was probably used to cut off his skin."

"Define crude."

"Like it was made out of sharpened stone."

"That's pretty crude."

"You talking caveman crude?" Benny said.

"Take a look in the microscope."

Matthew obliged, first raising the eye protection. Then, Benny took a turn.

"I found black shards of this rock scattered throughout the wound and under the skin." She stood up and rubbed the back of her neck. "I didn't think that was scientifically possible, but here it is."

"That's damn impossible." Benny took off his hat and whipped it across his legs. "When I skinned my deer last season, there was no way to take it off in one nice piece."

"I can't explain it, Benny, but check it out."

They gathered around the metal table with the skin. "Look at the area around the eyes and nails. Despite the rough weapon, it was sharp enough not to shred the skin. A very neat trick."

"You're right, Doc. That's fucking strange," Matthew said. "So what kind of stone?"

"I'm no rock hound, but it looks like obsidian."

"Obsidian can be very sharp," Benny said.

"How the hell do you know?" Matthew poked his ribs.

"From our time as Boy Scouts that summer before we got kicked out. We were studying Indian arrowheads."

"As I recall, the troop leader had good cause for kicking us out."

"Whoever did this knew what he was doing," Benny said.

"Like a doctor?" She barked out a laugh and raised her arms. "I didn't do it, Sheriff. And I have an alibi for the night Nick was killed. Just ask my girlfriend."

"That won't be necessary," Matthew said.

"The killer was skilled at, well, skinning, be it animal or human. And that is an unusual talent in any murderer's book," the doctor said.

"This is a terrible question, Rosemary, but was Nick Vargas still alive when he was flayed?" Matthew said softly.

"Because of the odd state of the body, I can't say. I really can't but I *hope* he was dead, or else he would have suffered something awful. Come on, let's get out of here."

She led them into an outer room where they shed their protective gear in the hazardous materials bin. Once in the hall, they all took a deep breath of air-conditioned air.

"I'll order tox tests as a matter of course. I'm also going to send the body and the skin to the state crime lab in Albuquerque to see if they concur or find anything else," Whitney said. "I'll tell them we want the results ASAP."

"Rosemary, thanks," Matthew said, and Benny nodded in agreement.

"After I finish up here, I'm heading home to share a liberal glass of wine with Selma. After what I've seen today, I may have two or three." She lit up a cigarette, despite the No Smoking sign in the hospital.

When Matthew and Benny stepped outside, the day's temperature had decreased, but only slightly.

"This has been the most extraordinary day in my whole life." He took off his tie.

"You said it," Benny said. "There's only one cure for that."

"Okay, but I'm buying because I make more money than you do."

****

At Joey's Bar, owner Joey Méndez brought two icy beers to Matthew and Benny, who sat at a booth in the back. Behind Joey's heavy mustache was the ready smile he reserved for the paying customers. "There you go, guys. Anything for the law."

"Thanks, Joey," said Matthew who had removed his jacket and rolled up his sleeves. He pushed the wedge of lime into the beer bottle. The brew was his second for the night, but after what he'd witnessed in the arroyo and at the hospital morgue, he wished it had been his tenth.

"How were those chicken tacos?" Joey said.

He gave a thumb up.

"Good, man." Benny rubbed a small circle over his belly.

Pulling up a chair, Joey sat at the end of the table. "So, is it true?"

"Is what true?" Benny asked the husky bar owner.

"Rumor around town is that Nick Vargas was peeled like a green chili. Come on, give me all the details. You can trust me." He put his elbows on the table.

"Joey, anything we told you would end up on your reader board like the daily special," Matthew said.

"Maybe I could help with the case. I hear a lot of gossip around this bar." He scooted closer and spoke conspiratorially. "Would you like me to tell you how many times I've heard people say they wish so-and-so was dead or how they'd like to kill so-and-so? It's very disturbing."

"We'll call if we need you."

Joey stood and shoved his hands in his jeans pockets. "Okay, but when the bodies start piling up, don't say I didn't offer to help." The bar owner waved to customers who entered and left their table.

Matthew drank his beer. Across the table, Benny knotted and unknotted his fingers.

"It's been quite the day, *compadre*," Matthew said.

"Yes, it has."

Matthew didn't use the term lightly. He and Benny were *compadres*. That's what people of Mexican heritage called those who became extended family through weddings and baptisms. Officially, Benny became his *compadre* when he stood up as best man at his wedding and when he and his wife Camilla had baptized his son Angel. Unofficially, he and Benny were family because they had grown up together, got drunk together. Protected each other. Matthew believed he could read Benny's mind about most anything, but not that night. Come to think of it, Benny's thoughts had become as shrouded as a morning fog over the Sangre Mountains to the north.

"Benny, you look like your head's going to explode at any second. What do you want to say?"

"We're just having a drink, Mateo."

"Don't jerk me around, Benjamin Manuel Ortega. It's late and I got heartburn from Joey's damn tacos."

"About this case. About Nick's murder." His head lowered. "I'm fucking lost, man."

"That's no surprise. What happened was pretty messed up."

"Yeah, it was."

"Prosecutors usually don't get involved at this stage of an investigation. So, tell me, Sheriff, why did you want me to see the crime scene? To go to Nick Vargas's house? And it's not just because I'm such fun to have around."

At that moment, Benny's massive shoulders drooped to his waist. He took a fast drink of beer and glanced around the bar, which was quiet for once with only a few customers. "Mateo, you know and I know that I'm not the smartest man in town."

Matthew held his lips together at the truth of it. Benny's intellect was no match for his good nature, loyalty, or his strength. A "C" student all through school, his friend seemed to get by because people loved him. Benny would laugh at your jokes, not try to steal your girl, and lend money he couldn't afford to lend.

"You've done fine, man. You graduated the police academy. You have to have smarts for that."

"Let's face it. I've always needed your help, even in school. I wouldn't have graduated if it wasn't for you. You let me cheat off you for years. Hell, you even helped me get elected sheriff." He downed his drink.

Benny, who was a deputy at the time, had won the seat nine years ago from Sheriff Mike Weathers. A man of infinite impatience, Weathers had nothing good to say in private—or public for that matter—about the substantial Hispanic population or the smaller black community of the county. While Weathers was in office, the number of profiling cases doubled, which outraged the public both Hispanic, black, and otherwise. Benny was encouraged to run for the office by almost everyone who knew him. Matthew ran his campaign, and his friend won by a landslide and then some.

"I'm in way over my head on this murder. You can see the big picture when I can barely see down the street. I need your smarts to get through this. What do you say, *compadre?* Will you take the lead with me on this?"

Matthew admired his friend's ability to cut to the truth about himself. He sat back in the booth. His decision was made. He didn't have to think about it. This man was his brother, despite the fact they didn't have the same blood in their veins. "Well, sooner or later I'd have to get involved when this murderer is charged, so you have me until I report to my new job. And if we don't solve the case by then, we're never going to solve it. After all, we're no damn CSI."

"Or FBI." Benny's grin came back in force and he stuck a toothpick in his mouth.

"Or any of those other damn acronyms." They clinked beer bottles.

"What's an acronym?"

Matthew let out a spurt of a laugh and was happy to see the old Benny return even if it was temporary.

"Any ideas?" Benny said.

"Hey, I just got on the job."

Benny motioned to Joey for two more beers.

"Let's tap the FBI guys over in Albuquerque and see if they've got any info on other skinned victims," he said.

Benny gave a twisted smile. "See, I got the right man for the job."

"Anything else going on with you?"

"*¿Por qué?*"

"Cause you're acting like you're constipated with worry. Is it Camilla? I'm here for you, bro."

His eyes lowered and then he looked up at Matthew. "I can handle it. And thanks for helping me with this case. I can tag drunk drivers and break up fights day in and day out, but this case is like trying to do algebra in Mrs. Gómez's class in high school."

"That's because when we were growing up, you never watched enough of those crime shows on TV." He grinned.

"I liked football better. And westerns."

Matthew paid the bill because he *did* make more money. Outside, a rare cool evening breeze brushed by them as they left Joey's Bar and headed back to the courthouse where their cars were parked.

"Geez, what a day." Benny wiped his forehead with a handkerchief.

"It won't be so good tomorrow, either."

Benny cocked his head.

"Isabel's story about the murder is coming out in the morning paper. People are going to get scared and paranoia will set in," Matthew said.

"Hell. I'll talk to Chief Wilson about boosting police patrols in town and I'll put on extra deputies."

"That's good. And to set the record straight, Benny, you didn't need my help getting elected. Everyone likes you much better than they like me."

Benny slapped Matthew's back with his powerful hand. "That's true."

Chapter 15

The bat cracked and Angel Riley took the bases with the zeal and energy of a nine-year-old trying out for the pros. Sitting in the stands, Matthew shot up and shouted, "Run, Angel, run," as his son slid on his butt into home plate.

The boy got up dusty and triumphant, smiling and waving at his dad. Matthew tugged down on his baseball hat and tried to concentrate on his son's game, but the flayed body of Nick Vargas stuck in the corner of his eye like a piece of grit. The FBI had reported back with little information on killers who skinned victims. The last one was in 1979 in Boston.

He sat back against the bleachers. He and Benny had no suspects. All he had was an increasing feeling in his intestine that this case was not going to end well for anybody.

He tried to clear out the negative. A breeze flowed over, easy as a lover's lips against his. He breathed in as much air as his lungs could hold. Probably to convince himself that he really was alive.

Angel was at bat again. This time he struck out. The boy's face sank with disappointment and Matthew knew exactly how he felt.

On the next play, his son skidded into third base on his hands and yelled, "shit." Then glanced up at his dad and mouthed, "sorry." The coach tended to Angel's scuffed hands and smiled at Matthew to show the kid was okay. The kid was more than okay.

Matthew took pride and pleasure in the unwavering fact that Angel was a great kid. His son split candy bars with others and made pals instantly. Angel would walk up to children in the playground and say, "I'm Angel. Want to play?" and they would. His son loved to ask questions and was not afraid of anything, which scared him a bit. But he also thanked God that Angel wasn't one of those boys whose eyes never left video games. He actually liked to be outside. He played baseball and soccer and rode his bike with his best friend from down the street.

He loved going fishing with his dad.

Matthew hoped he had helped his boy become that way, but knew Isabel had as much to do with the makeup of their son as he did.

The city league game ended with a considerable point spread for the Warriors, which was Angel's team. To celebrate, Matthew bought a hot dog and soda for his son and himself at a concession stand near the ballfield.

They sat at a picnic table. "How're your hands, son?"

Red streaks marked the palms. Angel grinned as if they were a medal.

"It doesn't hurt, Daddy. The coach sprayed them with some stuff that stung."

"Well, you were great today, Angel—a regular Sosa."

Angel rolled his blue eyes, which made him hoot. His son had Isabel's dark looks and hair color, but his blue eyes matched his dad's.

"You're just saying that 'cause I'm your kid."

"Hey, I'm a lawyer, and lawyers don't lie."

"That's not what it says on the news."

He feigned hurt and Angel laughed. "Eat your hot dog, buddy."

Angel chewed and swallowed. "These are my favorite. And I also like Mom's tacos and cheese pizza."

"You ready for your First Communion?"

Shoving the rest of his hot dog into his mouth, Angel shrugged his shoulders. "I guess."

"You don't look too happy."

"Do I got to wear that tie?"

"I'm afraid so. On the plus side, you'll get a party and lots of presents."

Angel deliberated about that. "Okay, I'll wear the tie."

With a napkin, Matthew wiped a spot of mustard off of Angel's cheek. "Your mom says you've been having bad dreams. Want to tell me about them?"

"They're pretty dumb. Just kids' dreams, and I'm still a kid."

"So tell me."

"I don't want you to laugh." Angel put his head down.

Matthew gently lifted his son's head in his hands. "I won't. I promise. So what do you dream about?"

Angel wiped his hands over his uniform. "It's the same one a lot of the time."

"The same dream?"

"Yeah. Some guys are chasing me at night. I can't see who they are, but I gotta run away 'cause they're going to hurt me if they catch me. They smell real bad. And they got zombie hands."

"Zombie hands?"

"Skin falling off. Bone's showing." He held up his hands and wiggled fingers like small claws. "Eyes like olive pits. Yuck."

"Good description, son."

"They kinda freak me out, Daddy, and here's the scariest part . . ."

"What?"

"The men howl like coyotes."

"Is that all?"

"Their howls change into something else. They turn into screams."

"Whoa. Stinky men who howl like coyotes with hands of the undead chasing you. That would scare the heck out of me, too."

"Really?"

"You bet."

"Every time I have that dream, those guys get closer and closer to me before I wake up." His blue eyes became wide as if he had seen the scary men in the daytime.

"How many times have you had that dream, son?"

"Like two times a week."

"How long has this been going on?"

"A month."

Matthew sipped his soda to hide his worry over the frequency of the dreams plaguing his son. Isabel always called Angel a special boy and not only because of his generous nature. The first sign was when Angel was six and they were having breakfast at their house. Angel stopped eating his pancakes and looked out of the kitchen window. When Isabel asked what he was looking at, he replied it was their old neighbor Mrs. Valentine planting roses in her large garden next door. "She was happy," Angel said and finished his pancakes. The trouble was Mrs. Valentine had died two weeks before. He and Isabel hadn't told Angel anything about the neighbor's death.

Isabel responded with the sign of the cross. He kept eyes on his son for the rest of the meal and the entire week. He read stories on the Internet about how children had paranormal experiences more than adults because they weren't hampered by grown-up realism. Matthew didn't buy that then, but couldn't figure out how to explain it away. His son never repeated those visions or whatever they were.

Now sitting near the ballpark, Matthew chalked up his son's bad dreams to his plans for leaving Guadalupe.

Monsters would come because he was moving away. That made him feel terrible.

"Angel, maybe you shouldn't watch scary movies and stuff like that."

"Mom won't even let me watch *The Walking Dead*. But the last time I had one of those crazy dreams with those scary guys, I woke up and I could still hear the coyotes. I ran into Mom's room."

He moved next to his son. "They're nothing. Most times, dreams don't make a lot of sense."

Angel suddenly hugged Matthew tight at his waist. "Daddy, if you come home I won't have no more nightmares." He gave a small smile, one of hope and trust in a father who would soon be gone.

Matthew wanted to cry. At that moment, he was the vilest father in the world.

"I can't come home. Your mom and I have told you why, son. It has nothing to do with you. We both love you so much."

When he and Isabel sat Angel down to tell him about their separating, their son got angry at both of them. Matthew had expected tears, but they got a scolding instead.

"You need to go talk to a priest. That's what Jimmy Conlin's folks did," Angel told them as they sat in the living room.

"Jimmy's parents ended up getting divorced," Isabel said.

"Well, that's them. You guys are smarter, right?"

"Mom and I just haven't been getting along," he had said.

Angel held up a hand. "I've heard you guys talking. I ain't dumb. Mom says you're too damn ambitious. You want a career and to leave us behind. And you tell Mom to 'comprise,' whatever that means."

"Angel, language," Isabel said. "That's *compromise*. It means to meet someone halfway."

"Well, I'm not giving up on you two, even if you give up," their son shouted and marched to his room. "Dammit," he yelled and slammed the door.

Since then, his son had reconciled to the separation, but still asked Matthew to return home each time they got together. He suggested Matthew live in the guest room until he and Isabel worked out their problems.

The kid would make a great lawyer, Matthew thought, but then hoped to hell his son wouldn't go to law school. The profession had brought him as much misery as reward.

At the ballpark, Angel made another argument for Matthew's staying. "Even if you don't come home with me and Mom, you can still stay at Grandma's house and not move so far away."

"This is a good job for me. I promise I'll visit every weekend and you're going to stay with me during the summer. We'll have a great time."

Angel didn't stop hugging. He hugged back and thought about Ronnie Calderón, the boy who went missing at the city park pool. The kid had been gone for a week. With that, he hugged his son tighter.

"You won't ever let anybody hurt me, will you?" Angel said suddenly.

"They'll have to get through me first. Even those nightmare guys with the zombie hands. Angel, I love you more than anything in the world, son. No matter where I am, I'll always love you."

Angel looked up, his eyes shining with tears. "Daddy, sometimes in my dreams, when those creepy guys are running after me, I call for you to help me and you don't come."

"I'll always come for you, Angel. Always."

"You promise?"

"Cross my heart and swear on a stack of Bibles or pancakes, whatever you like."

Angel smiled. "Okay then."

"How about some ice cream?"

The boy's head bobbed with enthusiasm.

"Good, but just don't tell your mom."

Chapter 16

"Son of a bitch."

Matthew's ball rolled into the gutter. He was trying to pick up the ten pin left behind from his first throw. The rest of his team threw catcalls and joked that they were glad he was leaving town because he was demolishing their chances to become city champs again.

"Sorry, guys. I'm tired. Unlike the rest of you, I work."

The four other team members didn't buy that and laughed.

He loved bowling night because he didn't have to think about anything except throwing balls and trying to hit the wooden pins at the end of the lane. He loved the beer drinking and dumb talk about sports with his teammates, who included Fire Chief Ben Smith and two other firefighters. But that night, Matthew's mind wasn't at the bowling alley. He missed another spare.

"Nice one, Matthew."

The remark came from Ray Sullivan, the owner of Magic Desert Lanes, who delivered a score of beers to a team of female bowlers a lane over.

Ben Smith got up and rolled a thunderous strike. "That's how it's done, bro."

"Show off," Matthew replied.

Determined to stop the laughter and get his mind on track, Matthew focused on the game and hit a strike on his next turn. He whirled around and gave a don't-give-me shit look to Ray, who had a belly like a ten-pound bowling ball.

Benny entered the bowling alley, ordered a beer, and looked at the telescore for Matthew's last game of the series.

"That sucks, *compadre*," Benny said.

"Get on some shoes, man, and see if you can beat me."

"Too bushed. Hard day at work. Weird day. Join me in the bar when you put on your street shoes."

Benny took a seat in the lounge area of the bowling alley. His friend carried a file, which he placed on the table. Matthew finished up his bowling for the night, which ended well below his usual 189 average. After putting away his equipment in his locker, he joined Benny.

"What you doing about the murder of Nick Vargas?" Ray asked Benny when he brought them beers.

"Everything we can."

"That's good because I don't want no killer skulking around town skinning people with the festival going on."

"Scoot, Ray, we got law business," Matthew said.

The owner left grumbling.

Benny looked like he was operating on two hours of sleep. "Have you gotten any rest?"

"Probably, not. Me and all the deputies and police officers spent the day chasing down tons of calls from people who claimed they saw psychos in every corner of the county."

"Anything check out?"

"*Nada.*"

Benny handed Matthew the file. "The report from the state lab."

Taking a sip of beer first, he sat and read through the state's findings about the death of Nick Vargas, which echoed Dr. Rosemary Whitney's examination. Massive blood loss. Flecks of obsidian rock scattered among the wounds on the body and inside the skin.

"She was right about that black rock," he said and then slurped his beer. "Nothing surprising so far, Benny."

"Well, read on." Benny's finger circled a paragraph. "Here, in the summary, which is all I can understand from that medical talk."

He read out loud. "Organic material recovered from under the fingernails of the deceased, as well as on the skin's surface consisted of decomposed flesh.'" He looked up at Benny. "Those lab guys must have been smoking crack."

"That's what I thought, too, but I called them. They swear the flesh came from a body that must have been in the ground for decades."

"This is fucking insane. Pardon my French."

"The lab guys were certain and pretty amazed, too. I guess the body still didn't cool off and get stiff from rigor mortis by the time they looked at it."

"Did any of that dead flesh have a match on the National DNA Database?"

"Another *nada* with a huge fat Na."

Matthew took another drink of the beer, which tasted bad because of the report. He let the beer settle in his mouth before swallowing. "All this medical mumbo jumbo aside, you realize what this is telling us?"

Benny's eyes tapered as if he was trying to come up with an answer.

"That a dead man wielding a rock knife killed Nick Vargas. That should narrow our suspects." Matthew was deadpan.

"Very funny."

"Okay, bad joke, but who handles dead people?"

"Funeral homes. Ambulances. The coroner."

"Bingo. And we already cleared Doc Whitney."

"So we check those other places to see if they have any suspicious people working for them." He grinned. "Or if any dead bodies are missing."

"Very good, Benny. See? You're getting the hang of this detective business. You don't need me after all."

"Yes I do. Damn, I hate this case."

"Get some sleep, bro. We'll start fresh tomorrow."

By the time Matthew got home from his league, his mother was sleeping. He crept into her bedroom and clicked off the television. She slept so serenely. He bit his lower lip because the world had been less than serene lately. He'd seen evidence of that at the morgue. He wished he could protect his mother and son from all the violence prowling Guadalupe like a mountain lion zeroing in on its prey.

After showering, he lay awake in his bedroom unable to sleep. After graduating law school, he and Isabel got married and lived at his mother's house until their new house had been built. They made love on the bed he had slept in as a kid and they giggled about it afterward like two teenagers sneaking away from parents. Then he moved back into that room following his separation. Same adobe color on the walls. Brown wooden blinds. Bedspread with Mexican peasant designs picked out by Isabel.

There was a comfort in the room similar to a force field in one of those sci-fi movies that Isabel loved. He needed that comfort badly. He took a melatonin pill to help him fall asleep and it helped, but he still dreamed.

He stands in the middle of the desert at night. All around him, coyotes howl but more than that. They communicate through their yips and shrieks and he's terrified they are talking about him. Behind him comes panting. He swivels. A huge coyote watches him with yellow eyes and he starts to run. Just as the coyote nears him, it shoots past and runs at Nick Vargas, who stands at the edge of the arroyo. The animal drags Vargas down into the blackness. A vivid full moon rises. Vargas climbs out of the arroyo with no skin and black cavities where his eyes are supposed to be. Vargas stumbles toward him with his hands out and mouths cries for help, but there are no words. He backs away from Vargas, whose hands wave about with a warning. He looks down. A decomposed hand grips his leg and yanks. He falls down as the hand hauls him into the chasm.

"Shit!" Matthew sat up sweating and gasping as if the dream lingered in the air.

He wondered if his son's nightmares had transferred to him. That was okay, though. Better him than Angel. In no hurry to get back to sleep, he got out of bed, went down to the kitchen, and drank two glasses of water. The last time he had a nightmare was months after his father left his mother and him when he was five. He was astounded he could remember it. He dreamed he was in the dark and kept following a yellow light, which he hoped would lead him home. When he reached the light and touched it, a sticky blackness crept over his hands and consumed his body. He woke screaming for his mother.

At six the next morning, Matthew went to his office, happy no one else was there. He couldn't seem to open his eyes all the way and the double espresso didn't do a damn thing to rouse him.

After catching up with prosecutor work, he called the Mesquite County Ambulance Service and asked the supervisor for a list of names of the paramedics and their work schedules so he could see who had been off the day Vargas was murdered. He didn't need to ask about whether the EMTs had criminal records. If they did, they weren't going to be hired in the first place. Still, one of them might have had a grudge enough to kill. He also made an appointment to meet Benny at the Guadalupe Funeral Home and Cemetery.

At eight, his staff began arriving and the phones started ringing. Matthew prepared for a meeting with his deputy attorneys later in the day. On the agenda was pending county legal issues and discussion of the criminal court cases on the docket. Previously, he had asked his chief deputy to take on more of his load, explaining his need to help out on the murder investigation. She understood.

"Besides, when I leave, you'll probably be doing this anyway," he had told her.

"Not if you stay, Matthew," she answered with a hopeful smile.

His secretary's rap on the door sounded like a battering ram that day. Holding messages and mail, Kitty Cardenas held one paper under his nose.

"Call this guy from the AG's office. Right now."

"Why?"

"Because he called twice yesterday, Matthew, and I'm getting tired of talking with him."

"And good morning to you, Kitty."

"Maybe, you'll piss him off enough so they won't want you anymore." She grinned.

"Thanks. Now get out."

She saluted and left.

Matthew called Stan Mason, who headed the AG division where he was set to work. A former college basketball player, Mason had rejected a draft offering to the NBA to go to law school. Matthew had never met anyone so fixated on the law, which was a tad intimidating.

"Heard you had trouble down that way." Mason had an impossibly deep voice.

"A skinned commissioner. Not every county can claim that."

"Any suspects?"

"I wish to God there were but I think we found a lead."

"We?"

"I'm helping out the sheriff on this investigation."

"Why?"

"Because he asked."

The seconds of silence on the phone buzzed like a jet overhead.

"I certainly hope that your assistance on that case won't interfere with your placement in our office." Mason's tone hinted that he considered murder old hat.

"Not at all, but it's vital we catch this killer."

"I daresay."

"And I'm going to give this investigation everything I can. Isn't that why you hired me in the first place?"

"We'll talk again."

Mason had the bedside manner of an iceberg.

After Matthew hung up, he swung around in his chair and looked out the large window facing the park. The day was as bright as he'd ever seen. The sky was clear and wonderfully blue as if the first one ever made by God. Residents walked in the park and on the sidewalks or drove about.

He didn't lie to Mason. And he was going to find this killer.

Chapter 17

Hector Bowden could have been called the king of the dead. He owned the Guadalupe Funeral Home, which was the largest mortuary in the county with franchises in neighboring ones. A barrel of a man in a tailored suit, Bowden exuded an air of condolence even when he was talking with a living and breathing person. Like his clothing, his office was immaculate.

He handed Matthew and Benny a list of his twenty-five employees.

"Who handles the bodies here?" Benny said.

"This is a funeral home, Sheriff. That's all we do."

Matthew blew out his breath at the man's condescension. "Hector, what we mean to say is which of your employees come in direct contact with decomposing bodies."

"I would, as well as my three assistants, but most of the bodies we collect for burial have not yet started the decomposition process. We usually pick up the deceased from the hospitals or homes within hours of their passing."

Bowden picked a piece of lint off of his jacket's lapel and shot it into the trash can. "Of course, once in a while we do run across a body that hasn't been found for several days. The last one was Mecho Hernández about six months ago. He'd been outside for almost a week before a neighbor found him. Poor man."

"His property is now the site of the Desert Rose development, so I hope the investors at least paid for his funeral," Matthew said.

"The county did." The funeral home director checked his watch.

Benny shuffled his feet, drawing him back on point. "Has anyone on your staff ever dug up one of the coffins either intentionally or by mistake?"

Bowden's head jerked as if he had been slapped. "Our business would never allow that."

"How about a person or persons unknown digging up a grave?" Matthew knew the question sounded screwy, but it well suited this case.

"Certainly not."

"You would have reported that to authorities, wouldn't you, Hector?" Benny said with graciousness.

"Absolutely, Sheriff. Are we finished? I have a family coming in to make arrangements for their dear departed."

"Just one more question. Where were you the night Vargas was killed?" Matthew said.

"How is that relevant?"

"Indulge us, please."

The man checked out his calendar. "In Santa Fe for a convention. I can provide documentation."

Benny looked at Matthew, who gave a slight nod.

"That's it for a while, Hector," Matthew said.

They left the funeral home, which was adjacent to the cemetery. With the temperature at ninety-four degrees, it was a green oasis with grass and trees. They walked to the shade of a large maple.

"So where else would people get their hands on decomposing flesh, Matthew?" Benny said.

"That's the four-million-dollar question. And I'll bet morticians aren't going to fess up so easily about whether their employees are mishandling bodies."

"Then we need to check with the other funeral homes in the county about people digging up a grave."

"First, let's have a look at that list to see who's working here." He held out the paper. "If any of them have records we can check their alibis for the night Vargas was murdered."

Benny glanced up at a backhoe rumbling out of a shed behind the funeral home. "Oh, man. They're probably digging a hole for Nick Vargas since his body was released for burial."

Matthew's eyebrows lifted. "Hey, I know one of these guys."

"Who?"

"John Juarez. Seven years ago, he got jail time for beating the shit out of two guys at a bar."

"I remember that dude. Belligerent as hell." Benny took off his hat and wiped sweat from his forehead. "But why the heck would he skin Nick?"

"He might have resented the guy for some reason, real or imagined. Let's go look for Juarez and ask him."

"We don't have to look."

"Why?"

"He's running that backhoe."

He and Benny hurried toward the machine just as Juarez noticed them. Juarez took off his sunglasses, threw them to the ground, bounded off the still running backhoe, and ran the other way. He sped through the cemetery, hurling over monuments.

"I'll stop that thing," Benny said.

Fueled on instinct, Matthew took off after Juarez. He glanced back. Benny leaped onto the backhoe, which was knocking down headstones in its path. He turned to his chase. Juarez ran a few yards ahead. He was built like a linebacker. Dense legs in jeans and muscled arms covered with sleeves of tattoos under his white T-shirt. Juarez had opened up a nice distance between them. Picking up the pace, Matthew prayed he wouldn't have a heart attack. He gained on him but realized he needed to do more cardio at the gym. Plus, he heard his suit rip.

"Dammit," Matthew said with what little breath he could manage.

Juarez made a severe right and headed toward the main gate of the cemetery. He hopped over a two-foot-tall monument, but the tip of his boot hit the edge and he slammed down on the wet grass with a grunt and swearing. Lungs searing from running, Matthew sped up to him. Juarez turned over, holding out a knife with a six-inch blade.

"Really?" Matthew said.

"Let me go." Juarez raged.

"Put down that knife. You don't want to add to your troubles."

Juarez swung the knife at Matthew. He stepped backward, but not far enough. The blade sliced the skin below his right knee. Although his leg was on fire, his foot crushed Juarez's hand until he released the knife. When Juarez tried to get up, he balled up his fist and let it fly right into Juarez's jaw. The man went back down to the ground with another grunt.

"Fuck," Matthew hollered from the pain in his hand and his leg. He hadn't hit anyone since high school when a drunk quarterback wouldn't stop bothering Isabel at a party.

Benny drove up with a screech. The sheriff burst out displaying his .44 Ruger Magnum Revolver. While his deputies and Guadalupe police officers carried the semiautomatic Glocks, Benny preferred that monster of the gun, though it was a single-shot. He did carry a Glock in his patrol cruiser, but used the Mag to scare the hell out of criminals.

Juarez did look scared with the silver barrel directed at his heart.

"You okay, Matthew?"

"No." He sat down on the grass checking out the cut on his leg. Blood soaked his pant leg and ran down to his shoe.

Juarez sat up, rubbing his jaw. "I didn't do nothing."

"Then why'd you run?" Matthew held a handkerchief against the wound that smarted like salted chili on a cut.

"I ain't saying," Juarez huffed.

"He beat the hell out of his girlfriend," Benny told Matthew. "Her brother came to visit her, saw the black eyes and bruises, and called it in. The office put out a BOLO on him about ten minutes ago." Benny cuffed Juarez and pulled him toward the patrol car. "And your girlfriend's brother is looking for you, too, *hombre*."

"Just because I went out gambling at the casino in Santa Fe and lost the rent money, she hit me with a frying pan." He pointed out a two-inch cut on his head. "She started the fight."

"Well, you gave her the worst of it with two broken ribs and a broken arm."

Placing a hand on a gravestone, Matthew stood up. "Juarez, you're facing a whole grocery list of charges. That includes assault on your girlfriend and on me, and I'm going to add digging up graves." He shot a look at Benny, whose eyes narrowed with questioning, and then widened with understanding.

"I didn't dig up no dead bodies. You're talking loco, dude." Juarez spit out blood from a split lip courtesy of Matthew.

"Whoever killed Nick Vargas left bits of dead body on *his* body. Who else has a record, likes to hurt people, and works at a cemetery. You're it, man," Matthew said.

"I didn't kill that bastard. And my girlfriend will tell you I was with her the night Vargas disappeared. Just ask her."

"You really think she'll give you an alibi?"

Juarez hung his head.

"She already vouched for him." Benny put Juarez in the back of the cruiser.

"Well, shit in a basket." Matthew's sliced leg ached even more.

Benny picked up the knife with a glove and placed it in an evidence bag. "Come on, Matthew. You're going to the hospital so you won't bleed to death at the cemetery."

"You're such a riot, bro."

Juarez laughed.

"Shut up," they told him.

"Before the hospital, I want to hear from Juarez's soon-to-be ex-girlfriend."

Back at the law enforcement office and with a towel wrapped around his wound, the girlfriend did declare Juarez was with her during the time that Vargas was snatched from the courthouse. She also agreed to press charges against him. As she signed the complaint, her bruiser of a brother gritted his teeth.

"I want that SOB," he said.

"You're going to have to wait until he serves time for hitting your sister," Matthew told him.

"I can wait." He left with the girl, and Matthew was glad he wasn't John Juarez.

"Since this lead petered out, my deputies will call all the other cemeteries and funeral homes in the county to ask about dug-up graves," Benny said. "We'll also have them send us a list of employees."

"Good thinking," Matthew said. "I already called the county ambulance supervisor about their employees. Can your people check up on them, too?"

"Definitely. Enough talk, Matthew. I'm taking you to the ER."

Dr. Whitney had heard about Matthew's injury from hospital staff and personally treated him.

While she tended to Matthew's leg wound, Benny sat on a chair in the ER cubicle.

"You should have seen him take off after the suspect, Doc. Just like a regular cop, even wearing his lawyer suit."

"Yeah, I ripped a hole in the butt."

Benny laughed.

"I'm just happy I put on clean underwear today. Ouch."

"Sorry." Whitney had cut away his pant leg and injected him with a local to stitch the gash.

A deputy called Benny on his cell phone. He hit the speaker function so Matthew could hear.

"Sheriff, we called every cemetery manager and funeral director in the county. None of them reported any digging up of graves."

"Anything on the county ambulance crews?" Matthew said.

"Only three paramedics were off duty the night Nick Vargas was killed. They accounted for their whereabouts."

"So where were they?"

"One was at home with her husband and kids. One was playing video games with his buddies. The other was home sleeping and his wife confirmed it. The paramedics were all where they were supposed to be."

He and Benny thanked the deputy.

"So you guys were checking funeral homes and ambulance crews because of those fragments of dead skin on Nick's body," Whitney said. "Nice police work."

"But that idea apparently didn't work out. Hey, what about hospital personnel, Rosemary? Can you vouch for your people?" Matthew said.

"I can't say. You're going to have to ask the administrators about who has access to the morgue."

"Wait, didn't the state lab say the dead tissue was pretty old?" Benny said.

"You're right. That'll eliminate the hospital's supply of dead people unless you keep them around for nefarious tests, Rosemary," Matthew said.

"Yes, we're attempting to reanimate flesh," Whitney replied with a heap of sarcasm.

"That's a good one, Doc," Benny said with a laugh.

"I admit, it was a long shot. Ouch. You almost done?" he asked the doctor.

"You big baby." She whistled. "This took ten stitches, but I'll give you a sexy scar, Matthew."

"Thanks a lot."

"So no suspect in the murder?" Whitney said.

"No, dammit."

She finished and wrote him a prescription for a painkiller. "You two stay out of trouble."

"I will for the rest of the night."

"Well, since you're all sewed up, I'm going home to my wife. And Matthew, good job taking down that son of a bitch." Benny added.

"My pleasure."

Matthew headed home. His body hurt from the cut, but also dragged with weariness and frustration about how the leads had dried up quicker than rain in the desert.

His mother's face lost its color when he entered the house and she saw the blood on his pants and bandage on his leg.

"My God."

"Just a slight altercation. Nothing to worry about." He kissed the top of her head.

"Go lie down, *mijo*, you need rest."

"I need to get back to work."

"Ay, Mateo, you're so damn *terco* I can't believe it." She crossed her small arms.

"Where do you think I got all that stubbornness from, little mother?"

He didn't rest. Instead, he searched the Internet about the behavior of psycho killers. That is, if one of them had indeed killed Nick Vargas. Alarming was the amount of information on the web. Thousands of the sites spotlighting killers from Jack the Ripper to Jeffrey Dahmer.

FBI profilers reported it rare that serial killers traveled around the country murdering people. The men—and they were usually males—didn't stray from where they resided. In many cases, they even kept the bodies of victims in shallow graves in the backyard or the basement of their homes. An exception to the rule was Ted Bundy, the tsar of them all, who swept over several states like a psycho plague that felled young women.

Matthew sat back from the computer. Dammit. He should have told Benny "no" when he asked for his help, but he couldn't because Benny would have done the same for him.

The leg where Juarez had sliced him itched and ached, but then again, that was how he'd describe this whole murder case.

Itching and aching.

Chapter 18

Tommy Day sang the last bars to "Whiskey River." He crooned loudly and out of tune because no one was around the Guadalupe Cemetery at that time of evening. Not the living who might complain or the dead who certainly wouldn't. The music played in earbuds attached to the iPod in his front shirt pocket. He expertly ran the backhoe in the Gabriel section, which was one of the newest in the boneyard.

Day spit on the ground in a bad mood. John Juarez would have taken care of this job, but the stupid jerk was in jail for hitting his girlfriend and cutting up a lawyer so he had to take up the slack. He wanted to hurry home where his new wife waited with dinner and maybe, a little more.

His German Shepherd Willie ran around the cemetery while he worked. He'd bring the dog when he knew his supervisor was going to be gone. Three-years-old and lovably frantic, Willie ran all over cemetery, occasionally peeing on the gravestones.

Day had lived in Guadalupe all his life and knew most everyone who was buried at the cemetery, or he knew someone who knew someone who knew someone related to the deceased. Here he was digging the grave for Nick Vargas. He'd gone to school with him and even back then, Vargas considered himself hot shit. He got the cutest girls and good grades, but was not above a bit of hellraising and taking short cuts to get what he wanted.

Day, on the other hand, didn't have the best grades and didn't get the girls.

After graduation, he worked labor jobs while Vargas ran around in expensive suits and cars, had a nice house, and won public office. His wife was also good-looking.

Whenever Day happened to see Vargas on the street, the commissioner just nodded and moved on as if he owned him money.

And now Mr. High and Mighty Nick Vargas was deader than a doornail. And he was digging his grave. Not a deep thinker, even that irony didn't escape Tommy Day.

He'd heard from an assistant funeral director that Nick Vargas's coffin was going to be closed because of what happened to him. His boss Hector Bowden was a genius at making the dead appear alive in their coffin, but he doubted that the funeral director could reattach Vargas's skin, which was going to be buried with him in a separate container. Day gave his head a shake. No matter how much of a bastard the man was in life, no one should go to their maker without a skin.

"Poor Nick. Poor dead son of a bitch," Day said to his dog Willie. "I wouldn't want to die like that, no matter how much money I made."

As the sunlight faded, he snapped off his music. He emptied out one more load of dirt from the grave into a pile that would be covered by a tarp to pour over the coffin later. Summoning his dog to join him on the seat, he backed up to take the machine to the shed. In a blink, Willie darted off the backhoe and ran back to the new gravesite. The dog barked incessantly.

"Willie, get over here."

The dog didn't obey and continued to bark beside the hole. He then sat on his haunches and yowled like a passing ambulance.

"Shut up, boy. You're gonna wake the dead." Day laughed at his joke. "Wake the dead, ha." He needed a sense of humor in this job that consisted of putting holes in the ground for all the dead people and taking care of the grass and greenery, the latter of which he much preferred.

He called again for the dog, which didn't move. Turning off the backhoe, he grabbed his flashlight. The cemetery was dark by then.

"What'd you see, boy. A rabbit?"

Day directed the light down into the grave. Large green lizards filled the rectangular hole. He guessed they must have been two-feet deep. They crawled over each other, bit each other, and began to climb up the dirt walls.

"God almighty."

Willie barked.

"Let's get the hell out of there." The dog followed his owner as they hopped up on the machine. In the headlight beams, the lizards climbed out of the hole and disappeared into the night.

****

Alma Chacon snorted awake after falling asleep in front of the television set. The TV played a love story, but she didn't enjoy romance so much after her husband Gilbert had died twelve years ago. As a result, it was hard for her to keep her eyes open ten minutes into the program. Besides, she was at the age when she'd fall asleep during a commercial.

This time, she was happy she woke up. Her dream had been horrible.

She hovered over the town like a bird of the night. Under the illumination of a red moon, people yelled in terror and ran with only one goal. To get away. Blood coursed through the streets and over the walls of homes and businesses as if a living entity out for revenge. The church melted into the shiny blood until it was engulfed up to the white crosses at the top of its two towers. People were smothered by the deluge, their bodies becoming wretched lumps in the blood.

Immune to the flood of red were two naked men. A small white-haired man in the park beckoned to a taller one in the middle of the street. The naked man in the street danced in the blood and talked in a foreign language. His raised hand held a black knife. Opening his mouth, nothing came out but the screams of the people as they were swallowed up by the blood. The short man laughed at the sight of the chaos and death.

Alma had lurched awake and her body shook uncontrollably.

With effort, she stood up and paced around her house. Her lungs could have been used-up sponges and she couldn't breathe. Her daughter Michelle worked the night shift at the mine so she was alone. Alma decided to step outside, hoping for the cool air of nighttime to enter her body. Mostly, she wanted to make sure the blood of her dream hadn't really invaded the town.

She flicked on the porch lights.

On her front lawn were the heads of more than one hundred feral hogs. Their blood sputtered black against the green. The snouts twitched even without bodies, and their piggish eyes fluttered as if trying to come back from the dead.

She crushed her hands against her mouth, backed into her door, and locked it. Please let this be a dream, she pleaded before peeking outside. The heads were still there.

During her daily devotions she prayed that evil would stay away from Guadalupe.

It had arrived nevertheless.

Chapter 19

With his mother Consuela, Matthew stood off to the side at the funeral service. While she held her head down in prayer, he tugged at his tie under the summer heat that also nagged at him about why Nick Vargas lay in that coffin.

Seventy people stood around the gravesite and more had attended the funeral mass. Benny was missing because he took a patrol shift for a sick deputy, which was why his deputies loved the guy. Due to the heat, Benny didn't want his delicate wife Camilla to attend.

Along with the deceased's numerous family members were representatives of county and city government, businesspeople, and members of the organizations to which Vargas belonged. Matthew hadn't liked the man in life, but remembered how Vargas's butchered body was sprawled over that rock in the arroyo.

"Pay attention, Mateo." His mother tapped his back.

"Sorry, Mama."

Glancing up, he saw Isabel looking at him. She smiled and shifted her eyes back to the services.

With final prayers, the last of Nick Vargas went into the grave and people headed to the funeral lunch at the church hall.

Father Henry Cantu shut his bible. The day heated up and the mourners already sweated into their black dresses and suits. The priest shook the hand of the widow and Victoria Vargas, Nick's mother. Like her son, she was short. Her build was stable as the mountains but not her constitution. Earlier in the service, the older Mrs. Vargas swooned from the heat and the grief so much so that relatives had to take her away to rest in an air-conditioned limo. She had only recently returned for the final prayers.

Vargas's widow was more stoic. Her grief seemed real enough. If not, she was a better actress than Matthew had given her credit for. She and the mother-in-law did wear what appeared to be designer dresses. Beautiful black numbers.

"Nick's wife is the best-dressed widow I've ever seen, and her mother is a close second." Matthew whispered to his mom.

She shushed him.

He had crossed Patty Vargas off of his list of suspects because she didn't look capable of murdering a piece of toast. Her mother did come off as a hard piece of fluff capable of bad things, but they were each other's alibis for the night Vargas had disappeared.

"That was a good service," Consuela said as she and Matthew walked back to his car. She had brought two homemade apple pies for the luncheon.

"Very nice."

"What were you thinking about, son? You weren't paying attention to the service—at all."

"I was just thinking about who might have killed Nick and why. Both paramount questions and I hope I can answer them."

"I hope you can, too," said a voice from behind them.

Alma Chacon came up to Matthew's chest, small as anything. So petite she was almost childlike, except that her light brown eyes were profound with wisdom and kindness. Her hair was wound in white braids around the top of her head.

His mom and the old woman hugged as if long-lost family members.

"You remember my son, Mateo. The county prosecutor." Consuela straightened when she pronounced his title.

"I knew you when you were this high." Alma's hand lowered to two feet off of the ground.

Matthew was happy that she didn't try to pinch his cheek.

"It is a sad day, isn't it Alma?" Consuela said in Spanish.

Placing a wrinkled hand to her eyes, Alma glanced up at the sky.

He and his mom looked up as well. There was nothing but the faded shadow of the moon against the blue.

"See it?" Alma said.

"What?" Consuela said.

"The red around the moon." The woman's voice deepened.

He and his mom looked up again, their hands shielding out the sun. There *was* a hint of a red shadow.

"Yeah, I see it," he said.

"I finally remembered what it means."

"What, the red moon?"

"There will be more sad days ahead of us. More trouble. More death."

"Death?"

"The signs are everywhere. In the red moon. In my dreams." For emphasis, the tip of her cane tapped at Michael's chest, leaving dust spots on his dark gray suit coat. "It even came to my house last night."

"What happened?" his mother said.

She told them about the heads of the feral hogs scattered over her lawn. Matthew tried not to give into his initial reaction. Namely, that she was certifiable.

"Terrible," his mother said.

"But of course, you've seen this trouble firsthand." Alma tapped his chest again with her cane.

"Oh, no," Consuela replied. "What can we do?"

"Nothing to do, but wait and watch and pray."

Alma rose up toward him and he lowered his head.

"You will be tested, my son." She whispered and then kissed his cheek. "There's my daughter. *Adiós*."

She walked away.

Sweeping the dust spots from his jacket, Matthew and his mother headed to his car. She asked what Alma had whispered and he told her.

"What the hell did she mean by all that?" he said.

"I have no idea."

He laughed. Consuela did not.

"Alma Chacon was a great healer when she was younger, a mighty *curandera*."

"Mama, for God's sake."

"She even healed you."

"When?"

"You were eight. I called her when you had a bad stomachache that lasted for a week. The doctor said it was nothing and told me to give you Pepto Bismol. I went to her and she rubbed your stomach with herbs and oils, and you got better."

"I don't remember that."

"You were only one of many she helped. She's also cured people cursed by *brujas*. People from all over the county called on her to help family members made sick by the spiteful witches. There was one man, what was his name?" Her eyes blinked while recovering the memory. "Yes, Samuel Montoya. He had these awful painful black bumps all over his legs. He didn't want to go to a doctor, but went to Alma. She prayed and made a paste of mud and herbs and spread it over the bumps. A day later they burst open and out came black beetles. She said a *bruja* had cursed him."

"You really believe that stuff?"

"I saw them, son. I even suggested he go to the doctor because they might be cancer."

"You don't even believe in those Mexican witch stories. You said and I quote, 'They are just magical tales from our tradition.' Unquote."

"Matthew, I've had my doubts, but as I get older it seems like anything is possible. And you may not know this, but Alma also knows the future. She feels it."

He blew a raspberry.

"She predicted that Mac Gómez would die in a car accident and he did. She did the same for Josie Rivera, predicting she'd end up rich. And what happens? Her father dies and leaves her lots of money."

"Mama."

"I hate when you don't believe in anything, Mateo."

"Of course, I do, but I also want facts. Let's get to the church hall. It's too hot out here to debate faith."

"Alma Chacon can read the symbols of life and death, but no one bothers to listen to her anymore." She touched his arm. "Next time, you should listen."

"Well, she's one scary woman." He opened the car door for his mother.

"She's scary because she sees the truth."

On their way to the reception, she asked him to drive by Alma's house.

"Why?"

"Just do it, *por favor*."

He could never refuse his mother and drove there.

In front of Alma Chacon's house, five trash cans overflowed with the heads of feral hogs. The brown animals were pests, according to the state Fish and Game because they messed up the habitat and contaminated water. The department even allowed hunters to kill them without a license.

He got out of the car to check them out, but his mother didn't. Clean cuts ran along the necks of the animals.

"Kids must have been pranking her, Mama. I'll have the police come out here."

"This backs up what she said, son. Trouble ahead. What more do you need?"

After they attended the funeral lunch, Matthew drove his mother home and insisted she lock the doors and stay inside.

"If a madman did kill Nick Vargas, he might still be hanging around Guadalupe."

"What would he want with a little old lady like me?"

"He's psycho, remember? They hear voices of dogs and shit."

"Don't cuss, *mijo*. Besides, if a stranger is hanging around I'd call the cops." She smiled. "Come to think of it, a stranger would stick out like a sore thumb."

He kissed her cheek. "You're a genius."

"I know. Don't worry about me, son. This killing is just a flash of lightning in life. And lightning never strikes twice in the same place."

Chapter 20

Deputy Jackson Rogers stomped on the gas pedal and the patrol car roared forward. The speedometer read eighty-five. He was determined to break his record of 106 on the county road south of town.

EIGHTY-SEVEN.

Just something to do whenever he was bored, like that night.

NINETY.

At ten-thirty on a Wednesday night, most of the good people in town and the rest of the county were already sleeping. Only the bad guys were running around.

ONE HUNDRED.

Headlights up ahead. Rogers lifted his foot off of the pedal and slowed. Damn. He couldn't be caught breaking the law. Not yet.

The deputy wondered how many more nights of patrolling he had left. He didn't mind the shift because nothing much happened. At times, he'd sleep in his car parked behind an abandoned barn a couple of miles from the courthouse.

Reducing his speed to seventy-five, Rogers concentrated on the headlights coming toward him in the other lane. A truck zoomed along doing eighty-five, he guessed. Loud Latino music blared from the open windows. He could have stopped the driver and issued a warning, but didn't want to work that night because he'd have to fill out reports, which he hated. After his shift and a shower, he was meeting up with the cute server girl from the cafe where he ate dinner four times a week.

He stretched. Almost done for the night. Making a U-turn on the road, he headed back toward Guadalupe.

The empty road laid ahead, a black hardened line to oblivion. Not even a coyote or rabbit to try to run over.

Rogers glanced at his watch. Five minutes until eleven. Almost done with the shift. When he looked back to the road, six men in long black robes lined up in his headlights thirty yards ahead. Hoods covered their faces.

"What the hell?"

Pumping down hard on the breaks, Rogers swerved to miss the men and skidded off the right side of the road. His patrol car kicked up dust as it slid to a halt twenty-five feet from the asphalt. The deputy cursed at what he figured were high schoolers playing a joke by dressing up like old-fashioned monks from the movies. Probably that cosplay crap. Whatever it was, he was going to put them all in jail for scaring the shit out of him.

"Fucking teenagers."

Rogers shifted about in his seat. In the red glow of the taillights, he saw no teenagers. With the car still running, he got out with his heavy flashlight in one hand and his Glock in the other. Lucky for him, the ground was hard enough that he'd be able to drive right out of there. He didn't want to be spinning wheels in sand and having to call a tow truck. Then, explaining to the sheriff what happened. He hated questions.

Still, he'd put the fear of God and Jackson Rogers into those little assholes.

Sprinting down the road, he swung the light all around. "Come out, you sons of bitches. You're all going down. You can't hide from me."

He fired his weapon into the air, which reverbed into nothingness.

The young jokers had vanished into the night. No sound of an escape car. No sound at all except for his breathing. They were probably hunkered down so he couldn't spot them. Walking up and down the road, he aimed his light on the ground on both sides. Nothing but sagebrush, yucca, and dirt. They scattered pretty effectively, damn them.

"To hell with it."

His shift was over. He was going home. Screw those kids. He'd get them next time and then they'd be sorry. He hated this job and counted the days until he could quit like they were precious stones in his hand.

The deputy got into his car and readied to put it in gear. With a curious whir and flick, the engine and the lights died as if someone pulled the plug on them. He was in darkness.

Rogers tried the radio. It was as dead as the car. He got out the cell phone from his pocket. No familiar warm light. For the last hour the only other vehicle he had seen was the truck playing Mexican tunes. That meant he was going to be stuck out there until another vehicle drove by.

The flashers on the car didn't work, but in the trunk were traffic cones and flares. He'd set them out on the road so someone would stop because he was out in the middle of freaking nowhere. He hated waiting like he hated questions and paperwork.

From his pocket, he took out a pack of cigarettes and lit up. Deputies weren't supposed to smoke in their cars, but he didn't give a shit. He drew in the smoke. As he exhaled, hands crashed through the windows on all sides of him, grabbing him. Holding him. Tearing into him with long jagged fingernails. They dug into his arms and legs, feeling of hot sharp metal. Yelling in agony, he couldn't push them off. He couldn't move. He could barely breathe. He was strong, but couldn't get loose from these bastards. Yanking at the hands with as much strength as he could rally, bones cracked. Not his bones. The skin of his captors squashed between his fingers. He couldn't tell how many men held him. When he managed to wrench one hand off of him, more took hold. He gagged from their smell. One of putrid and penetrating ruin.

Deputy Jackson Rogers batted his fist against the horn, which miraculously did work. Screaming, he held onto a desperate wish that he might be heard and saved.

No one came.

The night swallowed up the patrol car.

Chapter 21

Matthew was so sorry he went out there.

The naked body of Deputy Jackson Rogers, or what was left of it, sat upright in his patrol car. A trick of balance since his arms and legs were gone. The wounds on the torso were smooth and red, with a glimpse of white bone in the middle. The body's eyes popped and the tongue stretched beyond what Matthew believed a tongue could be stretched.

All the windows in the patrol car had been smashed in, which made the remains sparkle from the glass. The body sat on the seat right behind the steering wheel. Walking around the car, Matthew leaned into the open door. Out of Rogers's mouth crawled a large horned toad that vaulted out the far window.

Matthew fell back. "Jesus!"

The sturdy hand of a deputy caught him so that he didn't crash down onto the dirt. Matthew nodded thanks.

"This is fucking wild," the deputy announced.

"I won't give you an argument."

A van and SUV pulled up behind the sawhorses placed across the country road a half-mile up. Television crews got out and were held at bay by deputies. Isabel parked her truck right behind the van and rushed out to the barriers, taking photos as she walked.

Benny drove his cruiser around the sawhorses and parked. "How'd you beat me here?" he asked Matthew.

"Your secretary caught me while I was on my way to work. Ready to be freaked out?"

"Oh, no."

When he peered into Rogers's patrol car, Benny's mouth twisted like a rag.

"There's no blood—again. And no arms and legs. He must have been killed elsewhere—again—and then brought back to his car," Matthew said.

Benny waved over his chief deputy, Thomas Reynolds, who had fiery red hair and perpetually flushed cheeks. Although Reynolds's eyes were compassionate, his hands were fleshy anvils. "Footprints, Thomas? Tire tracks?"

"Just ours."

"Come on. Nothing?" Matthew said.

"When we arrived, there was a set of footprints heading to the road from his patrol car and then back. I think those belonged to Jackson, but there's no other footprints or car tracks around. How could the killer not leave any tracks? I don't get it." Reynolds scratched the back of his head.

"Neither do I. Who found him?"

"We did. When Jackson didn't answer his phone or radio this morning, we tracked the GPS from his cell phone."

"When was the last time he checked in?"

"Dispatch said about ten last night."

"Did he report anything?" Benny said.

"Only that he was bored," Reynolds said. "Jackson's shift ended at eleven and we figured he just went home. When we couldn't get a hold of him early this morning, we started to worry."

"That's not procedure, is it?" Matthew said.

"He's done this before. He'd just go home after his shift ended. I had warned him to call in and check out," Benny said.

"This is like a really bad dream out of the homicidal maniac's catalogue. I'm going to take another look around." Reynolds headed off.

Matthew and Benny were startled when Dr. Rosemary Whitney joined them. "Not another one."

"You scared the crap out of us, Doc," Benny said.

"Move aside, please," said Frank Cruz, the county sheriff's forensic officer who also arrived. "We should preserve the crime scene before the doctor's examination."

"You're right, Frank. Have at it." Benny waved his hand toward the patrol car.

They all moved back. Cruz began taking photos. A slender runt of a guy baring pockmarked skin, he was enamored with all of the forensic shows on TV and lived with his grandmother, who also loved them.

"Frank's the only deputy who wanted to take the forensic courses. The weird thing is he's pretty good at it," Benny said.

"He's dedicated to his work, I'll say that." Whitney wiped perspiration off of her face with a tissue. "I'm going to wait in the ambulance where it's cooler. Call me when Frank is done playing CSI."

Behind them, reporters shouted questions.

Benny looked like he had to take a pop quiz in math. "God, Matthew, what do we tell them?"

"As little as possible. Go ahead and get it over with." He bumped him with his shoulder.

"Why don't you say something? You're a better public speaker."

"They're going to ask why I'm doing the talking and not you."

"Shit, you're right, but butt in if I start sounding stupid." Benny straightened his tie and they both walked over to the reporters, which by that time included a TV crew from another station in Guadalupe.

Matthew stood behind his friend.

"What can you tell us, Sheriff?" one woman shouted.

"Only that a person is dead, but we're not releasing the name until the family has been notified."

Isabel pushed her way past the other reporters, which Matthew admired.

"This county hasn't had a murder for five years and this is the second one within two weeks," she said.

"I didn't say it was a murder," Benny said.

"Then what is it?"

Benny held up his hands. "Folks, that's all for the moment. Our investigation has just started, so you're wasting your time with more questions."

They walked back toward the crime scene. "That was pretty good, Benny."

"Think so?"

"Badass."

One side of Benny's mouth bent up.

"Did Rogers have family?" Matthew said.

"A dad in Colorado. From what Jackson told me, they didn't get along well."

Frank Cruz pulled off the blue latex gloves. "All yours, sheriff."

"Anything preliminary?" Matthew said.

Cruz looked at Benny for approval.

"Go ahead."

"Except for the broken windows, there were no signs of a struggle anywhere, which is odd as hell. Even his laptop wasn't knocked over. I did find a couple of Jackson's buttons on the floor."

"So?"

"Like he was dragged out of the car and his buttons snagged." Matthew supplied the answer.

Cruz frowned, apparently because he had stepped on his deductions, but Matthew did pride himself on smoothing the most ruffled of feathers. "Well, I'm really looking forward to what kind of prints you found, Frank. As well as anything else you discovered."

The frown eased. "I'll get those results to you ASAP, if not before."

"I'll have the patrol car transported to the office and you can have another look there," Benny said.

"Right."

"Your turn, doctor."

Before going to the patrol car, she crushed her cigarette under her foot and donned her protective gear. The physician scanned the cuts with a magnifying glass.

"I need to do lots more tests, but it appears the same crude knife made the cuts because I see the same flecks of black rock. No ragged flesh here. That obsidian knife or whatever it is, has to be as sharp as a scalpel."

"Same as the wounds on Nick Vargas?" Matthew said.

"Pert near, as my daddy used to say. The deputy must have died from blood loss given the severity of the injuries to his body. In particular, the removal of his limbs. I didn't see any other wounds." She stepped away from the car, removing her mask and gloves. "Sheesh. Can we remove the body now? The autopsy will tell us much more."

"What about his face, Rosemary?" Benny said. "Looks like he was strangled by fear."

The doctor sighed. Matthew could smell the cigarettes on her.

"I believe a person's face can reflect how he died. If he goes peacefully, there's a type of serenity, but for those who die horribly, it shows on their face." She glanced back at the patrol car. "And this guy went pretty horribly."

"Let's get him out of here," Benny said.

She supervised the crew loading the body.

Benny motioned Matthew away from Rogers's car and even farther from the waiting reporters. "This is going to cause hysteria."

"Probably. Just assure the public that your department is working hard to resolve this case. You're increasing the number of patrols in the county, although out here is too vast and desolate for it to do any good. We won't mention that last part. How about dedicating a phone line for news tips about the murders?"

"Good idea."

His friend had more to say. He kicked at the dirt. "I was positive we had a psycho on our hands, a guy who killed and left this county to kill again. But the bastard is sticking around."

The ambulance drove off, reporters taking photos and shooting video of it.

"Matthew, I'm not confident we can catch this serial killer."

"But I'm confident that we'll do the damn best we can to apprehend him. By the way, murderers aren't considered serial killers until they knock off three people."

"No shit?"

"I read it on the Internet."

"So that's good news?"

"It is so far." He checked his watch. "Oh man, I need to go to the office. I have a backlog of items staring me in the face since this thing has started and I've got to clear them away. Oh, and Benny?"

"What?"

"Don't call me for the rest of the day."

"You got it."

While heading back to their vehicles, a dispatcher's voice summoned Benny over the radio in his vehicle. He ran to answer. "Sheriff Ortega."

"The mayor and the commissioners want to see you and Matthew in the county meeting room," the dispatcher said.

"When?"

"Like now."

Matthew put his head between his hands.

Chapter 22

The previous year, the county meeting room had been remodeled to reflect the desert surroundings and make the public feel more comfortable during hearings. The commissioners even paid for an interior designer who suggested blue and cream colors and softer seats. Matthew smiled at that—as if the public could feel relaxed at any public meeting. Besides, the only people who turned up for the commission meetings were those complaining about their property taxes.

Despite the blue and cream color, Benny didn't appear so comfortable, either. His friend sweated under the air conditioning. Wet spots marked under his arms and down the back of his uniform.

Matthew sat in the front row next to Guadalupe Police Chief George Wilson, whose career was heading toward retirement faster than a speeding train. Wilson was a nice guy who looked more like a senior pro golfer than a cop. He was also one lazy son of a gun, notably because his career days were numbered. As a result, most of the city law enforcement work fell on his second-in-command at the police department and on Benny and his deputies.

Sitting at a table on a platform were the remaining County Commissioners Mary Lou Flores and Lonnie Dietrich. A replacement for Nick Vargas had not yet been named. Dietrich raised beans and corn at his good-sized operation west of town. His lean face was sunburned except past a line where he wore his cowboy hat—then it was a pale pink. That hat sat on the table, but it was not the white suede one he wore to official functions. This one was dusty, as if the commissioner had just come in from his farm which he probably did. He wore jeans and a work shirt. Dietrich was a fair and reasonable man, despite the fact he always boasted of never voting for a Democrat in his whole life and truly believing that kindergarteners should be able to carry guns.

Even in her severe CPA business suit, Mary Lou Flores flaunted curves and attractiveness. Her skin was perfect with blonde streaks highlighting dark brown hair. Before he dated Isabel, Matthew thought about asking Flores out, but she scared the hell out of him. She was as determined as a concrete dam.

Mayor John Stuart sat at the other end of the table. The three public officials were all business that morning. Benny stood in front of them.

"I'm glad those murders took place in the county and not in the city," Wilson whispered to Matthew, who wanted to hit him.

Dietrich sneered at Benny. "So, are we even close to arresting the person who killed Nick?"

"No, Mr. Commissioner." Benny held his hands behind his back as if ready to be cuffed for inefficiency.

"And on top of that there's another murder?" Dietrich shook his lanky head. "We have the festival coming up and the people must be protected at all costs. If anyone comes at all because of these killings." He spoke with a tinge of a southern drawl but had been born in Guadalupe, leaving Matthew to wonder where he had picked up the accent.

"And that will hurt this town's economy." The mayor constricted his eyes at what Matthew believed were visions of empty cash registers. "What are we going to advertise? 'Welcome to Guadalupe, home of a psycho killer'?"

Benny continued to sweat. "I've made arrangements for more reserve officers to patrol during the festival. The state police are also sending patrolmen to help. And George has promised as many officers as he can spare."

Wilson stood up. "That's right. The city force will provide its complete cooperation and manpower."

That consisted of seventy-five officers, not counting the support personnel, including Wilson's secretary, who was tough enough to be a cop. The county sheriff's patrol staff was a little larger. The deputies did have more square miles to be patrolled within county boundaries, although most of the population resided in Guadalupe.

"Excellent, Sheriff. That does make me feel safer already," said Flores who smiled.

Dietrich rapped the gavel and cleared his throat. "It's my opinion we should ask the state police to take over this case. Nothing against you, Benny, but they have more resources. Commissioner Flores and the mayor disagree. Matthew, I understand you're helping in the investigation. What do you think?"

As Matthew stood up, he glanced over at Benny. His friend held his eyes to the floor and his mouth went rigid like the last kid to be called in a game of basketball. "Benny and I know the locals. We understand this community. Those state guys will just get in our way. We can do this job."

"Aren't you leaving after the first of September, Matthew?" Stuart said.

"I'll stay until this case is resolved—one way or another. I promise you." The State AG would understand.

He hoped.

"Lonnie, if we ask the state for help, it will just bring us more unwanted publicity," Flores said in her throaty voice. "It sends a message that we can't handle our own problems."

"Well, maybe we can't."

"As much as I'm upset by these murders, I agree with Mary Lou. We certainly don't want or need that, and right before the festival," Stuart added.

"Matthew, I feel confident that you and Benny won't fail the county, or the town of Guadalupe. I have every confidence in both of you." The attractive commissioner winked at them.

Commissioner Dietrich huffed. "I can see I'm not changing any minds today. Okay, let's keep the investigation in local hands for the time being, but I want to see progress."

"You will," Matthew said.

Benny sighed with relief.

The meeting was over.

Dietrich put on his dirty cowboy hat. "Who wants to go to lunch?"

Everyone begged off.

****

On most days, the mood was light and friendly in the law enforcement office, but during that shift the deputies and police officers dragged feet and drank liters of coffee.

"What's wrong with them?" Matthew tossed a thumb in their direction.

"They're freaked out. They're not used to all this murder. And Jackson's killing hit too close to home. Suddenly, they're all vulnerable." Benny waved him into his office.

Compared to his office, Benny's was smaller and simpler. On the walls were photos of his wife Camilla alongside certificates from the state police academy and the Chamber of Commerce honoring Benny's service. There was also a photo of him and Benny each holding a mondo trout they'd pulled out of Twin Lake to the north. That was a good day. They drank and laughed and fished the hell out of those waters.

Matthew envied his friend's lack of ambition and pretension, things that he had way too much of.

"How was the funeral, by the way?" Benny sat back in his chair.

"Very final. It did draw a pretty good crowd. If Nick hadn't died, he would have been pressing flesh for votes." Matthew sat in the only comfortable chair in the office.

"Mateo." Benny clicked his tongue.

"Sorry." He set down the coffee cup. His lawyer mind was rebelling with logic. "Benny, I've lost sleep trying to make sense of the senseless."

"I can't sleep, either. And I'm having nightmares."

"You're not alone. But maybe that's the problem." He sat up, maybe a little surer of himself than he had been since he saw Vargas's body. "We're agonizing over this case because Nick's murder appears to have no motive and because of the horrendous way he was killed. The same thing with Jackson Rogers. But we need to regard these killings as straight homicides."

"I don't follow." Benny removed his cowboy hat and placed it on the desk. "They *are* homicides."

"Yeah, but psychos usually don't have a motive. Just a need to kill."

"Still don't get ya."

"We look for a motive. Why would someone kill a commissioner and then a deputy? We find a common denominator. We got nothing else, my friend, so I say we go with that."

Benny looked over his coffee cup. "I still say it's a sick psycho."

"If it is, then the killer might go after a certain type of victim. What drew this murderer to Vargas and Rogers? We find that out and we catch him." Matthew stood up. He was always better standing when making an argument, like presenting to a jury. This time he wanted to convince his friend about what direction they should take on this investigation. He dotted perspiration from his forehead because the air conditioning in Benny's office wasn't the best. "And something my mom said stuck in my brain."

"Your mom?"

"Stay with me here. Say an out-of-county psycho killer is wandering around Guadalupe; he would've been noticed, especially after Nick's murder. We were raised here. Everybody knows everybody else's business."

"That's for damn sure, but Guadalupe has 46,000 people. He might not have been noticed."

"I'll give you that, but I've also read that a majority of serial killers don't stray far from their home when they murder. So, if the killer resides in this county, why did he start killing now, and why flay one victim and remove the limbs from another? There's been no alarming rate of missing people who could have been his other victims. And as my beautiful and separated wife brought up, the last murder in the county was five years ago."

"Psycho killer," Benny said with firmness.

"Geez, *compadre*. Psychos are pretty damn uncommon, except in movies and on TV. Besides, we don't have many clues."

Benny had no answer except one. "Nick must have just been convenient. No sane person could have done that."

Matthew took a drink from the mug of now tepid coffee and quickly set it down. "Hold on one damn minute. Shit, why didn't I see this before?"

"What?"

"Why would the killer pick on a deputy who's packing a weapon? *That's* insane."

"Matthew, that's why psycho killers are called psycho."

"Granted, this guy is categorically deranged to do what he did, but maybe he thought he had a reason to kill those men. And that takes us back to motive."

Benny wasn't confused, only saddened.

He didn't blame him. "We either pursue that lead or wait for another murder."

His friend breathed out hard. "So what are you thinking?"

"More digging into Nick Vargas's life, in particular, his business and finances to find a reason someone might have targeted him. And we can start with the Desert Rose development."

"You're talking out your butt, Mr. County Prosecutor." Benny sipped his coffee, but missed his mouth, causing drops to run down the front of his uniform. "Dammit."

He handed him a napkin. "After the meeting about the development, Nick Vargas was on top of the world. Then Max Castro spots his body at seven the next morning. Isn't that too coincidental for a random killer? Here's another thing that's bothering me. At that same meeting, the developer Richard Wright and Vargas appeared to be bosom buddies. Yet, there was no emotion. It smacked of closing a deal."

Benny sat up a bit.

"What kind of deal did they have? And did it get the commissioner killed? You were there, bro. You saw it," Matthew said.

Benny tilted his head.

"There's a lot of money involved in that development, and money is always a good motive for murder. You have a county commissioner supporting the largest construction project to hit the county in decades. Could be that somebody doesn't want that development to happen, or, better yet, wants all the money from it."

"But Jackson Rogers had nothing to do with Desert Rose." Benny stood up to his full imposing height.

"That we know of."

"I worked with Jackson for six years."

"What about *his* finances?"

"That was his business." Benny sat back down. "But the way they were killed spells S-Y-C-O."

"That's such an easy explanation. I can't help but feel that Vargas's murder was so, so . . ."

"*¿Qué?*"

"Deliberate. There's always a reason for murder, Benny. The only prints in the deputy's car were his, so the killer wore gloves. That's damn deliberate."

Benny exhaled with frustration, but Matthew couldn't tell if it was because of the case or his speculations.

Probably both.

"Benny, this is a long shot but it's all we have to go on, so let's follow it until we can't or until I'm proved totally wrong." His voice grew more heated than he intended. His friend was the most amiable fellow he'd ever met, but when Benny's stubbornness kicked in, he could be immovable.

"Well, Sheriff? You're the one who asked for my help and here it is."

Benny knotted fingers together and then gave a deep nod. "Meanwhile, I'll keep up the patrols to catch the psycho. So where else do we look for a suspect?"

He smiled and Benny smiled back, which made him feel better. "At that development meeting, Josh Vale was very outspoken about the resort. He was downright angry."

"Josh is wacky, but not wacky enough to skin a commissioner and cut off a deputy's arms and legs."

"Maybe. Maybe not. He's a hunter. Ever see the walls at his garage? Norman Bates, man, Norman Bates."

"That don't mean shit. I go hunting."

"He knows how to use a knife."

"Everyone in Guadalupe knows how to use a knife, even the women. Mostly, the women." Benny grinned.

"But not everyone can skin an animal."

"*Ay, yi, yi*, Mateo. Josh doesn't use a stone knife."

"You got a better suspect, *amigo*?"

Benny didn't.

Chapter 23

Josh's Garage sat on the outskirts of Guadalupe. Cars in various stages of repair surrounded it. Before driving out there, Benny ran a report to see if owner Josh Vale had been in trouble with the law. The only items were citations from the city for weeds and unsightly property, and a misdemeanor for a drunk and disorderly on Easter Sunday.

The interior walls of the repair shop were indeed Norman Bates-ish. The stuffed heads and glassy eyes of a mountain lion, skunk, bear, deer, and coyote gazed down at them. Matthew's chin lifted to the furry wall décor so that Benny would get his drift. If Vale could skin animals, he could skin Nick Vargas. He could cut the limbs off Jackson Rogers.

When they entered, Vale was chewing on a sandwich at the dingy counter, defiance in his every bite. His wife Louise sat on a little stool in the corner and threw visual daggers at them.

"What do you two want?" Vale said.

"That's what I like about you. Right to the point," Matthew said.

Vale addressed his wife. "See, hon, it's what I've always said. Lawyers specialize in BS."

She grunted agreement and sipped coffee out of a chipped mug.

"You heard about what happened to Nick Vargas and Deputy Rogers?" Benny asked in his best sheriff's voice.

"She-et, everybody in town heard that. What do I look like, a moron?" Vale grinned. Bread stuck to his teeth.

Benny's face reddened. "Okay, okay, dumb question."

Vale grinned. "So the hell what?"

"That shows no respect for the dead." Matthew shot back. "And why would you say that, anyway?"

"Because all cops and elected officials are crooked."

Benny made fists.

"I got a better question. Where were you on the nights Nick Vargas and Jackson Rogers were killed?" Matthew said.

Vale's wife heaved her plus-size body off of the stool. "You don't have to answer, Josh."

"Oh yes, he does, Josh. Right, Benny?"

"You bet."

"You think they were killed because of that resort, don't you?" Vale dug into a bag of barbecue potato chips.

"You have a better reason? You were quite outspoken at the meeting about the development," Matthew said.

Vale crunched chips.

"Where were you?"

"I hate to disappoint Mr. Attorney, but you're barking up the wrong man." Vale threw the rest of the sandwich into the trash.

"You got an alibi?" Benny asked.

Vale stood. "Damn right. The night Rogers died, me and the wife were visiting her sick ma up in Santa Fe. She's in a nursing home."

His wife quickly thumbed through files in an overstuffed filing cabinet. "Here's the receipt from the motel where we stayed. You can check." She shoved a greasy bill in their direction.

"Don't worry. We will." Matthew glanced at it. The date fit their story.

Vale sat back on his stool and crossed his arms with annoying smugness.

"What about the night Vargas died?" Matthew said. "You were at the meeting."

"We went to the Cactus Inn after that and ran into some friends. We stayed there until eleven. Then we went home," Vale said.

"That would still give you time to pay a visit to the commissioner. He died between midnight and seven."

"That's more bullshit." Vale stood up.

"Anyone see you come home?"

"We saw each other," his wife volunteered.

"That doesn't count, Mrs. Vale," Benny said.

"Well, it should."

Matthew looked at Benny and then to Vale. "From your décor, you like to hunt and skin animals."

"Duh."

"Can we see what knives you use?"

"Don't you need a warrant?"

Matthew smiled. "I'm asking pretty please. It might remove you from our suspect list."

"I'm on a list?" He puffed out his chest. "What the hell? I'm innocent, so I got nothing to hide."

Vale pulled up his dirty pants and led Matthew and Benny out to a smaller garage in back. Mrs. Vale followed, her hate stares intensifying so much that Matthew wondered if her head might blow.

After opening a sturdy lock, Vale pulled back the double doors with a creak. He flicked on a light. A locked gun cabinet sat against one wall. Hanging on another wall were two bows and wicked-looking hunting arrows.

In one corner, a metal hook dangled from the ceiling with a drain underneath. Matthew touched the dark remnants of blood. He flicked off a bit with a small penknife he carried and placed it in an envelope.

"What you doing?" Vale's wife said.

"Just seeing what kind of blood this is."

"All deer," Vale said. "And elk."

He then spread out his collection of knives on a table. A dozen of them, some older, some newer. Some shiny-new from a store, others worn by use. All sharp.

Matthew and Benny examined them. No rock knife, but he didn't think Vale was so stupid as to keep a murder weapon in plain sight.

"You boys satisfied?" Vale said.

"I will be if you can verify where you were when Vargas died," Matthew said.

Vale sputtered. "Look, I don't want that damn resort, but I ain't gonna kill over it." Another grin. "I guess you boys are at square one."

"And I ain't voting for either of you at the next election." Louise Vale snickered with spit and satisfaction as she and her husband headed inside.

"Say goodbye to a suspect." Benny put on his cowboy hat once they were outside of the garage.

"You're right. If he didn't kill Rogers, he probably didn't kill Vargas, despite the fact he has no alibi for that night."

"Now where?"

Matthew adjusted his tie. "The widow."

****

Widow Patty Vargas was dressed in jeans and a stylish black T-shirt. She looked good. In fact, thought Matthew, she looked really good for someone whose husband had been recently flayed. Then again, how *should* she behave? He had phoned her earlier to say he wanted to check out her late husband's office to see if it held clues that would help solve his murder. This was not a request.

"How are you, Mrs. Vargas?"

"Numb and angry."

"That's probably to be expected."

"How else should I act when my husband's been horribly murdered?"

She led him to a grand study twice as large as his office at the courthouse.

"You mentioned that Nick was very excited about the Desert Rose development, and that your futures were set. Did he mention having any disputes with the developers or other business associates?"

"It can't be the people he worked with, Mr. Riley. Only a psycho would do that to him." Her breath did smell of scotch.

He pushed his lips together. What was it about psychos?

"Nothing about the development, Mrs. Vargas?"

"All he would say is that the project would be good for the county and the town. I should have asked him more about his business, but he was so successful he must have known exactly what he was doing." Her voice reflected pride in her dead husband.

"I'd still like to look at his office."

"I understand. You have a job to do too, catching his killer." She pulled a key from her jeans. "I found this and opened the drawers in the desk and credenza."

"I appreciate that. What about his computer? I'd like to look at his files."

"I'm sorry. I don't have the password."

"We may have to borrow the drive."

"I don't care."

He was happy she wasn't putting up a fight.

The doorbell's chimes sang like a children's choir.

"That'll probably be the sheriff," Matthew said. "He was out on patrol and said he'd join me here."

"I'll let him in and then be in my room if you need anything else." She left, swaying a smidge as she went.

He and Benny had already gone through Nick's desk at the courthouse, but it produced no clues. Vargas's file on the Desert Rose only contained copies of the informational pamphlet and proposed plans.

In the study, Matthew went through papers in the drawers of a mahogany desk. He glanced up. Benny stood in the doorway, slumped over like a melted ice cream cone. He suddenly felt guilty for not doing this himself and letting his friend get some rest.

"You look beat. I can handle this. Go home," he said.

"It's okay. I just need coffee." Benny walked over to the desk. "What are we looking for?"

"Anything related to the Desert Rose development. Please search that pile of papers on the desk and I'll look in the drawers. Tax returns and bank statements are good. Always trace the money."

Benny set to work. Matthew moved his search from the desk drawers to the credenza.

"At last," he said after a while.

"What?"

"Money, baby, money."

He had found a file of bank statements. The deposit column on one caught his attention and he snapped the paper with his fingernail. "Check it out. Vargas made a $60,000 deposit two weeks ago."

"What about it? I hear his construction business is raking in money."

"No doubt, but he made this deposit the same day he disappeared. If that's a coincidence, then I'm Oliver Wendell Holmes."

"*Who* Holmes?"

"Sherlock's brother."

"Asshole."

"Lighten up, bro."

Matthew called for Patty Vargas to join them in the study and asked her about the deposit. The petite woman's mouth opened at the amount and she had no idea about where it came from.

She held onto the bank statement. "It's nothing illegal, is it, Mr. Riley?" she said with hesitation.

"That depends."

"This serves me right for keeping house and not keeping in his business."

****

Jim Randall appeared capable of tossing cement blocks over his head with ease. Brawn crammed in a white business shirt.

Randall balanced reading glasses on his nose as he peered at the computer screen. He was Nick Vargas's VP at Vargas Construction. A photo of Randall and Vargas wearing hard hats and shaking hands hung in Randall's office. Matthew and Benny sat across the desk from him.

"Mr. Riley, Sheriff, we haven't signed a large contract in months that would have coughed up the amount of revenue you mentioned."

"What was your last major job?" Matthew said.

"The hospital renovation last January. Certainly, we've had smaller jobs, but nothing that would have cleared Nick that kind of profit. The hospital project would have, so maybe he just held onto the money." Randall's voice was surprisingly refined in contrast to his hulk.

"Did Nick mention this amount of money?"

"No, sir, but he kept his personal finances to himself." Randall gave an understanding smile.

"How about the Desert Rose development?"

"Oh, yes. He talked about how it would benefit the community. He also said he'd probably have to resign from the county commission."

"Why?" said Benny.

"So our company could bid for the construction."

"I mentioned that at the meeting, Benny. A conflict of interest," Matthew said.

Randall smiled. "The Desert Rose development would be a major undertaking, and needless to say, very profitable."

"One other thing, Mr. Randall." Matthew held up a printout. "This is a copy of the listing of the Desert Rose Development LLC from the Secretary of State's office. The only partners listed are Richard Wright and Samuel Uhlig, Wright's attorney."

"That's news to me," Randall said and he believed him.

"I'm sorry; this is an indelicate question, but it must be asked."

"I'll try not to be offended, Mr. Riley."

"Do you think that Nick Vargas received any payment from the developers to, say, help the Desert Rose project roll smoothly through the county system?"

Benny rolled his eyes.

Randall rocked slightly in his chair. He glanced at the photo of himself and Vargas. This smile was more of a shy one. "Nick and I worked together for eleven years, but that was it. We weren't friends in any sense. We didn't go fishing together or have barbecues at each other's houses." He crossed his arms. "We only interacted professionally, not personally. In some regards, he was stranger."

"I understand that very well. I worked with him, also. So what about the kickback?"

"I can't answer that. I really can't."

"Do you think he was capable of accepting a bribe?"

"You mean was he honest?" Randall chewed on one end of his glasses. "Mr. Riley, I never saw any indication he was overtly dishonest, but Nick was a businessman and a damn good one. He knew how to make money, and sometimes, that meant not always going in a straight line."

"Where the hell did you come up with that kickback stuff, Matthew?" Benny said when they were near his patrol car.

"You tell me where a guy could earn $60,000 in one day?"

"Sell drugs? Be a hired assassin?" Benny was not good with jokes.

"On the other hand, his mother-in-law thought Nick was always looking for the next big deal. He might have found one that was so big it ended up biting him in the ass."

Chapter 24

"BINGO!" shouted a woman a few tables over.

"*Ay.*" Consuela rapped the table at not hitting one win all evening. Usually, she was lucky at the game. That is, until that day. First, a murder, then a funeral, then another murder, and now a shutout of her favorite game, four corners.

She should have been depressed, but found it difficult to sustain the gloom. After her husband had abandoned Matthew and her, she had despaired for a full two weeks because she did love the man. But she had a boy to raise and only cried at night, and then not at all. Lying in bed surrounded by flowers of wet tissues from her sorrow, she had decided that life was too damn short to spend on tears. Her optimism was her sole virtue, specifically the ability to remember that no matter the misery of the night before, the sun would shine again in the morning.

"Ah well, maybe I'll have better luck on the next one," Consuela told Anita Rodríguez, her best friend since high school. She drove Anita to the game because her friend's eyesight was terrible at night.

"Win or lose, I just love playing," Anita said.

Anita was almost twice Consuela's size with a row of freckles over plentiful cheeks and a head of bountiful reddish hair. Consuela kidded Anita that she must be part Irish. Anita admitted with a horn of a laugh that her favorite cereal *was* Lucky Charms.

"We'll play another game in a few minutes, so relax and talk to your neighbors," announced the Moose member calling the numbers. He was a spry bald man whose chest was the size of a mini fridge. He winked at Consuela when his wife wasn't looking. The caller always tried to be funny when calling the bingo numbers, like saying "B-12, my favorite vitamin." Few people laughed.

A healthy crowd filled the remodeled Moose Hall on Diego Street for the bi-weekly bingo game. Players took their favorite spots at the round tables on the parquet floor. Consuela and Anita always chose a table in the corner so they could see everybody. They shared a love of gossip and cooking and had a relationship as close as sisters. They consoled each other when Anita's husband died two years ago and when Consuela's husband left long before that. A retired elementary teacher, Anita had baptized Matthew and never forgot to send him gift cards on his birthday. Consuela loved her friend's ability to make her smile.

"That Judy Robbins won again." Anita tore off the bingo sheet ready for the next game. "I think she must have an in with the guy who calls the numbers." She targeted her bingo dauber at the man who sat on the stage at the front of the hall. "I'm going to keep an eye on him."

"You're just sore loser, Anita."

"No, sir. I'd just like to win a jackpot once in a while."

"You and me both."

Anita reached for a handful of popcorn from a plastic bowl. "So how was Nick Vargas's funeral?"

"Sad as hell. Why didn't you go?"

"I never knew the guy. Don't forget, he only got elected because his cousin Victor ran against him and the cousin was worse. I heard there was no open coffin, so I guess ole Nick was really torn up. Least that's what I read in the newspaper."

"Yes, it was so scary the way he died."

"You betcha. Removing a man's skin as if peeling an apple. Gross."

"Anita, you're too much."

"Well, you didn't like Nick Vargas either."

"He was a greedy man. He smiled with his gums. God rest his soul." Consuela took a sip of coffee and smiled. The Moose Hall did make a good cup of coffee.

"And then that deputy got killed on the road." Anita raised her eyebrows up and down and whispered, "So what did my godson tell you about that one? The news only said the deputy was mutilated."

Consuela blew out her breath. "Isn't that enough? Besides, Matthew won't tell me a thing, but I don't think that deputy went peacefully."

"Why won't Mateo give you the juicy details?"

"He wants to protect me."

"That's sweet, but what good is having a son who knows everything happening in the county when he won't give you the dirt?" Anita grabbed another handful of popcorn.

The caller blew into the microphone and smiled. "This is game four. We are doing a Z formation."

The bingophiles twittered because that was another of their favorite figures. The white balls in the bingo machine tapped against the glass panels as the machine bustled. The caller picked out one. "B-15. Like the bomber, B-15."

"Oh, brother." Consuela motioned her thumb toward the announcer. "This guy needs new jokes."

"You said it."

"I-21, I'll never be twenty-one again. I-21"

Several people chattered at finding that number on their cards, but they hushed up at the successive pounding of thunder outside. The wall-to-ceiling windows in the front of the building flared with lightning and the whole place rattled with another thunder crash.

"Maybe we get rain this time, no?" Anita tightened her fist around the bingo dauber. "My flowers could use it."

"G-30. Could be the name of a bathroom cleaner. G-30," the caller said.

Consuela removed her left sandal and rubbed her toes. "Anita, it doesn't feel like rain. My corns don't ache."

"N-37," announced the caller. "I'll never see thirty-seven again, N-37."

With another rumble outside, the lights in the hall sparked out. With no electricity, the bingo machine also died. The players groused at not being able to go on with the game.

"Turn those lights back on," one player yelled.

"Just a power outage folks," shouted the caller. "We'll be playing again soon. We'll just go check the breaker box." Then he and another Moose member headed to a back room.

"Darn it. I had the feeling this was going to be my game," Consuela said above the complaints of the other players.

Another lightning flash sparked in the sky, vivid enough to momentarily light up the hall through the windows. Then the building went dark again. The hair on Consuela's arms stood straight up, as did Anita's short hair.

"You look like you put your finger in a socket," Consuela said.

Anita patted down her hair. "Must be the electricity from the lightning."

The metal roof of the building began to ping with a light rain. In seconds, the ping escalated into crashes sounding like buckets of nails hammering the roof.

"Must be a hail storm," Anita said loudly above the din.

Consuela looked through the windows. There was no rain. There was no hail. "Anita, there's nothing outside."

Her friend saw she was right and then made a slow sign of the cross. "God, I hope it's not a tornado."

The crashing on the roof amped up to a deafening noise. Many of the older people huddled together and held their hands against their ears. Consuela, Anita, and other players who were more curious than frightened stepped out of the front double doors. The sky was clear. Still, the crash of thunder and flash of a nonexistent lightning boomed against the building.

"Mother of God," Consuela said over the metallic racket.

"Sounds like hail," shouted Anita. "But nothing's falling. How loco is that?"

"Invisible hail? That is loco," Consuela shouted back and wondered if everyone at the hall was sharing a nightmare or hallucination.

The crashing thunder and lightning ended. The racket stopped. Consuela's ears buzzed with the stillness. She and Anita went back inside the still dark building. With a click, the electricity blinked on, causing a loud gasp at those frightened by the sudden light.

"I'm glad that's over so we can get on with our game," the caller announced, eliciting nervous laughter.

The bingo players took their seats, although a tad edgy. More than a dozen people left the building and drove home, giving up their chance for a bingo.

Sipping the now cold coffee, Consuela noticed that her hands shook. She looked over at Anita but the best friends dared not talk about what they had witnessed, just in case it might return.

"O-75," said the caller in a slightly shaking voice. "I wish I was seventy-five one more time. O-75."

The place calmed because after all, there was nothing that a good game of bingo would not cure, or so Consuela hoped.

****

In the kitchen, Matthew sized up his mother as if she sat on the stand. He really wanted to believe this witness, but was having the hardest time.

"Matthew Francisco Riley, don't you dare look at me like that."

When he woke that Saturday, he knew something must be wrong because breakfast wasn't ready. But he hadn't expected her story about the bingo game the previous night. He had worked late and she was asleep by the time he got home.

"Mama, that story is just incredible."

"You calling me a liar, son?"

"No."

"Ask all those people playing down at the Moose Hall if you don't believe me, Mr. Lawyer. Ask your godmother, Anita." She held out her arms. "I'll even take a lie detector test, Mateo."

He gave a smile and took her hands. "I think it was a freak storm. The desert can be unpredictable. That or kids were trying to scare you guys, and it seems these shenanigans have been going on too much lately. Like the headless hogs at Alma Chacon's house."

"You haven't heard a word I said." She dinged him on the head with her middle finger. When he was growing up and wouldn't listen to her she did that a lot.

"Yes, I have. Here's what's really happening." He patted down the hair she had displaced. "Guadalupe is usually a nice quiet town. Along comes these grisly murders and people are nervous. It's like when a house creaks at night and you think there's a burglar."

"*Mijo*, it was an omen, a sign that something evil has come to Guadalupe. Alma predicted it at the funeral. You want evidence. Here is evidence. That little boy disappeared from the pool. Two men were murdered and not in a good way. Two other men saw a demon in the park. Hog heads were dumped on Alma's lawn. Then this mysterious thunder and lightning at the Moose Hall. That is a lot of strangeness, son."

Matthew gently guided his mother to a seat. "Mama, you're a very smart woman. An educated woman. Do you really think demons or evil spirits were throwing rocks on the roof of the Moose Hall during the middle of your bingo game?"

She refused to look at his face.

"The two guys who claimed they saw that demon are known to exaggerate. As for the killings, we're looking into that, but they were committed by a man, or woman, and not the devil."

"What about that little boy who vanished in the water?"

Matthew didn't have an answer to that. "All I can tell you is that there's a sensible explanation for everything."

"This is one of your lawyer tricks."

"It's just logic. We learn that in lawyer school." He hoped she'd smile at his joke, but she didn't. He took another tactic. "We'll find whoever killed Nick Vargas and the deputy, and then Guadalupe can go back to being the boring small town you love so much."

The older woman stood. Instead of starting to cook, she went into the living room. He followed her, curious since he knew his mother didn't give up so easily on an argument when she believed she was right. On a shelf near the door she had placed a foot-tall ceramic statue of the Christ child, the Niño de Luz, which was the unofficial patron of the town. He would bet almost every Catholic home in Guadalupe had the same statue. Around their statue's neck hung a rosary, a medal on a silver chain, and a collection of scapulars.

Consuela handed the chain to Matthew. The medal had the likeness of the Niño de Luz on one side and the crucifix on the other. "You used to wear this when you were a little boy to protect you from harm. Somewhere you stopped wearing it. Wear this medal for me now, *por favor, mijo.*"

"Mama."

She smiled. "Even if you don't believe any of this, what could it hurt?"

Matthew took the chain and put it on. On his neck, he felt the warmth of the metal from where she had held it. He kissed her cheek. "*Gracias.* And don't worry about anything. You're just letting your imagination get the best of you."

"It's possible that all the weird stuff is getting to me."

"Only bad people are responsible. Demons and the devil have nothing to do with this."

"Okay, son. I was afraid I was going to have to give up bingo."

Laughing, she drew pans from the cupboard and eggs and chorizo from the refrigerator to start breakfast.

Chapter 25

Proud family members packed the Niño de Luz Catholic Church on Main Avenue. The reason for the crowd sat in the two front rows. Boys in dark suits and ties and little girls wearing white communion dresses and veils.

Angel Riley sat among them.

Father Henry Cantu occupied his place at the front of the church for the homily. The priest was over six feet and slender with dark skin and darker eyes that lightened whenever he talked about God. He kept his longish dark brown hair in a ponytail which caused much chitter among the older parishioners who wondered about whether he was a hidden hippie. They said as much to Father Joe De La Cruz, the main pastor of the church. The older priest merely smiled with perfect teeth and replied that if Samson could wear his hair long, so could Father Cantu. They couldn't argue with such a Biblical reference.

That Sunday, the young priest wore white and gold vestments as befitting the welcoming of thirty new souls into the church.

"We have all heard the story of how the Indians found the statue of the baby Jesus in the desert and how the townspeople built this house of God to honor him." His voice was compassionate and convincing. "Through the years, many of the faithful have witnessed the miracles brought by faith in the Niño de Luz. The statue glowing with light and purity. Its healing of wounds and souls. Our Niño de Luz, the child of light. How it brings our community together. Then as now, those who believe in Him are healed and can bask in the radiance of faith."

Sitting with Isabel and his mother, Matthew studied the statue enclosed in a glass case on the right side of the dark wooden altar. The ceramic baby Jesus wore a crown and sat on a throne. Its feet had been rubbed to nubs by all the people who kissed them in hopes of healings and blessings. It was a beautiful statue, but the eyes always bothered him. They were the type that followed you even when you didn't want to be seen. They appeared alive and not made of paint.

The Niño was the town's soul, appearing in everything from store windows to tourist trinkets sold for the festival held in its name. The symbol would have also made its way onto the city seal, but the city attorney had advised the council against it, saying that amounted to a violation of mixing church and state.

Matthew had been raised to believe in God and the Niño's protection of Guadalupe, but he had stopped going to church right after his separation from Isabel. His mom didn't bully him into returning. She had once told him she could never force him into faith. He either believed or he didn't, though he suspected he disappointed her. Did he lose it when he lost Isabel? When did he become cynical about miracles? When did he stop believing? The statue's eyes stared as if daring him to answer those.

"We wonder if we are worthy, but the test will not come in happiness but in times of trouble." The priest wrapped up, his voice rising and his hands tight together. "These days can be challenging for all of us. We worry about the future and regret the past, but faith will bridge that and take us to a new and better place."

Matthew hated when the priest seemed to be talking directly to him.

Father Cantu spread his arms. "So, it is very appropriate we welcome these young people into the church so near that holy festival dedicated to the Niño de Luz. These children are lights in our community."

Later in the mass, the children lined up to receive their first host of Christ. Many shuffled feet, others twitched with nerves, or walked stiffly as they drew closer to the priest. A professional photographer had been hired to capture the moment when each kid was presented the host. Matthew and Isabel moved into good positions to see their son. Angel stood straight, his hands held in prayer as they had coached him. After their boy received the communion wafer, he grinned wide at his parents. At that moment, Isabel took his hand with such tenderness it was going to be near impossible for him to leave town even though they were apart.

After the ceremony, the crowd moved to the adjoining parish hall. Women of the church league served a lunch of Mexican and American foods. Chicken enchiladas, Spanish rice, sliced turkey and ham, and mashed potatoes. Desserts covered a long table. Besides coffee and lemonade, wine was offered to the adults, because, as Matthew concluded, any Catholic celebration had to include wine and not just at the mass. If it wasn't Canon Law, it should be.

"Good turnout," he said to Father Cantu.

"Yes, it is. I just wish the other masses would be so packed."

He laughed.

"Still, after five years as a priest, I've learned to be happy with what I get and pray for the rest."

Within minutes, the boys had taken off their ties and jackets, and the girls handed veils to their moms and dads. They barely ate lunch and darted around laughing and playing.

"They make me tired just looking at them." Matthew sat at a table with Consuela, Isabel, Benny, and Camilla.

"Were we ever that young, Mateo?" Benny said.

"Yes, and you were both troublemakers," Consuela added.

Everyone laughed, although Camilla started to cough. Benny handed her a glass of water. In the last year, his wife had grown frailer. Her face wilted from discomfort, and her thinning hair was more white than brown. Benny would only say her heart had weakened, but no more about her medical problems. He didn't push him for more information. He figured the subject of Camilla was too painful for Benny to discuss. Benny would talk when Benny was ready.

The change in her was striking, however.

Benny had loved Camilla when he spotted her in a senior English class in high school. She was vivacious with a kind face. At their wedding reception at this very same church hall, Benny had told best man Matthew how damn lucky he was to have such a woman love him. Matthew had agreed.

Benny waved Angel over to the table.

"Camilla and I have something for you." He handed the boy an envelope.

Angel pulled out two $100 bills and waved them about. "Geez, this is great. Thanks, Uncle Benny and Aunt Camilla." He hugged them. Although they weren't related, Angel called them that for all their gifts and love.

But Matthew and Isabel traded glances.

"Benny, Camilla, we can't accept that," Isabel said.

"Yes, too much." Consuela said.

Matthew nodded, took the bills, and attempted to hand them back to Benny.

He pushed his hand out, refusing to take the money. "Nothing is too good for our godson."

"Don't hurt our feelings," said Camilla, whose smile was still pretty despite her waning condition.

"Please, Mom. Please, Daddy. Please *Abuela*," Angel said.

They relented.

"But it goes into the bank for your college," Isabel said.

"Can't I buy a new Lego police station set?"

"Okay, but the rest is for higher education," Matthew said.

"Oh boy! I want to show the money to the guys." Angel grabbed it away.

"No, I'll hold onto it, baby." Isabel held out her hand.

Angel gave up the bills with a pout. "All right, Mom." The brooding over the money didn't last long. "Hey, Dad, can you take me out to the old pueblo? Jimmie Montez says it's haunted. His dad told him that Indian ghosts are running around out there."

"Afraid not, son. It's dangerous and it's private property," Matthew said. "Don't go anyplace near there."

Angel kicked at the floor. "I can't do anything."

"You can do lots, son. You can go play with the other kids."

Angel smiled with contentment and ran to join his friends.

A four-piece band began playing as the floor filled with couples. Consuela excused herself to go help a group of older women clean up the hall kitchen.

Camilla coughed delicately into her handkerchief. She raised her head to see Benny, Isabel, and Matthew looking at her with concern. "I'm fine. Benny, ask Isabel to dance. That's an order."

Benny held out his hand. "Come on, Isabel, let me step on your toes."

"I'd love to." She took hold of his hand and they headed out to the makeshift dancefloor.

Camilla watched her husband. "Poor, Benny. I'm a burden to him."

Matthew placed his hand on hers. "No, you're not. You're the best thing that ever happened to Benny. He loves you so much. In fact, you're a blessing to all of us."

"I hate being like this." Camilla gripped her tiny legs. "Every breath, every move is full of pain and fatigue. I get up in the morning and wonder why this is happening to me." She smiled, her old beautiful smile. "Then I remember I'm so grateful for the life I've had each day."

"That's the way to think. Listen, if you or Benny ever need anything, I'll be there for you."

She waved a tiny hand. "Benny is taking me to a heart specialist in Albuquerque next week."

"Is that going to be expensive? As it is, the county insurance plan sucks. I have some money set aside I can lend you."

"Thank you, Mateo, but Benny says he has a little nest egg that he's been building."

"He never mentioned that."

"He's a very proud man. You know that better than any of us."

"Yeah, I do."

Two boys bumped Camilla's chair as they ran past. "Hey guys, be careful," he told them.

"Sorry, Mr. Riley," they yelled and ran in a different direction.

Camilla smiled sadly. "You and Isabel are so lucky to have Angel."

She and Benny had discovered soon after they were married that she was unable to have children. Matthew had suggested that they adopt but his friend said he could never warm to the idea. He and Camilla had each other and that was good for a lifetime.

"Yes, we're lucky to have Angel, and Benny is lucky to have you." He kissed Camilla's cheek.

Benny stood over them. "Hey, quit making time with my wife."

Camilla laughed.

"Go be useful. Dance with Isabel." Benny pointed to the kitchen.

"I know when I'm not wanted."

He found Isabel with Consuela and other women. "Isabel, how about stepping on *my* toes?"

Consuela playfully bumped Isabel with her hips. "Go ahead. We're done here. We're just chatting."

Isabel took Matthew's hand and they danced smoothly, like the couple they used to be. Angel zoomed past them, a happy kid.

He took in her flowery perfume, the one he had jokingly called Ode de French Whorehouse. Whenever he did, she had good-naturedly punched his arm. Damn, he had missed that smell. He was becoming blind to all but the murder case.

"How's your leg, Matthew?"

"A little achy, but better. My first knife wound. I should get a medal or something. And please don't quote me on that, whatever you do."

"Okay, off the record, even though I didn't cover your knife fight." She squeezed his hand.

Because Isabel was still married to him, another reporter had written up the news story about Juarez's knife assault and called him for a quote. He didn't have anything to say.

"I've got to ask. Why did the newspaper publish that story about the invisible storm at the Moose Hall? That's *National Enquirer* crap."

"We went with it because we had lots of calls about what happened out there. Even your mom told me about it, but I didn't quote her."

"Thanks. How's Angel?"

"He had another nightmare."

"I didn't feed him bad shit at the baseball field, I promise."

Her hands tensed up.

"What's wrong, Isa? This is supposed to be a happy occasion."

"I'm worried about him and these nightmares. I'm thinking they might have something to do with us." Her eyes blinked tears. She didn't cry often.

"I talked with him. He wants me to stay."

"Will you?"

"I don't want to go, but . . ."

"I know. Your career."

"Isabel."

She relaxed in his arms. "Well, no matter what was bad between us, we did something good, Matthew."

"Yes, we did. He is one great kid." He twirled her around and she laughed.

They noticed Benny help Camilla to her feet. Benny waved goodbye before they headed out the door. Matthew's skin itched under his shirt and he wriggled.

"Anything wrong, Matthew?"

"Nothing."

"Something is clicking in that lawyer brain of yours." She tapped his forehead.

"You're always so suspicious." He twirled her twice.

She threw her head back and laughed again. "Let's just enjoy the tranquility. It may not last long."

Chapter 26

FUTURE HOME OF THE DESERT ROSE RESORT
RICHARD WRIGHT, DEVELOPER
NO TRESPASSING

The plastic sign was the newest thing on the place.

To get there, Matthew and Benny had headed north out of town, drove fifteen miles on the state highway, and another five miles on a dirt road, which was not in bad shape. The sign stood at the entrance to a road leading to the property. After a half mile, they passed a row of aspen trees, entered a clearing, and parked.

The desert view of cactus, dirt, and yucca was replaced with a setting that even captivated Matthew. A blue-green mountain range ascended in the distance. Hardy stands of firs, palo verde trees, pinon pines, and aspens triumphed out of yellow and green grasslands. A creek wider than three cars end-to-end cut the property almost in half. The water was so clear he saw a trout dart past. Slim-fingered willows graced the creek banks. The whispering of the hastening water complemented that of a breeze shuffling over the tips of the trees. He blinked hard to quell emotion he didn't want to feel. Not to leave all this beauty.

"I can understand why Richard Wright wanted this property."

He removed his suit jacket, placed it in Benny's vehicle, and began to shoot photos with his digital camera. He had had his secretary call Wright's office to tell them they would be out there as part of the investigation into Vargas's murder.

Benny put on his cowboy hat. "Yeah, it's pretty. But I can't really understand why we had to come out here."

He obviously wasn't impressed by the scenery.

"I needed to see it," Matthew said.

"There's nothing here but dirt and dreams."

"That's poetic, bro, but Nick Vargas died after throwing his support toward this development. And that's what may have gotten him killed."

"Lots of people are backing the resort, and nobody else was skinned."

"Indulge me. Besides, I've always wanted to see the ruins." He started toward them with a grin and jaunt.

The property formerly owned by the late Mecho Hernández was known for more than its panorama. The remains of an old Indian pueblo swept out over the north side. From a distance, they were a phantom emerging out of the grass. He and Benny crossed a wooden bridge over the creek. As they approached the ruins, rabbits and lizards scampered in their path.

The village consisted of a dozen adjoining adobe block houses. Stacked on them were four more levels of houses, narrower than the ones below. The structure appeared taller, almost an optical illusion. Wooden logs sticking out of the top of the structures created sundials on the walls. But neglect and nature had worn down the buildings on the ends and reduced them to jagged bones. Still, there was a mystery to the pueblo, as if belonging to another world just out of reach.

Almost shyly, he and Benny peeked into the intact houses. The dilapidated wooden doors were askew on tired hinges or missing altogether. Sunlight came through little windows and created the appearance of a cell rather than a home. Inside laid remnants of life. Metal bedsprings. A spoon on the uneven wood floor. Overturned chairs and tables. A baby's broken crib.

Grasses and other weeds were the only inhabitants.

Matthew imagined the heartache of the indigenous people who had abandoned their homes. The Puebloans who resided there had departed in the night, or so went the town rumors. People claimed they were spooked off by evil spirits or that their wells ran dry. The real reason for the exodus was unknown, even to the members of the Mesquite Historical Society who claimed to know everything about the county's past. They only reported that the land had been given to Mecho Hernández, who knew the whole truth about the Indians. He didn't talk then and couldn't talk now.

The pueblo had been uninhabited for as long as Matthew could remember, but he hadn't gotten this close before. Hernández had allowed no tourists or town residents anywhere near. But every kid in Guadalupe had wanted to check out the old pueblo. Who wouldn't? The ruins appeared ghostly even in the daylight. A southwestern version of a haunted mansion. As kids, he and Benny made up their own stories about why the pueblo was empty. Their conjectures included mass murders, zombie attacks, or his favorite: the Indians had all been abducted by aliens. Many kids had attempted to slip onto the property for a peek inside the ruins, but Hernández scared them off with loud warnings about a shotgun that he wasn't afraid to use on trespassers and occasionally shot it in the air to back up his threats.

In junior high, Matthew suggested to Benny that they politely ask the old guy if they could tour the ruins instead of sneaking onto the place. They rode their bikes there, planning on what to say to the old man. They decided Matthew would talk since it was his idea. Once there, they didn't get past the gate. Hernández brandished his legendary shotgun. Diminutive and lean, he wore a clean work shirt and khaki pants held up by colorful suspenders. Over skin that resembled a well-used football was a short beard. He looked old even then. Yet, his eyes were as forceful as bullets.

Pointing the barrel at them, Hernández had called his land a sacred place and ordered them to get out—all in Spanish. He added a few Spanish curse words, all of which Matthew knew. Still, he tried to assure Hernández that he and Benny would touch nothing and be respectful.

"Get the hell out," replied the old man.

He could not be persuaded otherwise.

A few times after that, Matthew would spot Hernández shopping in stores in Guadalupe. Hernández spoke to no one and no one greeted him. There goes a lonely grouchy guy, he had thought.

Years later, he and Benny stood at the pueblo at last, and he had to confess the wait wasn't worth it.

"If nothing else, we finally got to go inside," he told Benny.

Benny chewed on his toothpick. "All that time we wanted to come here and there's not much to see." He picked up a broken adobe brick and then tossed it to the ground. "Kinda disappointing."

"Let's check out Hernández's house."

Despite the sunny day, his friend's mood lingered in the dark.

"What's up, man?"

"Nothing. Just tired." He gave a half-smile. "Maybe I need more vitamin D or something." He walked on.

The single-level white house stood five yards from the clearing where they had parked. A row of aspen trees provided shade. Dried up rose bushes lined a stone walkway. In the back of the wood-framed house were chicken pens and corrals, all empty. Lines of yellowed cornstocks, and tomato and chili plants bent over dead in an abandoned garden. A scarecrow wearing a plaid shirt and patched overalls lay face down in the dirt. Although the plants were overgrown and weeds sprouted, the place showed the old man had taken care of it when he was alive. The exception were the bodies of a junker car and truck near where Benny had parked in the clearing.

The door of the house was not locked, a bad sign to Matthew. The interior was indeed a wreck. Chairs had been thrown about and the couch lay on its side. Dishes were smashed on the floor. Cupboards and drawers opened and the contents strewn about. The linoleum had been ripped up from parts of the kitchen floor.

"Damn vandals," Benny said as he stood in the doorway. He didn't go inside the house.

"The front door doesn't look forced open."

"Mecho was outside when he had his heart attack."

"So he probably didn't lock it, then the vandals arrived."

"That's what happened, I guess."

Through all the destruction, Matthew saw that Hernández led a simple life. The suede couch in decent shape, wooden desk, older TV with even older VCR recorder in the living room. He was a Clint Eastwood fan because a collection of the actor's movies on videotape were also scattered on the floor. In the kitchen, a plain wooden table and two chairs. A tin vase with dried flowers had been knocked to the ground. Despite all the vandal wreckage, the kitchen appeared clean.

Putting on latex gloves, Matthew sifted through the papers on the floor in the living room. They had probably been stored in an old-school steel document box chucked in a corner of the room. One by one, he let the papers drop from his fingers. Nothing, but bills. He kicked a chair across the floor and then picked it up.

In the only bedroom in the house, the mattress had been sliced open and the chest of drawers knocked over. Matthew checked under the bed but saw only new slippers.

Work shirts and pants hung in the closet. Three pairs of work boots and one pair of nice dress shoes had been thrown under the clothes. He removed the shoes. In one corner, a floorboard had a square grove cut into it. Going back outside, he asked to borrow Benny's crowbar.

"What the hell are you doing in there?"

"Searching for treasure."

Matthew placed the crowbar in the grove and pushed down. The piece of laminate floor lifted. In a space underneath sat another locked metal box. He used the crowbar to open it. Inside, stacks of hundred-dollar bills were bound with rubber bands.

He whistled.

Also in the box was a title to the land and a silver key.

Benny stood under an aspen tree drinking a bottle of water. "What's in the box?"

"There's got to be $30,000 in here."

"Where'd he get all that money?" Benny was going to touch the bills but pulled back his hand.

"He probably saved up all his paychecks and Social Security. Or, he was a good gambler."

"What do we do with it?"

"Vegas?"

Benny didn't laugh.

"I'll take the dough to Judge Howard and see what he thinks. Wright owns the property, but this money belongs to Hernández's estate." Matthew closed the box. "And estate law is not my thing."

"Find anything else?"

"Just the title to the land and a key."

"For a safety deposit box?"

Matthew held out the key. "More like one to a lock. Anyway, it's what I didn't see that's odd."

"Like what?"

He motioned his head back toward the house. "Not one crucifix, statue of Jesus, or painting of the Virgin de Guadalupe anywhere in his house."

"So?"

"How many Latino homes have you seen without any of those?"

"Like none."

"That's my point."

"Maybe, he wasn't Catholic. He might have been a Protestant."

"Could be, but it still gives me a headache."

"How come?"

"Unanswered questions always give me a headache."

Benny headed to his cruiser. "Ready to go? I'm hungry."

Matthew noticed a glint in the dirt a few yards beyond the clearing where they parked. A metal lock secured a four-foot-square wooden door in the ground. The wood was warped with age and weather.

He gripped the key he had found in the house. "The plot thickens."

Benny laughed.

The key opened the door. He knelt down and looked in the hole. "Got a flashlight, bro?"

Benny retrieved one from his vehicle. "What is it?"

"A kiva. So cool." He was almost giddy. "And check it out. An extension ladder against the house."

"Kiva? Who do you think you are, Matthew? Indiana Jones?"

"Don't you feel adventurous, *compadre*?"

"I feel tired. And haven't we outgrown this sort of thing?"

"*Pollo*." He clucked.

"There's nothing down there."

He clucked louder.

"Who you calling a chicken?"

"You, baby boy."

"I'm no chicken, *pendejo*. Let's go see the damn kiva."

"Well, all right."

He couldn't help it, but he was excited at the prospect of doing something besides standing around in court. He loved being a lawyer, but a locked secret kiva was more than he expected that day. The pueblo ruins had been a letdown, so this was realizing a childhood dream of exploring the unknown. Shaking hands with the inexplicable.

They lowered the aluminum ladder into the hole. Three feet stuck out.

"The kiva's about twelve-feet deep judging by the length of this ladder," Matthew said.

"You first, Indy Riley."

He almost lost his footing because of the stink in the kiva as he climbed down. "Damn, smells like something died in there." He retched from the odor of decomposition. "This is what it must feel like to be at the bottom of a grave."

Benny cussed as he climbed down. When he reached the bottom, he pulled out his handkerchief and tied it around his nose and mouth.

With only tissue in his pocket, Matthew had to put up with the stench. Such was the price of exploration. He clicked on the flashlight. "Hell. A lot of things must have died down here." He held his arm up to his nose.

"The old man might have used this for his toilet or to dump trash," Benny said.

"Great."

He swept the light over the ground. Thankfully, nothing there but dirt floor and a worn wooden ladder with a few missing rungs.

The opening provided muted light. Past that was dimness. He inched the flashlight around the circular wall that he estimated to be about thirty feet in diameter and formed by compacted dirt and flat stones. Long wooden logs held up the ceiling.

Matthew stepped forward. Plaster had been spread over the entire rounded wall of the kiva. On the plaster were painted images of ancient Pre-Columbian gods. With dead eyes and jarring teeth, the creatures appeared angry at the interlopers. A snake deity with the head of a man was curled up and ready to strike. A blue-colored man laid spread over a stone with his chest sliced open, while another man wearing an elaborate feathered headdress held a heart aloft. The paintings gave Matthew an uneasy feeling of being surrounded by an enemy.

"These don't look like anything Pueblo Indians would paint. They're Aztec or Mayan, something like that."

"How can you tell?"

"I watch the Discovery Channel a lot. Jesus, Benny, just look at them. This isn't Norman Rockwell material."

On the floor in front of the images were the stubs of hundreds of burned candles and incense that stank of sage. He handed the flashlight to Benny and began to take photos.

Benny retreated to a spot under the daylight coming in from the opening. He was sweating, although it was twenty degrees cooler down there than outside.

"What's wrong, Benny? Afraid of a little kiva?"

"Shut up, and where's that stink coming from?" He gave the flashlight back to him.

"My God. There's another room. I think it's coming from there." He pointed the flashlight to an arched opening into dark.

With the light held out in front, Matthew had to stoop as he passed under the arch. The second round room was also formed of stone and dirt but smaller. The horrendous smell originated there, so dense it created an invisible wall he had to step through. Rows of animal skulls had been cemented together and stacked the full height of the wall. They covered more than half of the room. Their empty sockets stared as if caught by permanent surprise.

"Shit. Benny, you got to see this," he called.

Using the flashlight on his cell phone, Benny entered the smaller room with slow steps but cursed after striking his head on the low entrance. "This is so screwed up. It smells worse than a sewer in here."

Matthew touched one of the skulls. "Rabbit. And there's a coyote, cat, deer, cow." He studied another skull. "Oh, hell. This looks like a dog."

"You're right, bro."

In front of the skulls stood a waist-high cement block. A large jagged black spot covered the two-foot-square top. Down the sides and around the block were more ragged dark stains hitting the smooth dirt floor. Matthew gathered up a bit of the dirt and held it to his nose. "This is dried blood."

He moved the light farther along the arched walls. Across from the skulls were decomposing heads of different kinds of animals impaled upon wooden stakes and stacked one on top of the other. More coyotes, dogs, cats, and deer.

"Whew, that's why it smells so bad," Benny said.

"That Mecho was one sick old man."

"Can we get out of here? This makes me want to puke."

"Let me get a few more photos."

With each flash from his camera, the skulls and decomposing heads appeared to come to life, more than willing to leap at them.

When they climbed out of the kiva, Matthew and Benny took in a lungful of the fresh air.

"Mecho Hernández was sacrificing animals like the Aztecs sacrificed people." Matthew took a deep breath and let it out before he spoke. The stench of death was still in his nostrils and he knew he was going to have to get his clothes dry-cleaned once again. "That was totally fucked up."

"Still want to be adventurous?" Benny smirked.

"At least not until tomorrow."

Chapter 27

Nine o'clock.

Matthew couldn't believe he was still at his office, which was dark except for the light on his desk. After wrapping up pending work for his county prosecutor job, he read through the growing file on the murders. Leads were dropping like flies. The blood from Josh Vale's garage turned out to be deer blood, but the hunter who was angry over the Desert Rose development hadn't really been a good suspect to begin with.

He cursed his decision to help Benny with the investigation. Yeah, it was taking a lot of his time and the killings were awful. As unsettling was what the murders revealed. The wounds on both victims held the same bits of obsidian and decomposed flesh. The same guy killed both men. The same sick fuck running around his town.

"Shitshitshitshitshit." He pushed back into his chair.

Then there was the horror show in the kiva at Mecho Hernández's land. The bundle of money the old man kept under the floorboards. The whopping chunk of money Nick Vargas had deposited the day he was killed. And if he was going to stick with his focus on the Desert Rose Resort development, where the hell did Deputy Jackson Rogers fit in? He had to answer that question or his whole line of inquiry would fizzle like a wet campfire.

The front door squeaked.

Matthew froze.

Another squeak, then another. Footsteps in the lobby. Dammit, he didn't lock the front door. Someone coming towards him. Maybe the killer wanted another victim.

He needed a weapon. There. His two-foot-tall bowling trophy on a shelf by the door. His team had only come in second place, so the trophy was expendable. He tiptoed over so he wouldn't tip off the assailant. He was ready to defend himself, though he still sweated. Grabbing the trophy by the base, he knocked over his pathetic philodendron plant, which crashed to the floor.

"Fuck," he said out loud, but didn't mean to. "Fuck."

"I heard that, Mateo." The voice came from the outer office.

"Mama?"

He hit the light. Consuela carried a cardboard box. She was backlit from the lights on in the hall. "How'd you get in the building?"

"Through the sheriff's office. They know I'm your mom."

"What are you doing out at this time of night? A murderer's on the loose." He took the box, which smelled of spice, chili, and salt.

"I brought you something to eat. And don't worry about me. Your Uncle Ramon drove me here."

"Uncle Ramon is seventy-eight."

"But he's very fast on his feet."

Matthew laughed and looked in the box that held a plate with two tamales and a helping of rice.

Tired of sitting in his office, he suggested they take the food to the porch of the coffee shop next to the courthouse. The place closed at three in the afternoon, so they sat at one of the patio tables.

Music came from the church across from the park. A choir sang a hymn, but he couldn't remember which one it was.

"Listen to the singing. How beautiful," Consuela said as he ate. "I wanted to go to the vigil, but I knew you wouldn't eat otherwise."

"I'm not ten-years-old, Mama."

"Eat your dinner," she said with a smile.

The hymns grew louder. "Here they come," he said through a full mouth.

Led by the two Catholic priests, a procession ambled down the street. He guessed there must have been more than one-hundred people following the statue of the infant Jesus. On a platform decorated with purple velvet and gold fringe around the edges, it was supported by four men in suits. The statue was in its glass box and well secured. Two police cars lead the way to clear any traffic. The faithful carried candles which created a soothing light.

"Maybe I'll join them," she said.

"It's late, Mama. There will be more processions when the festival really gets going."

When the statue passed in front of them, his mom got to her feet. He didn't, so she tapped him on the head. He stood up. He recognized many people, their faces lit by the candles they held. They mouthed the Our Father in Spanish. There was a peace to them. They had faith in something they could not see.

While they walked, the statue swung back and forth like a ship on a dark sea. The eyes of the baby Jesus seemed to drill into Matthew and say, "Will you have the strength to do what you must do? Will you have the faith? Will you?"

"Belief is beautiful, isn't it, Matthew?"

It *was* on his mother's face. "*Sí*, Mama."

"When did you lose your faith, *mijo*?"

He almost choked on the food from such a direct question. "When I didn't think I could afford to let hope in."

"Then I'm sorry for you, son."

He wished his mom wasn't so damn honest.

The procession continued on. He checked with her for an okay to sit and finish eating. She nodded and then touched his hand. "You didn't lose your faith, Matthew. You just misplaced it. But what's lost can be found again."

He smiled. "Great tamales, Mama."

"Did you save me some?" Isabel came up the sidewalk, wearing a pretty summer dress.

He couldn't help but still be knocked out by her looks.

"¿Consuela, *cómo estás?*"

"Good, except for what's happening around town." They hugged.

Matthew sighed at how well the women got along. Even after he and Isabel had separated, she and his mother had lunch once a week.

"He's working too hard so I brought him dinner," his mother said.

"That's not surprising," Isabel answered.

"Where's my grandson?"

"At the movies with his friends." Isabel checked her watch. "I'm going to pick him up soon. And I'll bring Angel by this weekend."

"You're a good girl." Consuela looked right at Matthew as she said that. She glanced down the street and stood up. "I better go home. Uncle Ramon's falling asleep in the car. Good night, Isabel. Don't stay too late, Matthew, and don't forget to bring home my dishes."

He kissed the top of his mother's head before she left.

Isabel took the empty seat and a bite of his food. A smile over her pretty face. "She's still an incredible cook."

"Too bad you weren't," he joked.

Isabel didn't laugh, and in fact, took on such a powerful expression that he almost looked away—almost.

"Matthew, you were never home long enough to eat my cooking. You were too busy with work." Her voice was more accusatory than angry.

A silence pushed between them. He licked his lips in embarrassment at the truth.

"I'm sorry for being bitchy. I guess that's behind us." Her voice held finality.

His mouth dried at that.

"Can I ask you something?"

"Go ahead."

"Matthew, just what in God's name is going on in this county? I'm carrying a baseball bat in my car and I installed more locks at the house."

"I'm going to goddamn find out. And cliché as it sounds, I'm not going to rest until the killer faces justice."

She smiled.

"What are you grinning at?"

Isabel's face softened to one of support and love with a little mischief on the side. "I've always loved it when you talked like Matlock."

She placed a hand on his shoulder. Her touch still transmitted the warmest of shocks to his system.

"Okay, I'll leave you alone. I've got to go pick up our son."

"Wait. I'll go with you. Who knows what's hiding in this town."

Chapter 28

Matthew let out swear words at taking another wrong turn. He had already stopped twice to consult a map showing the two properties that bordered Mecho Hernández's land. Although the property was owned by Richard Wright, he couldn't stop thinking of it as belonging to the old man, despite the fact he was long dead.

He had borrowed the map from the county assessor's office where he also obtained the names of the property owners. But after getting lost, he gave up on the paper map and used the map app on his phone. He hated to rely on technology, but there were times when he couldn't avoid it.

While driving around, he had a vague hope the old man's neighbors might have information on the development, anything to help solve this case. He and Benny didn't have a suspect, and though he might be spinning wheels worse than a NASCAR driver, it was worth the trip. Unable to join him that day, Benny was still convinced a traveling psycho was responsible. Perhaps his friend was right. Yet, the skulking possibility that there was purpose to the madness followed him like a shadow.

"I sound like Alma Chacon," he said out loud. "Next thing, I'll be seeing the *Llorona* and the *cucuy* hanging out on the corner."

When he was a kid, his mom had told him all those Mexican ghost stories passed down through families like jewels, albeit murky ones. Tales of Mexican witches, the *brujas*, who'd curse people with whacky whammies like putting snakes in their stomachs or insects under their skins. The only people who could check the *brujas* were the healers, *curanderas*, who cast their own spells to reverse the weird afflictions. The

Llorona was a woman who killed her children, was transformed into a monster by God, and doomed to search the night for her kids, wearing white rags and animosity. The *cucuy* hid under beds and fed on the souls and bodies of sleeping children. He laughed that his mom shared such terrifying tales with her little boy. Such was tradition.

Now, he needed technology. The map app told him to make another turn down a country road. Nobody resided behind the proposed resort development property because it was up against the mountains. Abutting its right border was a three-hundred-acre cattle operation owned by Bob and Betty Johnson. As with the Hernández property, the Johnson land offered a lovely view of the mountains and a lush pasture thanks to the sizeable creek passing through.

He pulled into their dirt driveway. Their house appeared right out of the Ponderosa, as did the white-haired couple who stepped outside as soon as he rolled up.

Gruff was the best description for them, even after he introduced himself and the reason he was there: the investigation into the murders of Nick Vargas and Jackson Rogers. Before he could ask about the development, they started grousing about their late neighbor Mecho Hernández.

"We weren't on friendly terms with the man," Bob Johnson said. The guy appeared to live on a diet of prunes and bad moods.

"He wasn't neighborly at all," added his wife, who was only slightly less grumpy than her husband.

"What'd you mean?"

"Whenever we saw him come down the road, we'd wave at him like neighbors are supposed to do, and he never waved back. We lived next to that guy for more than forty years and he never waved," Johnson said.

"And I think he killed our dog, Butch." Mrs. Johnson dug her hands into her jeans pockets. "Butch would wander over to his property sometimes hunting for rabbits. Last year, he went under the fence and never came home."

Matthew nodded with understanding. That was entirely possible. Butch was probably among the skulls he saw down in the kiva. "Did you ask Hernández about your dog?"

"No, I should have."

"He probably would have lied," her husband said. "Who's going to admit they killed a dog?"

"You must be aware of the planned resort development next door."

"Oh, yes." Mr. Johnson swiped his cowboy hat against his leg. He glanced at this wife, who lowered her head.

A tell if there ever was one. These people were hiding something and not very well. "Has anyone offered you money for your land?" Matthew said.

The couple looked at each other.

"Yes, sir," Mr. Johnson said.

"I didn't see your land anywhere on the proposed map of the development."

"Well, Mr. Wright . . ."

"Richard Wright."

"That's him. He said the main part of the resort would be built on the Hernández land, but he wanted our place for another golf course and condominiums."

"Too bad. We spent our whole life raising cattle here," his wife said, a bit wistfully. "But then again, we're getting too old, so maybe it's time we get out before it's too late."

"So, you sold?"

They nodded.

"When?"

"January of last year."

More than a year before Mecho Hernández had died.

"Mr. Wright said we didn't have to move right away. He didn't even want to record the property sale until they started to build the resort," Mr. Johnson said.

"Did he say why?"

"No, sir."

"That resort is going to be a class act," Mrs. Johnson said. "Too fancy for me, but real nice."

He thanked them for their time.

"No problem," Bob Johnson said. "You impress, sir."

"Thanks."

"And you seem like a decent man. I'm sorry I didn't vote for you."

Getting in his car, Matthew headed the other direction, troubled by the information from the Johnsons. Why would Richard Wright buy their land before he had Hernández's property?

A fifty-acre place lay on the left border of the development property. The owners were Edward and Vicky López.

He stomped on the brakes.

"Dammit." He had missed the road. Jerking the car into reverse, he drove down an unpaved road for another six miles. Unlike the scenic property of the new development and that of the Johnson property, the López parcel was more desert in appearance. Dry and unyielding.

After Matthew parked, he took off his tie and chucked it into the car.

Chickens strutted around. Six cows grazed in a pasture. Painted a turquoise blue with adobe-colored trim, the house appeared a refuge in the desert. Stands of red maples, aspens, and cottonwoods surrounded it with stillness. On the other side of the house stood rows of apple and cherry trees. Orange and yellow marigolds lit up the walk to the house and grew in pots everywhere. A bush of red roses saluted a tall statue of the Virgin Mary in the front yard.

A three-year-old boy with lots of black hair and dark eyes the size of quarters giggled as he chased chickens. The kid fell. Matthew picked him up and brushed him off.

"There you go, kid," he said in Spanish.

The kid laughed and hurried around the back of the house. No sign of his parents.

"Hello? Hello?" He honked the car horn.

"Who the hell are you?" A voice came from behind him.

He spun around. A young man in work clothing held a rifle aimed at his chest. Clearly the boy's father. Same hair. Same eyes. Only this guy wasn't smiling.

"What you doing on my property?"

"You can set down your weapon. I'm Matthew Riley, Mesquite County Prosecutor."

"I hate lawyers."

"I don't blame you."

A young pretty woman peeked out of the screen door. "Eddie, don't be so rude," she said in Spanish, and in the most lilting voice Matthew had ever heard.

"Well, what'd you want?" the man said.

"To talk about Mecho Hernández's property."

The man lowered his gun. "It's about goddamn time."

****

Vicky López poured Matthew another glass of lemonade and took a seat beside her husband at their kitchen table. He sipped the drink. Their house was a real home, smelling of good cooking and family. Their son, the little spark named

Joseph, bopped around in circles until his mother narrowed his eyes at him. Joseph giggled and sat down. She gave him an apple. They were an attractive couple that reminded him of Isabel and himself when they first got married. So in love with each other and their future together.

He unbuttoned his jacket.

López glanced over his shoulder. "Mecho could be pretty cranky and even a little scary. We lived out here for years before we even got up the nerve to talk to him."

"He was a lonely man, I think." Mrs. López's eyes saddened so much that Matthew felt choked up just to look at her. She passed a plate of homemade pumpkin empanadas in his direction. He took one.

"Every year on Christmas, she used to take a bag of tamales to Mecho. It took three years before he finally came over and talked with us," her husband said with a smile.

"After that, he became like an extra grandfather to us. He gave us chickens, eggs, vegetables from his garden. He even sent us a lamb," she said. "When we got to know him, he was very generous."

This was a different man from the one who sacrificed animals down in his kiva. The two sides didn't mix. Then again, everyone had a little bad and good in them. He had learned that while prosecuting the ones with too much bad. Pure evil was a rarity.

"That man was full of stories," Mrs. López said.

"I'll bet. About the abandoned pueblo?"

"Definitely. At night, he said he could hear the ghosts of the Indians roaming around and the spirits speaking in their own language," López said.

"Did he ever mention why the Indians left? I've always wondered about that and no one really knew why."

The couple smiled.

"That was one of his favorite stories," Vicky López said. "He told us he was eleven when he hitchhiked from Mexico after his parents died. He was an orphan on the road, but he happened to stop at the pueblo and the Indians took him in. They helped him renovate that house on their property. When he got older, he worked at the mines and he bought food for them. They took care of each other."

"This is where the story gets good," her husband said.

"Then one of their elders or holy men or whatever kept having bad dreams about what would happen if their people stayed. It was like the world was going to collapse into nothing." Her fingers wiggled for illustration.

"And one night, after he came home from work, everybody was gone and he had no idea where they went," López said. "But they had signed over the property to him. He found the paperwork in his house."

"That is a good story." Matthew placed his hands on the table. "I read the sheriff's report that you found his body."

The young couple held hands.

"When we didn't see Mecho around for a week, we knew he was in trouble," López said.

"Eddie went over and found him dead, right out on the ground. He had no one. *Pobrecito*." A tear skidded down her cheek. Their son outstretched his arms and she picked the child up.

"He wasn't completely alone. He had very good neighbors," Matthew said.

She blushed at the compliment. "We went to his funeral. No one else came."

"According to the autopsy report, he died of a heart attack."

"I guessed that," López said. "He must have hit his head on a rock when he fell because his shirt was covered with blood. Poor old guy."

"When I introduced myself as the county prosecutor, you said it was about time someone asked about Mecho. Why was that? Did he mention anything about the development?"

Mrs. López nodded.

Her husband tightened his hands and his voice intensified with anger. "Mecho told us people were trying to kill him, Mr. Riley."

"Matthew, *por favor*. Who was trying to kill him?"

"That developer bastard."

"Richard Wright."

"That's him. *Cabrón*."

"Isn't that why you came out here to talk with us, Matthew?" Mrs. López said.

"This is the first I've heard about any threats against Mr. Hernández."

"Three months before he died, Mecho told me that someone was poisoning his sheep and putting manure down his well. Another time they trashed his house when he was in town," López said.

"Didn't the sheriff investigate the vandalism?" Matthew said.

He spit on the floor.

"Eddie, *ay*." His wife chastised him.

"Mecho said the sheriff's office didn't do *nada*. Some deputy came out and wrote down the information, but nothing happened," the young man said. "After a week, he called to see why they didn't arrest Wright and they told him they had no evidence that he did anything wrong."

"Did he tell you the name of the deputy?"

"No, he just said it was a brute of a guy with short blond hair. Like a Marine cut."

And that described the newly dead Deputy Jackson Rogers. Matthew's mouth was parched. He drank more lemonade.

"That real estate guy wouldn't leave him alone. Mecho said he and some fancy lawyer came out all the time and made him offers. Even Nick Vargas, the mayor, and that lady commissioner tried to convince him to sell. They all told Mecho that the resort would help the town and the whole county."

"But Mecho refused. He loved that place," Mrs. López added. "He told us Mr. Wright wanted to push him off of his land, but he wasn't going to sell at any price. That land was all he had. It was his life."

"He was a stubborn old man. He could have been rich." Her husband took another empanada.

She gave a deep sigh. "At least he died where he loved." She hugged their little boy, set him down, and he scampered off.

"What about your land? Did Wright make you an offer, too?" Matthew said.

"I wish he would have," López said with a smile, to which his wife tapped him on the arm. "My dad left us this place. I work in the mines because it's not good for much like ranching or farming or subdivisions. Too damn dry. The nice creek that runs through Mecho's land doesn't cut through ours. Hell, if that developer guy *would've* thrown lots of money our way, we wouldn't have said no."

"Our place isn't as pretty as Mecho's, but we still like it out here. It's a good place to raise our boy," Mrs. López said.

"Eddie, Vicky, thank you very much. You may have just given me a motive," Matthew said.

They appeared confused, but then smiled.

He stepped outside, the sun still white and beating down. The couple followed. López had his arm around his wife's shoulders. Mrs. López looked over in the direction of Mecho Hernández's land.

"May God rest his soul." She crossed herself.

He swiveled around.

"I don't believe Mecho Hernández believed in God, do you, Vicky?"

Uncertainty crossed both their faces. Then, she gave a slight nod to her husband.

"He had another religion," López said.

"What kind?"

"Mecho told us he kept to the old gods of Mexico. His father, grandfather, and great-grandfather had taught him about them before they died and he never forgot. He said the Christian god had no power for him."

"I've seen how he kept to them. I've been down in the kiva. Have you?"

"I didn't know there was one," López said. "I would've liked to see it."

"No, you wouldn't."

"A mess, huh?"

"Yeah, a horrible mess."

"Mecho had boasted that he had pure Aztec blood in his veins," Mrs. López said. "He even spoke their language. What did he call it, Eddie?"

"Nahuatl. I asked him to say something, but he said he saved it for his prayers."

Vicky López's face became troubled. "Mecho told us there was only one way to honor those gods and keep them alive."

"What was that?" Matthew said.

"Blood, Mateo. Blood keeps them alive."

"Did you understand what he meant?"

The lovely young woman touched his arm. "No, and I didn't want to."

Chapter 29

Mike Rand chewed the turkey sandwich his wife had packed, enjoying the still night and time without the TV blaring and his kids yelling and carrying on at his house. In the light of the full moon, he spotted a rabbit race across the lawn, stop for a second, and speed on.

"Have a nice night," he told the animal.

At more than six feet and three-hundred pounds, he was daunting even sitting down and didn't mind giving that impression. During high school, he was equally feared and loved as captain of the football team. He and the other players dominated the hallways. People actually parted for them. After he graduated, the admiration had dropped to nothing. He became a regular guy with a regular job and regular life, which irked him to no end. He missed the damn glory.

This night job held no glory, either. He'd been hired to guard the spacious house belonging to Mary Lou Flores located two miles outside of Guadalupe's city limits.

The commissioner was a rich, snotty bitch, but she paid good money for watching her rich, snotty house. He was going to earn more in one night than in a week as a parts clerk in the car dealership in town. She didn't tell him what she was afraid of, but one commissioner was already murdered so he figured she didn't want to be victim number two, make that three since a deputy also was killed. Flores did tell him to bring his rifle. It rested against the house near where he sat. But this was going to be the easiest money he'd ever earn.

The door opened with a whoosh. He almost fell off his chair.

"I'm not paying you to take it easy, dammit. You're here to watch my ass. Take a walk around the house."

Flores wore a long sheer white robe and nightgown that exposed everything she had, which was a lot. But, a stony personality made her as appealing as the Wicked Witch of the West.

"Yes, ma'am," he replied.

"I heard a noise in the backyard."

"I'll check it out."

"Then check it out, moron." She slammed the door.

He sat back down. Even though she *was* paying him good money, she could damn well wait until he ate his dinner. He finished his turkey sandwich.

****

The plans for the Desert Rose Resort spread out over the cream-colored carpet in the stylish living room of Mary Lou Flores. She poured two large glasses of wine—expensive wine. Sipping on hers, she started up a disc of Lady Gaga. Mayor John Stuart emerged from the bedroom wearing only a towel around his waist. He took the wine glass from her. The muscles in his neck were tauter than a knotted rope.

"John, you get any tenser, your heart will explode," Flores said.

"People are dying all over Guadalupe. I don't want to be the mayor of Deathville."

She laughed.

"Come on, aren't you nervous, Mary Lou? The sheriff thinks it's a random psycho killer, but it doesn't feel random. We *know* who was murdered."

She drank the wine. "That's why I hired that monster of an ex-football player. Even though he's dumb as a pool of mud."

"You're always thinking. And I liked your performance at the meeting." He imitated her voice. "And we don't want state people coming here for a closer look." He grinned. "Very effective. We can handle the sheriff."

"And Matthew?"

"He's getting ready to leave Guadalupe. He won't give a shit in the long run."

"Still, we ought to get out of town for a while." She slipped off the robe.

"That's a fucking great idea. We can go to Puerto Vallarta till this all blows over." He stepped up to her and stroked her hip. She moved her body into his. "I've always had a thing for corrupt public officials." His hand moved around her waist.

Her voice stayed strong. "We've got to remain focused. We're so close."

"Let's get even closer." He roughly kissed her and pulled her to the floor. He ripped off the sheer nightgown and then his towel. They made love on top of the plans for the resort.

****

Nearing midnight, Mike Rand clutched his jacket tighter around him. That was one thing about the desert, hotter than hell during the day and a chill to his bones when the sun set. He battled sleep and settled into the chair up against the wall. He'd just nap for a minute or two or three. The lady commissioner wouldn't bother him anymore. She was humping the mayor inside. That was pretty obvious from the whispery moans he heard through the door.

Just as his lids went down, he opened them again at a sharp bad smell. His eyes wetted from the stink. He gagged and coughed.

"What the shit?"

The porch light over him sparked and went out. For such an expensive home, the electrical was for crap.

Squinting in the radiance from the full moon, he walked to get a flashlight from his truck parked in the driveway. As he was about to return to the house, hands seized him. Men seemed to materialize out of the night. They covered his mouth. He couldn't yell for help. He couldn't break their hold on him. He couldn't see faces, only the unbelievable. Skeletal hands covered with remnants of skin clutching his arms and legs. He felt cold meat. The bones of the hands scraped at his face. He struggled with every muscle but it did no good. His mind couldn't accept what he was seeing. And the smell. He began to cry.

Lord help him, let this be a dream, he prayed as the hands tore into his flesh.

****

Mary Lou Flores shot out of bed where Stuart still slept. Donning a white silky robe, she headed to the bathroom and turned on the light. It extinguished with a flash.

"Dammit," she uttered.

"What's wrong?" Stuart came out of the bedroom, pulling on his underwear.

She put a hand over his mouth. "Listen," she hissed.

He did.

"It's nothing, Mary Lou."

"Shut up."

He heard it that time. A brushing against the house. No. More like metal scratching against the walls and windows. The scraping came from one side of the house, then another, and back again.

The scraping ended. Replacing it was a low howl, which escalated into a human scream. Men were screaming. The noise was pitiful and frightening.

"What the fuck?" Stuart whispered.

"I'm calling for help." Flores picked up a cell phone.

The same screeching came over her phone and Stuart's when he tried.

"Dammit. That moron is probably asleep outside," Flores said.

From a drawer, she pulled out an automatic handgun and a large flashlight. Stuart followed. She stepped cautiously down the dark hall to the front of the house.

At the window, she slightly opened the curtain. Under the vivid moonlight, a few feet from the front door, six men in robes squatted around the prone body of Mike Rand like hawks tearing at prey.

She dropped the flashlight. One of the men in the robes raised his head. His face was obscured by the robe and the night so that just gloom stared at them. Then the rest of the men looked up.

"Oh, fuck!"

"Let's get out of here," Stuart said.

In an instant, fists beat at the door. The pounding became deafening. Flores spun back and fired several shots through the door.

Hands crashed through the windows. In the pale light, they looked like they were made of just bone. Flores wiped at her eyes because that couldn't be real.

The front door crashed open.

"Get to the garage," Flores said.

She and Stuart sprinted through the dark house. She grabbed a key from a hook. They dashed into the garage and into her car. She jammed in the key to start it. Not one spark, not even the battery light.

"What do we do?" Stuart said.

Flores hurled herself out of the car. She swung open the back door of the garage, saw nothing, and ran out.

"Wait, damn you. Wait for me." Stuart followed and banged his toes into the door frame. He cried out.

Flores dared not look over her shoulder. She would circle around, follow the old arroyo near her property, and end up at the highway. She'd flag down help. She didn't wait for Stuart. He never would have waited for her. In fact, he would have left her to the maniacs breaking into her house.

Behind her, more screaming. Stuart's voice. She sped up.

As her white nightgown flapped around, she stumbled over a yucca plant and fell on her face onto the dirt.

"Goddammit." A stench belonging in slaughterhouses throbbed in her nose.

She slowly rolled over. Standing around her were six figures in shredded robes. Her skin chilled. They pulled back the hoods that covered their faces.

Mary Lou Flores, the ever-professional businesswoman and county commissioner, shrieked for help until she had no more breath left.

Chapter 30

For the last eight miles, Matthew and Benny hadn't spoken, which was a record for them. They could talk all night, as they did when they went fishing at the Rio River outside of town, but on the ride out to the Flores house they said little. Benny drove his patrol vehicle while Matthew tapped his fingers on the seatbelt.

Mayor John Stuart and Commissioner Mary Lou Flores had failed to show up for several appointments that morning and didn't answer their cell phones. Their respective secretaries called to report their no-shows and express worry in the face of the two murders that had already taken place. Then the wife of Mike Rand called in to say he hadn't been home that morning after he'd been hired by Flores as a bodyguard.

Off they went to check her house.

Along the way, Matthew stopped tapping. His face flushed with the question he had to ask. He hoped it didn't catch in his throat.

"Benny, why didn't you tell me that Mecho Hernández was being harassed? That someone was fouling up his well and killing his livestock?"

"I didn't believe him, Matthew."

"It doesn't matter whether you believed him. The information was vital to this investigation."

Benny gripped the wheel tight one moment and then extended his fingers the next. "Mecho Hernández was crazy, Matthew. Yeah, he reported that someone was bothering him, but he also kept saying some old gods would take revenge for him and bring about the end of the world."

"Jesus. Did he really say that?"

"He was lucky we didn't start procedures to commit him to the state hospital."

"But didn't Hernández accuse Richard Wright of badgering him?"

"And everybody else in the county. He was paranoid as hell. We investigated but couldn't find evidence showing that Wright was to blame." Benny looked straight ahead as he talked. His fingers tightened up on the wheel.

"Did you interview Richard Wright about the allegations?"

Benny's nod was sharp.

"Well, what was his story?"

"He said he did make several offers to buy the land but didn't harass the guy. Wright also claimed that Hernández pulled a weapon on him but he didn't want to press charges."

"You should have told me anyway."

"You're right. I'm sorry. I screwed up."

"I'd like to read the incident report."

"It's at the office. I'll send you over a copy."

"Did Jackson Rogers interview Hernández?"

Benny turned his head toward Matthew. "How did you know that?"

"From Hernández's description to his neighbors."

Benny shifted in his seat, clearly uncomfortable. That made Matthew's stomach twist like he'd eaten a bad meal. They both knew Benny had totally fucked up on this count.

"I just pray Flores and Stuart are safe. If they are, then we're going to question them about the resort." He then told Benny that the commissioner and mayor had both visited Mecho Hernández and urged him to sell.

"Mary Lou's going to be pissed," Benny said at last.

"Let her. She and Stuart are mixed up in this somehow." The conviction in his voice surprised him.

His friend exhaled so hard that Matthew wondered if he had any air left in his body. "What a mess."

"The word 'mess' doesn't quite cover it, Benny. Not with one skinned public official and a deputy with no limbs." He laughed. "Man, that sounds demented as a bag full of rabid armadillos."

Benny joined him, although his hinted of nervousness. "Why *are* we laughing?"

"As my mom says, if we don't laugh we'd be crying."

"I need a drink."

"You and me both. But no matter how weird they died, it's still murder."

They stopped laughing when they pulled up to Mary Lou Flores's house.

The front door was open. A rifle lay on the ground. Several plants had been trampled and a pricey ceramic pot knocked over. The windows were broken in.

All signs of trouble.

John Stuart's expensive truck was parked out front with its MR MAYOR customized plates. Behind it was parked Mike Rand's beat-up truck.

"Could be Mary Lou and Stuart just got to drinking, screwing, and are hung over." He hoped that was the explanation. "Rumors are that they're having a hot affair. Least that's what my secretary told me."

"Yeah, that's it." Benny said.

He wasn't really convinced, though, and from Benny's voice, neither was he.

Benny spit out his cinnamon toothpick and called for more deputies. He drew out his Magnum and motioned for him to stay behind as they headed toward the house. Matthew had no problem letting his armed friend go first.

They stepped inside the door, which was marred by four bullet holes. Benny stayed in the lead. "Mary Lou?" he called. "Mr. Mayor."

No answer. They proceeded slowly. When death stopped at a home, there was a tangible quietness to the place as if life had not only left the body of the deceased, but also the house itself. That unnerved him more than anything.

Their footsteps echoed like cannons bouncing off of a marble floor as they continued.

He blinked a bit as his eyes adjusted from the bright day to the dark house. Farther on they stepped. Benny whipped his intimidating gun around the corners.

His head echoed with the silence. "Smell that?" he whispered to Benny. Metal. Copper. "Blood. A lot of blood."

When they reached the living room, they stopped at the source of the smell and the lifelessness. On the carpet lay the naked body of Mesquite County Commissioner Mary Lou Flores. A horizontal cut covered the entire length of her chest. The skin and ribs pulled back. Her chest cavity was missing a heart.

In the chair nearby sat Mayor John Stuart wearing only shorts. He was dead. His eyes stretched open. His mouth and right hand covered in blood. Unlike the previous murders, this time there was a massive amount of blood. Red soaked the light carpet a profound scarlet.

"Dear God." Benny lowered his weapon. He touched Stuart's shoulder. Something in the body's hand dropped to the floor.

A half-eaten heart.

Chapter 31

Dr. Rosemary Whitney stood up, medical bag in hand. From her void stare, she could have been hit by a stun gun. For all the death and damage she'd probably seen, it took a lot to shock the woman, Matthew guessed. She slowly removed her gloves and the rubber coverings to protect her shoes from all the blood.

"It's probably a good thing you're leaving this town, Matthew. There might not be anybody left."

"Nice sentiment, Rosemary."

"It doesn't take a medical genius to see Mary Lou died from blood loss considering her heart had been cut out of her chest."

"What about Stuart? I didn't see any wounds on him."

"Me neither."

"So what killed him?"

"He probably died of fright," Benny murmured. "Just look at his face."

"That might be entirely correct. Anyway, we'll have more answers after the autopsy. I hope so at least." The doctor pulled a cigarette from her bag and lit up. "Yeah, yeah, it's a crime scene, but I need a smoke." She took in a deep draw. "I'll be talking to you after I examine the bodies at the hospital."

"I'll bet a set of steak knives the same weapon used on Mary Lou also killed Vargas and the deputy," Matthew said.

"That's a bit preliminary," Benny said.

"What are you talking about? It's the same sick shit."

"Whatever's going on, I'm going to have to start charging the county hazard pay for dealing with this," the doctor said and punched Matthew in the arm.

The men thanked her and she left.

The bodies were removed by the county coroner's crew. Wearing gloves, one of the men gently peeled paper off of the back of Flores's body before placing it in the familiar black plastic. He was coming to hate this sight and wondered if the morgue at the hospital was going to run out of space from all the victims.

He should have left months ago, but then Benny would've had to handle the investigation himself and he wasn't convinced that he could. Not with Camilla's illness and the complexities of these crimes. Not that he was doing any better, but these murders added heft to his supposition that the Desert Rose Resort was at the core of these killings. If only he could figure out why.

The house bustled with the forensic deputy lifting fingerprints off of doors. Outside, more deputies searched for the missing guard, Mike Rand. As Benny instructed his other deputies on where they should be looking, his eyes were half closed and he pushed his fist against the wall. He worried his friend was going to become physically ill from all these gruesome deaths.

"Okay, man?"

"Yeah."

"You look a little *verde*, my friend."

"Never have liked death. And with Camilla's not feeling one-hundred percent. I can't stand the thought of mortality."

"I didn't think you'd be afraid of dying."

"I'm not, but I don't want to see it visit anyone else." Benny put on his cowboy hat and went out the front door.

Death had definitely visited and left a calling card. A sizeable blood stain on the carpet. He joined Benny outside.

His friend rested against his cruiser and watched as the bodies were loaded into the ambulance. His hair appeared to have grayed even more during the last weeks.

Crime tape and deputies encircled the house. Another deputy kept the news people away at the road leading into the property. When the coroner crew slammed the doors to the ambulance, Matthew flinched. His nerves were becoming unraveled as a worn sweater.

A helicopter buzzed overhead.

"That's probably from Channel Seven." Deputy Rueben Salazar glanced up and then looked at Benny. "Sheriff, please come to the backyard." He wore the resolution of a grave.

That indicated he didn't have any good news.

The backyard was as striking as the house with a pool, patio, and an elaborately landscaped yard. Beyond the landscaping and a row of decorative rock, however, was the desert in all its desolation.

"Check it out," said Salazar, who was as sturdy as a tank. He showed them a single pair of footsteps heading out into the desert. Small bare feet. "We only found one set, Sheriff Ortega. It appears the victim was running fast from the look of those prints, but unless she was being chased by ghosts, she was alone. Even if she was caught and carried back to the house by an assailant, there would've been footprints."

Deputy Salazar never exaggerated.

"We can't tell if she made those footprints last night or some other day," Benny said.

"They look pretty fresh to me." The deputy grunted slightly.

"Murder weapon?" Matthew said.

"Nothing, Mr. Riley."

"Any sign of Mike Rand?"

"We didn't even find *his* footprints."

"Keep looking," Benny told the deputies. "Get Cal Napier on the horn and see if he can bring his dog out to help in the search."

Salazar nodded. He and other deputies set off in different directions, studying the dirt as if it held answers.

"Dammit, I've got to notify Mary Lou's mom back in town. Then, I'll call Stuart's family." Benny told him. "Want to come with me?"

"I want to look around here."

Benny shuffled off.

Matthew returned to the house. Careful not to step in the blood soaked into the carpet, he crouched down for a look at the papers that had been under the body of Mary Lou Flores. Borrowing gloves from one of the deputies, he picked them up. The maps of Mecho Hernández's land were wrinkled and red.

The stunning home was decorated with the kind of modern and overpriced furniture he disliked because it was better suited to a store than a house. But the dead commissioner didn't buy from Acero Furniture in downtown Guadalupe.

One room was a home office. He opened a laptop on a desk. It needed a password. A short filing cabinet was also locked. Checking the house for Flores's purse, he found a key that might fit. It did. He hoped to find the password for the laptop; if not, he'd take it to his office and let his secretary try. She was an outright genius with computers.

The late Commissioner Flores had been organized. Files with tax returns and receipts in her desk were clearly marked, but no bank statements. One file held $800 in cash, so burglary wasn't the motive because nothing of value had been stolen. Not one chair or table had been upset in the office. Not one broken lamp. Other than the shattered front windows and bullet holes in the door, the upset inside had been minimal.

He placed the cash in an envelope, which would probably go to Flores's mother. At the back of the cabinet, a file held brochures for the Desert Rose development and drawings similar to what had been presented at the informational meeting by Richard Wright.

"Ever since that resort, there's been nothing but blood," he said out loud.

"What'd you say, Matthew?" asked one of Benny's deputies, who was passing down the hall.

"Nothing."

He stripped off the gloves.

"Hey." Isabel stood in the doorway.

Matthew came out of the funk. "How the hell did you get past the deputies, Ms. Reporter?"

"There's a back road. I parked and walked in. I think keeping me out is the least of their worries."

"No photos inside or *I'll* throw you out."

"I already shot some but probably can't use them. Too much blood."

He didn't have the strength to threaten her. He even felt comforted she was there. Isabel let the camera hang down on the strap around her neck, as if tired, also.

She placed her small hand on his. "Matthew, you look exhausted."

He took her hand and moved her gently toward his chest. "I used to pride myself on having all the answers or knowing where to find them. Maybe it turns out I don't know anything at all. In fact, the more I ask, the more I don't know."

"It's a maniac killer. You and Benny can catch him." But from her voice, she didn't sound certain.

"How they died appears to be the work of a lunatic, but there's a pattern to this insanity."

"What's on your mind?"

He put on a wry smile. "I could share my theories with my wife, not with a reporter."

She nodded. "You always did want everything neat, like a file that fits in your briefcase."

"That makes me sound pathetic."

"No, Mateo. You're doing the best you can. As you always do."

"What if that's not good enough?"

"And I won't even quote you on that." She smiled, a forlorn one amidst the death and chaos. As if it was going to be her last smile ever.

That struck Matthew as tragic.

Chapter 32

As Richard Wright listened to Matthew, he didn't sweat. Not even after Matthew mentioned he could be the next victim.

"Aren't you alarmed, Mr. Wright? If I were you, I might be."

"You're making a grand assumption here, Mr. Riley."

He bit the inside of his lip and wondered whether Wright had sweated at all or ever. He and Benny questioned the real estate prince at his office, which was in the newest and swankiest building on Main Avenue. Even the First Bank of New Mexico, renovated two years ago, appeared shabby in comparison.

Wright's office had thick carpet. Leather chairs. Actual art on the walls instead of prints.

"Why would anyone even oppose this development? It will only be a windfall to Guadalupe and the surrounding county." Wright sat behind an expensive desk.

He was acting so cool Matthew believed ice crystals would form around his body.

"Nick Vargas, Mary Lou Flores, and Mayor John Stuart were all proponents of the Desert Rose development, and they're all dead…and in a most gruesome way. And Mike Rand has disappeared," he said.

"Mike Rand?"

"Mary Lou had hired him as a bodyguard. I believe he was collateral damage. In the wrong place at the wrong time." Benny spoke at last. He had encouraged Matthew to conduct the questioning since he was the one who came up with the resort-as-motive idea.

Wright's mouth became a line. Then one end curved slightly. "Hey, what about the deputy?"

"Jackson Rogers," Benny said. "What about him?"

He was amazed his friend could talk. Benny grinded teeth in clear annoyance at the businessman's seeming indifference to the deputy's death.

"He had nothing to do with the Desert Rose," Wright said.

"We haven't finished investigating his background, but that resort is a common denominator among four victims," Matthew said.

Wright concentrated on Benny. "You agree with all this, Sheriff?"

Benny straightened to his full height. "As Matthew said, it's our best lead at this point. Have you received any threats, Mr. Wright?"

"Just from Josh Vale at the informational meeting."

"He has an alibi. Anybody else?" Matthew said.

Wright gave a full-on smile. "Other than him, I haven't heard one negative word about this project."

"On the day he died, Nick Vargas deposited a large amount in his bank account."

"So? He was a great businessman."

Matthew was taking a chance with the next question, but it was a logical one. "Did you pay Nick Vargas for his support of the project? And I might as well add, Mary Lou Flores and John Stuart?"

"You accusing me of bribing public officials, Mr. Riley?"

"I'm asking a question."

Wright pushed his chair forward and seethed with so much animosity Matthew expected his ears to eject steam just like angry cartoon characters. All that businessman coolness was suddenly gone.

"Well, did you?"

"No." Wright's answer foamed with hostility.

Matthew didn't believe in intuition, but his fingers tingled as if he had grabbed an exposed wire. What was that Shakespeare saying? He doth protest too much. Okay, not a "he" in the quote, but it fit the situation.

Wright took in air and breathed out slowly. His persona of the frosty real-estate agent and entrepreneur resumed. "If I'm in danger, then I demand protection."

Benny gave a nod. "I'll assign deputies."

"See that you do. We done here?"

Matthew stood up. "For the moment."

Once outside, Benny stood in front of Matthew. "See? I told you there was no bribery."

"Where else did Nick Vargas get all that money?"

Benny shrugged and spit out his toothpick.

He wanted to spit, too. "The trouble is I can't prove anything, but this whole thing stinks like yesterday's burritos."

****

"Matthew."

He didn't stop.

"Matthew."

His secretary Kitty Cardenas held a stack of messages out as he passed her desk. "You going to take these or do I have to staple them to your suit?"

"What? Oh, it's been a rough day." He took the messages.

"I know, Matthew, I know." She gave a supportive smile. "Two of those messages are from Mr. Stan Mason at the AG's office. The snooty guy."

"Kitty, really."

"Well, he is. Anyway, he called twice and he was extra snooty."

"Sorry."

"Not your fault."

He handed her a laptop. "Kitty, this belonged to Mary Lou Flores. Please, see if you can get into this thing. I want to see her files."

"At your service. I do love those *Law and Order* assignments."

She was a fan of the show.

Shutting the door to his office, he sat behind his desk and rubbed at the headache digging a hole in his temple. Before the murders, he'd been counting down the time until he started his new job in Albuquerque, but since he became involved in the investigation, he'd forgotten to count. He'd only been thinking about the killings and his responsibility to help solve them. Benny had asked him to help, but *he* had to solve this thing.

For the victims, for the town, for the sake of justice.

Who might be next to die if the murderer wasn't caught.

He picked up the phone to call Stan Mason. He was supposed to be at his new job in two weeks and had no suspect. What he had was four bodies.

"I haven't heard from you lately, Mr. Riley."

His secretary was right. Mason was a snob, but he didn't appreciate how much until then. And he had to work with this guy.

"I didn't think I was supposed to check in until the day I started the job, Mr. Mason." His answer wasn't smart-ass, but there was sharpness to his voice.

"That is in two weeks."

"I realize that."

The silence over the phone had the weight of an aircraft carrier.

"Are you still joining us, Mr. Riley?"

"My work isn't finished here." It wasn't much of a response.

"I've read what's happening. Four murders. That is quite a disarray."

"And it must be cleaned up."

"Bluntly, Mr. Riley, will you be here in two weeks?"

Matthew took in the last of the air left in his office. "All I can say is that I will make every effort to be there. So if you'll excuse me, Mr. Mason, I've got to catch a killer."

Chapter 33

"Get out of my chair, Matthew." Dr. Rosemary Whitney entered her office at the hospital.

"Sorry." He got up and sat next to Benny across the room.

She swept into her seat, placing down a backpack, and picking up her coffee. She sipped as if to keep them in suspense.

Shaking his right leg, he couldn't stand it. "Well?"

"Matthew, you're getting more impatient the older you get."

He stopped the shaking.

"Mary Lou Flores died of massive blood loss."

"And don't tell me. A sharp primitive knife created the wounds. The same shards of black rock."

"Yup."

"I asked you not to tell me."

"Then don't ask, Matthew."

"What about the mayor? How'd he die?" Benny said.

"From a heart attack."

"You were right about that, bro," Matthew said.

Benny put his head down to hide a smile.

"Did Stuart have any heart problems?" Matthew asked the doctor. "I mean, he wasn't *that* old."

"I looked up his records and he had no such coronary troubles. I believe the mayor died of fright. And you're really going to hate this, but we found a bit of Mary Lou's heart in his stomach."

"Yucko," Benny said.

"Yes, but the killer must have held the knife on Stuart and made him eat it," Matthew said. "I don't think he would have volunteered."

"You guys find Mike Rand?" The doctor took gum out of her desk and offered them a piece. They declined. "My girlfriend says I'm smoking too much because of this case. So, what about him?"

"Still missing, Doc," Benny said.

Matthew wanted to sleep. He wanted a drink. Maybe a lobotomy as a chaser. "Anything else, Rosemary?"

"No, praise God."

Benny pushed back his hat. "This is a nightmare, Mateo."

"I tell you it's that damn development."

"You guys want me to leave so you can talk police?" Whitney said.

"No, a fresh outlook is welcome."

"Good, I've always had a hankering to play cop. So, what do you have?" She sat back and drank her coffee.

He started in on his theory that the development might be a factor in the killings. The paycheck Nick Vargas deposited. Mecho Hernández's complaints about being pressured by Wright, Flores, and Stuart to sell and how his well had been poisoned and his animals killed. He didn't mention that Benny neglected to tell him about the harassment.

"That's an interesting speculation," the doctor said.

"According to what we found on her laptop, Mary Lou Flores was also doing accounting work for the developers of the Desert Rose Resort," Matthew said. "That teetered on unethical since she was a commissioner and could be voting on the project."

"What about John Stuart? The guy owns a ranch. He's not hurting for money," she said.

"I've seen his house."

"My point, too," Benny said.

"So, we'll check out his finances."

Benny put his hands into his belt and chewed on his cinnamon toothpick. "Well, I'm not ruling out psycho killer."

"That's fine, but according to state records, Richard Wright owns the land and he and Samuel Uhlig own the company developing the land. We're talking a multimillion-dollar investment. And money is always a good motive for murder. Vargas, Flores, and Stuart might have been silent partners or paid to move the project along through government channels."

"So why kill them?" Benny said.

"Tying up loose ends."

"This isn't some damn TV crime show, Matthew," Whitney said.

Benny rubbed his eyes. "If by any stretch of the imagination you are right, I don't think Uhlig and Wright had the guts to kill Nick and the others."

"They probably contracted out the job, and you can guess to whom."

"Not Jackson Rogers?"

"The deputy? He's dead, Mr. County Attorney," Whitney said.

"Granted, his murder is the hitch in my theory." He wasn't going to hide that.

Benny waved his hands about. "Did you just pull all this out of your ass?"

"No matter what you think, there's a kind of logic to this." He rubbed the cut on his leg courtesy of John Juarez. It ached like a son of a bitch.

"Logic? You're shitting me."

"In law school, we learn deductive arguments. It's drummed into our little lawyer brains."

"We don't need that in medical school." The doctor grinned.

"If the premise of something is true, then it's impossible for the conclusion to be false," Matthew said.

"I see where you're coming from, Matthew." Whitney widened her eyes as if invited to play a game.

"Three out of the four victims supported the Desert Rose development. It's only logical the development is at the center of all this."

"How are you going to prove that?" Benny said. "Where's the evidence to support it?"

"By checking the accounts of Flores and Stuart to see if a huge amount of money came their way. And who wrote those checks to them."

"That makes sense." The doctor relaxed back in her chair.

"One other thing."

"Oh, God," Benny said.

Matthew got up and walked to the window. He raised the blinds. The moon was clear and whole, as if nothing bad had happened in town.

"Well?" Benny and Whitney said.

"These murders feel like ritual."

"What do you mean, Matthew? You said the murders were related to the development," the doctor said.

"That was why they were killed. But how they were dispatched is more than a guy blowing away another guy with a gun. These murders had an almost ceremonial quality about them."

Benny's head went back and forth. "Bullshit, bro, bullshit."

He was getting a little angry that Benny was adamantly fighting this lead, which was really the only one they had. He had to practically drag his friend along on the investigation.

"Tomorrow, I'm going to the library."

"What are you going to do? Check out a book about how to find a killer?"

Matthew glanced at the moon again before closing the blinds. "I was just thinking about what we found in the kiva at Mecho's land."

Benny grinned. "All that Mayan stuff?"

"Aztec."

"Whatever."

The doctor's eyes brightened. "What'd you find?"

He told her.

"Wow, that's revolting," she said when he had finished.

"Yeah, it was. And it stunk to high heaven," Benny added.

"May I see the photos?" Her eyes brightened with curiosity.

"I'll email them to you," Matthew said.

"They're pretty disgusting," Benny said.

"What we found in the kiva seems to echo what's happening in town."

"Rituals, resorts. Your thinking is all over the place." Benny stood up and tried to rub the wrinkles from his pants.

"It'll make sense in the end, I promise." He hoped so anyway and then looked in his wallet. "Shit."

"What's wrong?"

"I don't have a library card."

Benny and the doctor laughed so hard they choked.

Chapter 34

"Here's more, Matthew." Librarian Susan White placed down a load of books on the table where he sat. The large woman huffed from the exertion. "You doing a book report?"

"I'm making a case."

"Just don't make a mess." Immediately disinterested, she left to shush loud patrons.

The Guadalupe Community Library was located in one of the oldest buildings in town. While the official history stated the building was the first courthouse, local historians knew better and didn't like to talk about it. That's because the library had also served as the town's one and only brothel before it became a courthouse. The top two floors housed the rooms of the prostitutes, while on the bottom floor was a bar, dance hall, and office of the madam supposedly named Jenny Jones. Jenny had a great trade until the wife's mayor shadowed her husband to the place and forced him to shutter it in 1899.

Matthew could understand why the library made a good whorehouse. The building had an easy air to it. The interior turned all flowery when the sun shone through the stained glass of roses. Closing his eyes, he smiled at the johns of yesteryear having a damn good time. Anything for a little reprieve from the murder and mayhem in his home county. He opened his eyes and got back to work.

Benny skipped the library and bank visits because he said he had work to finish at his office, including planning patrols for the festival. Then he wanted to go home and spend time with Camilla. Matthew suspected his friend was also fatigued from talking murder. So was he, but he also experienced a voracious need to resolve the unresolved.

His nerves sparked like electrical wiring and his body felt a thirst only quenched with a suspect in jail.

Several books lay open before him. They were all about the history of Aztecs. The pages illustrated the wonders of the ancient people. Most wondrous—the magnificent Tenochtitlán, now the site of present day Mexico City. In the fifteenth century, the city was an architectural wonder. It had been built on an island on what was then Lake Texcoco. Bridges and causeways wide enough for ten horses connected it to the mainland. The people designed levees to keep out the bad waters of the lake and bring in fresh water via aqueducts.

Tenochtitlán became the largest city in the pre-Columbian Americas with an estimated two-hundred-thousand residents.

"Wow," he whispered to himself.

He studied the imagined drawings of Aztec life. The resplendent emperor's palace held one-hundred rooms, a zoo, aquarium, and botanical garden. The Aztecs were craftsmen, artisans, poets, and mathematicians residing in an almost futuristic construction of temples, floating gardens, and expansive markets. One walled square contained forty-five public buildings. He'd never been to Mexico City and this history gave him an itch to go and see the remains of the city.

Scholars only guessed at the exact origins of the Aztecs, but the once wandering people had a vision of building a great city on the spot where an eagle stood atop a cactus with a rattlesnake in its mouth. They saw that vision realized on the island in the middle of the lake in the year 1325. No wonder the eagle, snake, and cactus was depicted on the Mexican flag. Wherever the Aztecs came from, they knew how to raise an empire. At its zenith, it ruled over eighty-thousand-square miles of Central Mexico. The people who resided under them paid tribute to the Aztec rulers.

He smiled. They were truly amazing.

He flipped another page and lost the smile.

Here was a different side of the Aztecs.

The human sacrifices.

Up to twenty-thousand people were killed each year the empire reigned.

Twenty thousand.

Sacrifices took place atop the splendid stone temples painted by blood. In drawings, Aztec priests in capes and feather headdresses dug out hearts with razor-sharp obsidian knives as the victims were straddled across sacrificial stones.

Obsidian. The same stone used in the knives that killed people in his county.

In another illustration, an Aztec priest held up a human heart in triumph and religious ardor. If that wasn't enough, the priests cut off heads and limbs of victims. What remained of the bodies were then rolled down the steps of the temples, some almost two-hundred feet tall. Skulls of the sacrificed were embedded in walls and heads set on spikes. From his briefcase, Matthew pulled out the photos he had taken down in the kiva. Mecho Hernández had created a miniature version of the horror with sacrificed animals.

In other drawings in the books, Aztecs wore the skin of the conquered people or fed on the flesh of victims. His mind zipped to Nick Vargas's skinned body. Mary Lou Flores's heart removed from her chest, and how the mayor took a bite before he died.

In the kiva, Hernández had painted an image of Huitzilopochtli, the god of sun, war, and human sacrifice. The sacrifices and blood nourished the many and hideous Aztec gods. The people believed that without the murders, which was what they really were, the sun wouldn't rise and the world would die. Even infants and children were sacrificed to bring rain. The Aztecs believed their tears wet the earth.

The description of another god gave him goosebumps. Chalchiuhtlicue, the goddess of water, rivers and seas, whose tears once flooded the world. Once a year, a child was sacrificed to her in the water. He thought of the boy who disappeared in the city swimming pool weeks before. His body still was missing.

Most of the sacrifice victims didn't go willingly. Bands of Aztec warriors captured them among other tribes. They were ferocious fighters, dressing in jaguar skins and feathered helmets who blew whistles sounding like human screams probably to scare anyone who might resist.

Human screams.

In his son's nightmares, the howling of the scary guys chasing him had become human screams. Unrelated. It had to be.

Because of the Aztec raids for sacrifice victims, they created many enemies, which in the end led to their downfall. Spanish conquistadors became their allies to crash down the empire.

With each drawing, he perspired, despite the air conditioning of the library. He wiped at his forehead. He licked his fingers to turn the page, but had no spit.

He closed the last book.

"It's all here, dammit! It's a goddamn match," he said loudly and received one dirty look from the librarian.

"Put a plug in that language. Don't make me throw you out, Mr. Riley," the librarian replied in a loud whisper.

He gathered the books.

"Ready to check those out?" she said.

"I'm not checking them out. They're evidence."

Chapter 35

Angel and his friend, Billy DeAngelo, skidded their bikes up to the property, jerking up dust.

FUTURE HOME OF THE DESERT ROSE RESORT
RICHARD WRIGHT, DEVELOPER
NO TRESPASSING

Billy, who was taller and a year older than Angel, was far less brave than his friend. He tapped the sign with his hand. "We can't go in. The sheriff'll arrest us and that'll make my dad freak out."

"My dad's a lawyer. He'll get us out of jail."

"Yeah, really funny."

Angel walked his bike past the sign. He would, of course, be yelled at if his mom and dad ever found out, but the excitement of checking out the place would be so worth it.

"I don't see anything cool here," his friend said.

"We got to go inside a little more. I heard my dad and Uncle Benny talk about an old Indian village out here. They didn't think I was listening, but I was. They just said it was dangerous and that means there's something cool to see."

"We're going to get in trouble."

"Nah. My uncle *is* the sheriff." Angel grinned and continued on. His friend followed, though slower.

The boys parked their bikes in a clearing.

"Is the owner going to kick us out?" Nervously, Billy glanced at the house off to the side.

"Nah. He's dead. I heard that from my mom when she didn't think I was listening, either. And I read her newspaper stories." His feet were already headed toward the ruins in the distance. "Wow. Come on, let's check 'em out."

Once in front of the pueblo, Angel looked up at the abandoned structure. "This is great."

Billy brushed dirt off of his jeans. "There's nothing out here but old houses on top of each other. So boring. Let's go to my house and play video games."

"What are ya talking about? I bet we'll see Indian ghosts in there."

They ran up to one of the rundown square homes. The adobe was yellow and cracked. Angel hesitated a bit before entering one house, wondering if he really would see a ghost. He didn't tell any of his friends about his bad dreams. And he wasn't going to tell them about the ones where the creepy guys chased him in the dark. His dad was right, though. They were just nightmares.

He walked from the white-sunned day into the dim house. No ghosts inside. Just gloomy nothingness.

"See, I told you. This is boring." Billy hung back by the door.

"Yeah, there's nothing here, but maybe we can find arrowheads or Indian treasure." Angel searched the ground as he walked outside. All he spotted were old tin cans, dried up cow pies, and cracked bottles, but he didn't stop looking at the ground as they headed back to where they parked their bikes.

"No treasure." Billy took a slug of water from the bottle on his bike.

Angel ignored his friend and continued surveying the ground. Something shiny was wedged in the dirt. He hurried towards it. Could be a Spanish coin or old arrowhead belonging to a famous Indian. He picked it up.

"What do you got?"

Angel opened his hand. "It's a bullet, but it looks new." He put it in his jean's pocket anyway. "Look over there. That's a kiva."

"What's that?"

"Billy, you never listen in school. It's where Indians held their ceremonies and stuff. It's kind of like a big round hole in the ground." He led his friend to the square door. "Probably lots of arrowheads lying around. Maybe even a bow. Let's go down. Better than a video game. It'll be our adventure."

"It's locked, Angel."

"Crap."

Billy showed interest at last. "We can break the lock open with a rock. And I saw a ladder near that house. We can climb down with that."

"Now you're talking, dude. Look for a rock."

Angel didn't watch where he stepped. His shoe caught in a hole and he went face down. "Damn." He pronounced the word he heard his dad often say when he watched football on TV.

"Nice one," Billy laughed as Angel hit the ground.

Angel raised his head. A few inches from his left hand, a black scorpion emerged from the dirt. Six-inches long, it clicked its front claws together. Angel didn't dare move. A dozen more scorpions dug out of the dirt near Angel's other hand and all of them began to scamper toward him.

"Oh shit! Angel, get the hell out of there." Billy took off toward their bikes.

Angel bolted up and leaped over the insects. He raced to his bike. He had to turn around. More and more scorpions dug out of the dirt until the ground appeared to be a black creeping carpet.

"Shit," Billy shouted again.

Soon, the mass of scorpions moved toward the boys.

"Whoa!" Angel said.

"If we get bit by them, we're goners."

"It's like one of those old monster movies on TV."

"Now can we go home?"

The boys raced off. They didn't see the black scorpions dig themselves back into the dirt.

Chapter 36

Maxine Santiago clicked her tongue and crossed arms so broad she could have been a bouncer at Joey's Bar. She threw in a dirty look for good measure as Matthew ate a fast-food taco in the courthouse basement.

"You better not be getting your greasy fingers over all my files, Matthew."

"I swear I'm not, Maxine." He wiggled clean fingers and the clerk laughed. "This all the info on Mecho Hernández's land?"

"That's it. The old guy always paid his taxes on time. He didn't have any relatives, so when he died the land reverted to the county and Richard Wright snapped it up."

"Snapped is right."

"Yeah, but he's done that before. He must watch the obituaries or something. He buys the property of dead people and flips it. Just like on that TV show." Maxine placed files into a cabinet. "When an opportunity comes up, you had best take care of it quickly. I guess that's why Wright is such a rich bastard."

"Did Mecho Hernández leave a will?"

"Nothing that's been filed anywhere because I looked. It was like that man wasn't even born. Kinda sad, huh?"

"Kinda sad."

"Need anything else, Matthew?"

"A listing of all of Richard Wright's properties in the county."

Maxine exhaled irritation. "Really, Matthew?"

"Really, Maxine."

"It might take me a few hours."

He smiled. "You're the best."

"Then next time, bring me a taco."

****

Ross Conrad scowled. "This is highly irregular, Mr. Riley."

"It's part of a murder investigation, so don't make me get a court order, Mr. Conrad, because I will."

Conrad managed the largest branch of the First Bank of New Mexico in Guadalupe. He was as stiff as a teller's pen wearing the kind of suit all bankers seemed to wear. Dark and pressed. Boring tie on a white shirt. With much grumbling and pursing of pudgy lips, he agreed to show Matthew the accounts of Mary Lou Flores, Mayor John Stuart, and Deputy Jackson Rogers.

Matthew and Benny had searched the homes of the dead and discovered they had all been customers at the bank, which was the largest in town and the state. They had found checks but no bank statements, which Matthew thought strange, so that warranted a visit to the financial institution.

"I don't want a fuss or scandal. I'll handle this myself," the banker told Matthew.

In his office, Conrad searched the bank's computers. "If these customers were alive, I don't think I would have been so accommodating, Mr. Riley, but since they are all deceased, it is not so egregious."

"This is very important to the case, Mr. Conrad."

He huffed as he checked the records.

In the last year, no huge deposit had been made to John Stuart's checking or savings accounts, which threw a rock into Matthew's theory. Stuart's holdings were even modest. The mayor had no say on the county commission board that would approve the resort development, so maybe he was wrong about whether Stuart was involved. He might have indeed been collateral damage that night like Mike Rand, the bodyguard.

"That's everything on John Stuart, Mr. Conrad?"

"Wait a minute." The manager checked out a few other computer screens.

"It appears the mayor added a $40,000 contribution to his stock portfolio a month ago. Sorry, I didn't see that notation."

"Now, we're talking."

Flores had deposited $60,000 into her savings account three weeks before Nick Vargas's death.

"Can you tell me the source of the money? Was it a check or a bank transfer?" Matthew said. If the check was written by Richard Wright or the Desert Rose LLC, he had the proof he needed.

"The deposits were all in cash."

Matthew bit the inside of his mouth. Deposits or not, Benny was right. He still had no proof whether Richard Wright had bribed Flores or Stuart to help the development along, not to mention Nick Vargas.

The banker then called up the accounts of the late Deputy Jackson Rogers. Four months before Vargas had died, Rogers added $75,000 to his savings account.

Whatever Rogers did, it earned him more than what the public officials had received.

"Another cash deposit?"

"Yes."

"Shit."

"Pardon me, Mr. Riley," Conrad said.

"Nothing."

And everything. He would wager that Rogers got a big payday for doing something really bad, perhaps killing Nick Vargas. Why then was he killed? The deputy might have wanted more money from the conspirators and got cut out of the deal entirely—not to mention losing his life and limbs.

"Mr. Conrad, please don't mention my research to anyone."

With a handkerchief from his jacket, he dotted his forehead. "I don't want this to get around. People must be able to trust our bank."

Matthew placed the bank printouts in a file. He didn't have evidence linking the money to a suspect, but dammit, this supported his premise.

The Desert Rose Resort was the key.

Chapter 37

The band tuned up and started right into a cover of Selena's "Bidi Bidi Bom Bom."

People crowded around the stage that was set up at the northeast corner of the park. Sitting at outdoor cafes or strolling along sidewalks, they sang along. A few danced to the popular and lively song, moving hips to imitate the Tejano star. Everyone had room to celebrate. The streets around the park had been closed to traffic for the Niño de Luz Festival.

Matthew sighed. This was only day one of the four-day event. Religious processions, masses, and vigils in the park were the spiritual side, but the rest of the time was going to be filled with non-secular activities ranging from barbecues to dances. Recently added was a car show with vintage autos and lowriders displayed around the park, where most of the festival action took place.

Vendors sold tamales, tacos, drinks, burgers, and hot dogs. In one corner a beer garden had been set up where patrons could drink, but within the confines of an area marked with rope and police barriers. The festival perfume was cooking meat, chili spices, and Coors.

Each evening included a procession around the park. People followed the statue of the Niño de Luz carried on a platform and then ended up at the center of the park for a mass. On the final day, the Lions Club members hosted a large dinner, as they had for a decade. One year, the Elks had tried to take over the concession, causing a mini-controversy, but the Lions Club remained victorious in serving up the prime rib feast.

Each year, he, Isabel, and Angel attended as many events as they could and had a great time. As he watched the people having fun, it struck him that this would be the first time they wouldn't be together.

"You have to love the festival," Benny said.

"What? Yeah, you do. For all the hassle." Matthew afforded a small smile.

He wanted to talk about the case, but Benny insisted they meet at the park. His friend and the police chief shared responsibilities for patrolling the festival and keeping it peaceful and safe. So every available deputy and officer worked the event. But it still was a demanding job as demonstrated by a near accident at an intersection.

"*Ay!*" Benny pronounced.

"People are acting rowdy and it's only the first night."

Benny spoke into the radio attached at his shoulder. "Jim, this is the sheriff."

"Go ahead," the dispatcher answered.

"Find Jose and tell him to do some traffic control on Main Avenue and Cordova Drive."

"Yes, sir."

"Pronto."

As they walked around, Matthew told Benny about what he had found at the bank. He couldn't tell if he wasn't interested or just surveying the festival for trouble because his eyes constantly shifted about.

The dispatcher called again.

"Sheriff, Richard Wright wanted me to tell you that he doesn't need a deputy for protection anymore."

"Good, more manpower for the festival." He walked on, talking to Matthew. "Wright probably hired a Navy SEAL to protect him."

"Or maybe he doesn't need it. You saw how he acted when we talked with him, like he didn't really believe he was in any danger. That makes him a person of interest."

"Matthew, you're the lawyer. We can't charge him with any wrongdoing."

"Don't you think I know that? But what about those bank accounts of all the murder victims? The money deposits? That's pretty damn suspicious."

"Wright is a respected man in this town. I can't believe he's going around cutting people up with a rock knife. He's never been in any trouble with the law."

"The guy's still an enigma. His parents died young and left him money, which he generated into *more* money. He's not married, has no best friends I could find, and seems to breathe profit. Money and power turns people into monsters."

"This is so nuts, Mateo."

"Then who do you think killed everyone?"

Benny's voice lowered. "We must have a friggin' cult at work here. Like the Manson family. Only these guys worship Aztec shit."

"Benny."

"It doesn't make any sense. Why would Wright kill those people? They all supported the resort."

"Here's one explanation."

"Oh, I can hardly wait to hear this."

"My friend, sarcasm doesn't suit you."

"Just get on with it, Matthew."

"Wright got rid of his partners in the resort deal, specifically Nick Vargas, John Stuart, and Mary Lou Flores. With them gone, he and his attorney, Samuel Uhlig, keep all the money from that development."

"What about my deputy?"

"I'm sorry for saying this, but I think Rogers killed Nick, got paid, wanted more, and had to be eliminated."

"Matthew, I love you like a brother, but you're talking shit."

"It does make sense. The grotesque way the people were killed is just misdirection, and very imaginative if I do say so. I mean, imitating how the Aztecs murdered their victims. Flaying, digging hearts out of bodies, chopping off limbs. And it nearly worked because it looks like a lunatic is responsible."

"Isn't this all too complex? Why not simply bump them off?"

"Because then it would've been more suspicious. First thing, we need to exhume Mecho Hernández's body."

"Why for God's sake?"

"Wright had been after that land for months, and then the old guy suddenly dies of a heart attack? How convenient. If a heart attack really killed Hernández, I'll take Richard Wright dancing on a Saturday night. I'm also going to have to find a way to obtain a search warrant for Wright's office, home, and records."

Benny stopped walking and his eyes finally set on Matthew's face.

"Almost one year before the death of Mecho Hernández, Wright and his legal thug had set up a corporation for the resort development. Like they knew the old man was going to die and they were going to get the land. They even purchased an adjacent parcel for the project," Matthew said.

They stood in the middle of the street, but hadn't noticed. They'd been yelling. The last time he and Benny had a fight was in the fifth grade when Benny refused to go camping with him out in the desert. He called him a big chicken and Benny pushed him. Taller and more muscular, Benny sent him toppling backward, smacking his back on the parking lot at the school. His friend couldn't stop apologizing.

He supposed that he knew everything about Benny, but he couldn't understand his friend's stubbornness at what seemed a logical explanation. He had to try to make him understand.

"Wright only wants us to think a psycho is mimicking Aztec sacrifices," he said in a somber voice. "It's all subterfuge, dammit. But I give you this, the killer is still pretty fucked up in the head to do in people that way. My theory may sound far-fetched, but it fits the facts."

Benny's radio sparked up.

"Sheriff, there's a fight over at the beer garden."

"I'll handle it," he told the dispatcher.

"Matthew, if you really want to convince me that's what happened, then prove it." He stomped off.

He called after. "Don't worry. I will!"

Chapter 38

Every time Isabel Sánchez Riley entered the county courthouse, her feet headed automatically in the direction of Matthew's office. A matter of habit. That's what came from being married for almost ten years. Memories of those years, those very good years, caused her bones to throb. Their love had been so intense, she wondered how the walls of their house didn't blow apart. They seemed to share the same air and thoughts. Their life together had been made up of a million great moments.

"Hell," she breathed out.

Then there were those last four months before they separated. The silences and the fighting. The prods that drew invisible blood. How Matthew had applied for the Attorney General's job without talking with her. When he was offered the position and finally told her, she blew up at his concealments. He knew she didn't want to leave Guadalupe, so he wanted to make sure he had the job first, he said. Bullshit, she replied. He always wanted more and didn't seem to be satisfied with what they had together, which was great or so she thought. That was her accusation and it split them because he didn't deny it. Sometimes, she wished, foolishly so, that he'd been having an affair. Another woman she could fight. Ambition was a whole lot tougher competition.

Those latter and painful memories made her walk past the stairs leading up to Matthew's office and right into the office of Bailiff Greg Trujillo. It was located directly across the hall from the city-county law enforcement agency.

"Hey, Greg." She carried a drink holder with two coffees and a box of assorted doughnuts.

His grin was broad and welcoming.

Isabel had found out long ago the best places to gain information were not necessarily from official sources. Greg was one of the best of those. He heard everything because people didn't pay attention to him. Once a week, she bought him coffee and doughnuts, which he shared with the other bailiffs. Nearing retirement age, he didn't care if anyone knew he was talking to Isabel the reporter.

Greg was buff for an older man and boasted about lifting weights even at that age, though they were twenty-pounders rather than the fifties he used to raise up in his youth. He had deep green eyes that glinted with intelligence. On his desk always sat an open book. He read only biographies. That week it was about Ulysses S. Grant.

"With two commissioners and the mayor dead, they might put me in charge." He brushed powdered sugar from the doughnut off of the front of his dark blue uniform.

"Dream on." She sat on the edge of his desk. Through the open door, she could look across the hall and right at the side door of Benny's office. It was closed at the moment. That meant the sheriff was out or in a meeting and didn't want to be disturbed.

"So, anything good for me?"

"Isabel." Greg blew out powdered-sugar breath. "Four people have been killed. Ain't that enough?"

She suddenly felt stupid for asking the question. "Well, you can't report about murder every day. Any exciting lawsuits going on?"

"Nothing. It's the festival. Nobody sues anybody during the festival."

Across the hall, the door to Benny's office opened. Out came Benny, then Richard Wright and his attorney, Samuel Uhlig. They were in a heated conversation based on the tight expressions on the faces of Benny and Wright. Uhlig, however, held onto calmness. Benny glanced up and saw Isabel. He smiled briefly at her and motioned to hush the men. Wright and Uhlig headed off. Benny nodded to Isabel and then walked back into his office, his head down. The bailiff watched her watching them.

"They look thick as thieves, don't they, Isabel?" Greg slowly chewed his doughnut. "That's the old saying isn't it?"

"Yes, it is."

"One night I had to come back here because I forgot my cell phone. I saw those two going into Benny's office way after hours. The late Nick Vargas joined them a few minutes later."

"So?"

"So, Wright and his lawyer have been pretty frequent visitors to the sheriff. Maybe Benny's getting free legal advice."

"Most likely, Wright and his attorney are yelling at poor Benny because he hasn't solved the killings. People don't want to live in a town with lots of murders."

"Whatever you say." He straightened his tie. "And thanks for the doughnuts."

She barely answered and left the courthouse.

Matthew and Benny had been good friends since elementary school. He trusted Benny with his life, his son's life, and hers. But Isabel had always been troubled by the big man, whom everyone had considered less than smart. She was one year behind Matthew and Benny in high school and always watched them. Mostly, she watched Matthew because she had had a crush on him even back then. Matthew stood up for Benny and protected and helped him. When he did so, Benny stood back, observed all, and just smiled. She never mentioned her feelings to Matthew, who loved Benny like a brother.

Isabel, you're always suspicious, she told herself as she walked back to the newspaper office. It was the reporter in her. The two men probably shared more than what Matthew told her, things only brothers share.

Still.

"Thick as thieves," she repeated out loud.

Chapter 39

The diminishing sun wrapped the house in a muted red that matched the dismal mood inside. Father Joe De La Cruz had hurried over when Junie Mondragon called about her husband Philip's descent into the final crossing, but he'd been across town anointing the sick at the hospital. Nearing sixty, the priest was in good health, but the busy business of the parish could be exhausting.

He arrived too late.

All that was left to do was pray for Philip's departed soul and comfort the living.

Philip had died from age and COPD. As disease tends to do, it reduced the once burly construction worker into a shrunken and sallow being lying on the double bed in their bedroom. A smoker since the age of fourteen, Philip had made it to seventy. The priest considered it a miracle that he lasted that long, considering how many packs he went through in a day.

Before the terminal diagnosis, Philip had been a kind, generous religious family man. A painting of Jesus touching his Sacred Heart hung above the bed. A large crucifix was over the door of the bedroom. This was not surprising for the family who never missed Sunday mass, unless they were out of town. Even when Philip became ill and couldn't attend church, Junie would bring him the communion host.

But he had been in denial about his situation and declined final confession and rites, although the priest attempted several times to change his mind. As death closed in, the kindhearted Philip became cruel and short-tempered with his family. More than once did Junie sob to the priest about the change in her husband. He told her that was probably because Philip was angry and scared that he was going to die, though he still didn't admit it.

But death was the great leveler, and Philip gained serenity when he passed. The rest was up to God.

"We were married almost forty-six years." Junie gripped the priest's hands.

"A blessed life," he replied.

Junie kissed her dead husband's cheek, as did their three grown daughters, and then held his hand in a goodbye. Gently, a young hospice worker removed the oxygen mask from Philip's face and pulled the sheet over him. The family stood around weeping and soothing each other with hugs as they waited for the funeral home staff to arrive. The sunset's rosy light poured into the room from the windows.

"He's at peace," the priest said. The words apparently held no comfort because the family kept crying. At times like that, he felt like a failure.

Father De La Cruz took off his dark purple stole, kissed it, and placed it in his valise. The family thanked him and walked him to the front door.

He blessed the surviving Mondragons and left. He didn't get ten steps to his car before he heard screaming from inside the house. Not screams of grief.

Screams of terror.

He hurried back inside.

"What's wrong?"

The yelling came from the bedroom. The priest hurried down the hall and was almost run down by the daughters helping their mother out of the room. Junie swooned. Her head rolled back, her legs barely moving. The hospice worker stood immobile by the door.

"Please, tell me what's going on," he said.

The women didn't answer. They just continued to scream and cry.

He entered the bedroom. A bloom of red grew out of the sheet covering the newly-deceased Philip Mondragon. The color spread everywhere.

The priest took the sheet away. The eyes of the body were nothing but ragged red pits. More blood emerged from the open mouth and still more oozed from a fist-sized hole in the chest right over the heart. The red dripped to the floor.

The priest sat down before he fell down.

Chapter 40

Isabel drank coffee and made a face. Cold and biting. She threw the rest of the stuff in the sink.

She had knocked off work early that day. Her editor hadn't said anything and he shouldn't. For the past week, she'd put in extra hours with the reporting on the murders. Earlier that day, she finished a story that would run Sunday about how the sheriff's department had no new information on the grisly killings and how the crimes might affect the festival attendance. In today's paper was an article she had written about how the resort was ready to break ground any time after county zoning approval and the final okay by the county board of commissioners, according to Richard Wright. The only hold up would be the commissioner vote because the board was short two members. New commissioners would have to be appointed by the governor.

She reached for the coffee pot to pour another cup, but didn't. Instead, she leaned against the counter and gripped the edge. What she had seen at the courthouse lodged in her mind like a piece of sand. Benny, Wright, and Wright's attorney, Samuel Uhlig. What the hell were they up to? Benny appeared uncomfortable that she saw them together.

It wasn't her imagination.

Benny looked guilty.

She had never trusted Wright. In high school, she heard he sold pot to kids. At first, she believed it was gossip, but then he offered her a joint when they had one date. She was a freshman and he a junior. Sighing with humiliation, she hated to think about that episode. Back then, he was cute and had a nice car because his grandparents were wealthy. His parents had died. After a movie and a burger, they parked outside of town and he tried to put his hand under her sweater and then between her legs. Other boys had tried such a move, but with Wright she sensed he felt entitled to feel her up. She pushed him away, flew out of the car, and walked home, gagging with shame that she'd ever agreed to go out with the guy.

She had never told Matthew, but every time she'd interview Wright for a news story, he shot her a wicked smile as if she let him go all the way. That pissed her off.

"I should have asked Benny what he was doing with those guys," she said out loud.

That's what a good reporter would do.

She called the law enforcement agency and asked to speak with Benny, but was told he was on patrol at the festival.

"Please have him call me as soon as he can."

The dispatcher took the message.

When Isabel first went to work for the newspaper, an older reporter advised her not to make friends with sources because sooner or later they would ask her not to print something. Or she'd be tempted not to run a story that might hurt them. She and Benny were friends and he was Angel's godfather. Yet, she had to ask him about that meeting with Wright, if nothing else to alleviate her uneasiness.

She glanced out of the window over the sink. It was dark outside and she clicked on the porch light. Since the murders, nighttime became as impenetrable as a wall of steel teeth. If she ran out into the night, she'd probably be chewed up by it. Rinsing her coffee cup in the sink, she tidied the house. You're being dramatic and morbid, she told herself, but that didn't calm her anxiety that something dangerous and extraordinary hid outside in the dim.

As a kid, she and her younger sister Monica loved to play outside in the nighttime. They'd scare each other with stories about monsters running after them. Their own game of chicken to see who fled inside first. Her sister always lost.

Last year, her parents moved to Raton to live near Monica, who was coming out of a horrible marriage. Monica had a good job as a clerk for an insurance company and didn't want to leave town, so they offered to go live with her. She welcomed the idea. Her parents hated to leave Guadalupe, where they had been born, but they confided to Isabel one evening that the real reason they were moving was because her sister would always need their help, financially and emotionally. Isabel, on the other hand, could take care of herself. She got into college on her own and found a career as a reporter. Monica hadn't finished college, had trouble managing money, and was drawn to men who liked to exploit her sweetness. Her parents wanted Isabel to know that they held no preference in their love.

Still, her parents and sister called once a week to check on her and had been calling twice a week after the murders started. She was glad they weren't around for all the deadly weirdness.

Isabel wanted to get out of this mood, and the only cure was keeping busy. Laundry should do it and there was a hamper full. She always checked Angel's pockets because he tended to put everything in there from rocks to dried-up grasshoppers. One time, she forgot and the whites came out a nice pink from a cinnamon candy. From the pocket of one of Angel's jeans, she removed a rock, three pennies, a chewed piece of gum, and a bullet. Her hand clutched the bullet and she strode to his room.

Angel was putting together a Lego set of a race car on the floor.

"Where did you get this?" She opened her hand.

He barely glanced at it and returned to figuring out how the bricks fit.

"Tell me, young man. I'm serious." She used her mommy voice.

"At that old pueblo." He didn't look up from the small colorful blocks.

"Your dad told you to stay away from that place." She knew how to get to her son. Ever since Matthew had left, Angel had been ultra-sensitive about him.

Angel set down the bricks and reeled around. "Please don't tell Daddy. I'm sorry, Mom. I just wanted to see it. Me and Billy thought it might be haunted or that we could find arrowheads."

"So, was it haunted?"

"No, and I didn't find nothing but that bullet. There was a kiva, too, but it was locked and we couldn't go down there."

"A kiva? I never heard about that."

"The place was scary."

"Why?" She kneeled down next to him.

"I tripped and a bunch of black scorpions came out of the dirt. We freaked out, but it was also kind of cool." He beamed pride at the exploit.

"Oh God, they didn't sting you, did they?"

"No, but the ground was black with them. Please don't tell Daddy."

Isabel threw her son her best most-furious mother look, but she couldn't hold it for long. "You're too curious." She kissed the top of his head. "Just like me."

"Isn't that good?" His smile was impish.

"Not in this situation." Her smile disappeared. "Angel, I don't want to catch you out there again. It is dangerous." There was that word again.

"And fun," he dared to say.

"That's even a bigger reason to stay away."

He held his hand out. "Can I have the bullet, Mom?"

"No."

****

By nine thirty, Angel had been in bed for an hour. The laundry was folded and put away, the dishes washed. Pouring a glass of white wine, Isabel sat on the couch and read the novel for book club. It didn't hold her concentration at all.

A yell came from the other room. "Help. Help me, Mommy."

Spilling the wine, she sprinted down the hall and switched on the light. Her son sobbed, while hunched down in the corner of his room.

"*Mijo*, what is it?" She wrapped him in her arms.

"Another bad dream, Mom."

She wiped sweat from his hair and slicked it back off of his face. "That's all it was, baby, just a dream."

"Men were chasing me. They were ugly. I was so scared." Angel cried as if a boy younger than he was. "This time they caught me. They pounded on me, right here." He placed his hands on his chest.

"Shhhh." She kissed his cheeks. "Dreams aren't real, baby. They're stories your mind makes up. And sometimes, those stories aren't happy."

He took in quick breaths. "It was so real."

"Close your eyes and I'll stay with you until you sleep."

After an hour, Angel finally drifted off. With bones tender from fatigue, Isabel kept on the hall light and opened his door a smidge. Returning to the living room, she wiped up the spilled wine and poured another glass. She'd never been afraid in Guadalupe. She loved this town. Was born there, grew up there. She fell in love, married there. Her son was born there. She had a connection to the people and setting. The mystery of the desert, splendor of the mountains. The place was a rung in her DNA strand and she wished with all her might that Matthew would have felt the same.

Matthew.

Like her son and this town, he was part of her DNA. She touched her lips. She felt him on her body. She *should* go with him to Albuquerque. Yet, she was raw, hurt, and mad that he accepted the state job without discussing it with her. When he finally told her, tempers erupted powerful as those volcanoes she saw on TV. They should have talked more.

Was she being too stubborn?

All those reflections and questions made her more miserable.

Lights from a car flew over the curtain. A car door shut. Grabbing her son's baseball bat she had placed in the corner, she looked out the window. Matthew sat on the porch. She stepped outside.

"What the hell are you doing here, Matthew? It's late." She kept her voice soft so as to not wake Angel.

Matthew didn't answer, but even under the porch light, she could tell trouble dusted his handsome face. "How is he?"

She motioned him inside to see for himself. Angel had kicked off his covers. Matthew replaced them and kissed the top of his son's head.

"I love you," he whispered.

Isabel watched from the doorway.

They went into the kitchen.

"Want some wine, Matthew?"

"Forget that." He opened the refrigerator and got out two beers. "Follow me." He led her back outside to the porch and they sat on the steps.

Isabel pulled the bullet out of her pocket and handed it to him. "Your son went to the old pueblo and found this."

"Dammit. I told him to stay away from there."

"Don't worry, I yelled at him. Kind of."

He held it up in the faint light. "Looks new."

"He and his friend were hoping to find arrowheads."

"That kid has no fear."

"He also said he saw a bunch of black scorpions. 'The ground was black with them,' to quote our son."

"Now I *really* want him to keep away from there."

Matthew put the bullet in his jacket pocket, but by the way he tapped his foot, she could tell he had more to say. "We built this porch. It took us two weeks and we fought every day, but it still looks good."

Isabel smiled. "Yes, it does."

He took her hand. Regret twisted her gut.

"Isabel, I'm sorry I never told you how much you meant to me."

"I knew."

They talked with familiar tenderness.

He breathed out hard and she thought he might cry. "I'm sorry for so many things, it'd be impossible to list them all. You know more than anyone how I fucked up. I didn't apologize because I thought I was right. I'm such a jerk."

She didn't answer right away because it took all her strength not to cry. She should have stood up, ran back into the house, and locked the door to keep out the hurt and hope. Her lips brushed against his cheek.

She didn't want to run away.

"Why the apology, Matthew? Why now?"

"Things are dearer to me than ever before."

"Because of those murders."

He glanced up at the moon, astounding in its brightness. "How fragile everything is." He touched his stomach. "I feel it here." He touched his chest. "And here."

She laughed.

"What's funny?" He looked hurt.

"I only laughed because that's exactly what I was thinking."

In the moonlight, he could have been ten years younger.

"It's like the night we met. You and me at that dance. Even though I knew you most of my life, it was as if I'd never seen you before. So beautiful. More than that, so full of life, light, and love," he said.

"Good alliteration, Matthew."

"I'm a lawyer, not an idiot." He gently shoved her with his shoulder.

"To tell you the truth, I liked you ever since I saw you play basketball in the seventh grade."

"I did look good in those shorts."

"You said it, baby."

They listened to the high bursts of tweets from a goldfinch. Crickets snapped legs in the bushes. Newly-cut grass and bitter sage scented the night air.

"Matthew, why'd you come here tonight?"

He took her in his arms and kissed her. She didn't fight it.

"We shouldn't. You're leaving town soon, Mateo," she said after they kissed.

"I'm not leaving tonight."

Chapter 41

Night manager Mitch Jacobs caught a smoke on the long wooden porch of the Guadalupe Inn Hotel. His favorite spot. He brought out a coffee can where he placed the butts, since the owner didn't like the sight of them. The whole town was asleep and he enjoyed the feeling of being alone. There was already too much noise in this world, which was why the night job suited him well. He had worked at the mining operation for a couple of years, but the clamor was enough to make anyone go off the deep end. No wonder that lots of the workers drank too much, probably just to drown out the noise.

As he crushed out his smoke in the coffee can, he heard a grinding noise coming toward the hotel. Like someone lugging a stone over the street. Several stones. He stepped away from the porch. A couple of yards away, a breeze stirred low to the ground, kicking up a swath of dust. A black alley cat he always saw running around at night rushed into the path of the small whirlwind. The animal went up on its toes and its belly burst open, crackling like a firecracker.

"Holy fuck." Jacobs headed inside, shutting the door behind him.

At the desk, the phone was ringing. Nervously glancing outside, he saw the call was from the man in room 310. He was tired of that guy. The guest had already asked for extra towels, complained the mashed potatoes from room service were chilly, and insisted on a change of sheets. The night manager was tempted to throw him out, but Samuel Uhlig only stayed there when he came to town and always wanted the most expensive room they had. Jacobs gave an ass-kissing nod whenever Uhlig complained and then complied with his dumb wishes.

Jacobs rolled his eyes and answered the phone. "Desk."

"This is Samuel Uhlig. My shower water is not heating up."

"Give it a minute, sir."

"I don't have all night long."

"Yes, sir. It will heat, I promise."

Uhlig hung up.

"Asshole," Jacobs mumbled.

****

Up in room 310, Samuel Uhlig put his hand in the shower water.

"Damn cheap hotel."

The Desert Rose Hotel would be constructed with luxury and profit. He'd have his own suite. Until then, he had to put up with this shithole. At last, the water heated to his liking.

He threw down the towel around his waist and stepped under the water. As soon as he did, his cell phone beeped with a call.

"Never fails." He stomped out of the shower to answer. "Hello?"

He gripped the phone and extinguished his impatience with everything. It was an important call.

"Don't worry, people have a short memory. When it comes to a good piece of real estate, it's very short. Then we'll all be very rich. The maniac terrorizing this town is making us richer."

In the mirror of the chest of drawers, he glanced at himself and sucked in his gut as he listened. "Well, you better take care of it. Earn your profits."

Uhlig placed down the phone and was about to go back to the bathroom. Through the door, he heard a loud creek down the hallway. Grabbing the handgun from his suitcase, he sneaked up to the door and peeked through the peephole.

No one was in the hallway.

"I hate this fucking town." He would be ecstatic when this business wrapped and he could move onto the next project, the next reward.

Picking up the towel from the floor, he headed to the bathroom and shut the door. The room was steamy from the long-last hot water.

Uhlig hung the towel over the tack and rubbed away the steam from the mirror. Someone stood behind him. The tall figure of a man who appeared to have been torn out of black paper. His eyes watered because the stranger reeked of fetid meat.

He had to get his gun. He'd push past him, get his weapon, and blast the hell out of the attacker. It would be self-defense.

He swiveled and stepped right into the arms of another man in a tattered black robe.

The lights went out.

One of the men took hold of his chest. Uhlig couldn't breathe from the grip. He just wanted the guy to rob him and get it over with. The strain on him tightened until he couldn't move his chest at all. He swore his heart was being flattened. Uhlig realized this man didn't want to take his money. The man was interested in only one thing.

The attorney began to weep because he smelled his death.

Chapter 42

Lettie Williams and Juanita García scooted out the side entrance of the Mesquite County Courthouse. They worked in the treasurer's office and wanted a cigarette and talk. Both in their mid-twenties, they sought any excuse to get away from the other female employees who were in their forties and fifties. All those women chatted about was the cuteness of grandkids and worry about going through menopause. Forget that. They had lived their lives. Lettie and Juanita were on the start of theirs.

While the alley was dotted with potholes and sometimes even dog shit, they didn't mind. It was shaded and private. They would have preferred heading across the street to the park, but they didn't have that much time for a smoke break. So, the alley would do.

Lettie lit up as they walked. "I told Jimmy that if he didn't stop betting on the Raiders he could just kiss my ass goodbye."

"What happened?" Juanita lit her own cigarette.

"He kissed my ass goodbye."

"Oh, no. I'm sorry, Lettie. How long were you going together?"

"Six months." Lettie's high heel hit a large rock in the alley. "Dammit."

"You okay?"

"Fine. And watch out you don't step in that, girlfriend."

Juanita sidestepped a big pile of dog crap. "Right, thanks. So, what you going to do, with Jimmy gone?"

"Nothing." She grinned, her red lips going wide. "Ramon Samuels is ready to take me out. And he is as fine as the day is long."

"I hear that."

They both laughed. Lettie took another drag of her cigarette and then spotted something behind Juanita. Her eyes grew into the size of ping-pong balls. She dropped her cigarette. She couldn't speak.

"What is it, Lettie?"

Embedded in the stucco wall of the courthouse were the heads of Samuel Uhlig and missing bodyguard Mike Rand side by side at eye level. Their faces were encrusted with mortar. Their lips parted, showing teeth. Their leaden eyes open and crumbling.

Lettie and Juanita yelled and dashed down the alley.

Chapter 43

Matthew lay in bed next to Isabel. He stroked her hair, which had a touch of red in the bare morning light. He hadn't felt that good in months. Like three months, since their separation.

"God, what time is it?" she asked.

He checked his watch on a chest near the bed. "A little after seven."

"Angel will be up soon."

"So, we have some time." He kissed her.

"You haven't been this romantic since your bowling team took first in the summer league." She pushed him away.

He laughed. "That *was* romantic. The cheap bottle of vino in the back of the bowling alley."

It was her turn to laugh. She was even lovelier.

He kissed her. "Man, how could I have forgotten how beautiful you are."

"You're so full of shit, Mateo, but I guess it's second nature to lawyers."

"No, Isa. I'll take an oath on it." He kissed her and she clung to him. He never wanted to get out of that bed.

"Matthew," she whispered when they came up for air.

"What?" His fingers traced her breasts.

"Mateo."

"Ummm?"

She withdrew his hand. "Last night, you were talking about gut feelings?"

"Yeah?"

She sat up in the bed. "Yesterday, I saw Benny, Richard Wright, and Wright's attorney coming out of Benny's office.

It looked like they had finished up a meeting and a pretty intense one judging from their faces."

"It was probably about the murders."

"They're hiding something. Benny was like a kid who got caught with his hand in the cookie jar. A bailiff told me he also saw Benny meet with them and Nick Vargas way after hours."

"What are you saying?"

She squeezed his hand. "Matthew, I think Benny is involved in all this."

He shot up in bed. "What the hell are you talking about, Isabel? You have a good imagination. I've always said that."

"Not this time, Matthew. Benny looked guilty."

"Of what? Did you ask him what they were up to?"

"I called him but he never called me back." She put her arms around him. "I'm just saying, be prepared, my love, for what you might find when you go digging."

He placed his hands on her arms. His chest deflated. "Sorry."

She kissed his forehead.

"Know why I'm really upset?"

"Why?"

"Because I think you're right."

His cell phone rang. They looked at each other and began to dress.

****

When Matthew arrived at the courthouse, an ambulance crew was trying to revive Juanita García who had passed out. She lay on a gurney in their rig. Lettie Williams also sat in the back, her eyes enflamed from crying. He knew them both as talkative and sometimes giddy. But in the alley, they had the appearance of people who spent the weekend in hell.

Police had blocked both sides of the street and alley, but a crowd still gathered outside of the barriers. After waking Angel and taking him to school, Isabel had followed in her truck, but wasn't allowed near the crime scene. Matthew threw her an apologetic look, but she flipped him off.

Guadalupe Police Chief George Wilson stood with his back against a wall taking deep breaths, whiter than a washed-out sheet. He threw a weak wave as Matthew arrived.

Standing in the middle of the alley, Benny and Dr. Whitney watched a forensic officer take photos. After what Isabel told him, he couldn't help but study Benny. How he stood. How he crossed his arms. He prayed her suspicions and his amounted to nothing. He joined them and had his first look at the faces embedded in the wall. They gazed back with open eyeballs.

When the photographer took his fill of shots, Matthew touched Samuel Uhlig's forehead. A bit of the skin crumbled in his gloved fingers like plaster.

"Fuck." He quickly wiped his hand on his pants, which left traces on the fabric.

Removing his pocketknife from his pants, he scraped away at the chin of Mike Rand. Under an inch of the crusted gray mortar was a white skull.

"Un-fucking-believable." He stepped back.

"Here's the weird thing," Dr. Whitney began.

"Doc, that's the understatement of the century."

She placed up a hand up to make her point. "These heads look like they've been part of this building for years." Her mouth bent slightly. "How I'm going to write this up in my coroner's report is beyond me. The state will probably drag me away to the mental hospital."

"Then we'll all meet you there." He glanced at Benny, whose stare penetrated the wall as if he had Superman's X-ray vision. "Benny, you're awful quiet."

"What can I say, Matthew? This is wacko."

Matthew motioned for the police chief to join them. The man didn't hurry. "George, this is your jurisdiction, but I think it might be related to the county investigation."

Wilson slowly stood erect. "Yes, yes. You and Benny take the lead on this. I'll provide whatever help you need in terms of staff or resources."

He wasn't surprised at Wilson's response.

A buff blond with forearms larger than Matthew's thighs came down the alley. He carried a pickaxe and bag of tools.

"I called Mickey Solonga," Benny said.

"Good thinking."

Solonga headed the county's maintenance crew and could fix anything. Putting on safety glasses, he asked everyone to step back and then took a pickaxe right next to Uhlig's head. Matthew cringed.

Whitney lit a cigarette and passed it to him and Benny while they waited.

"I don't smoke anymore, but I may start up again." He took it, inhaled, and started to cough.

"Lightweight." Benny also took a drag and also coughed. Meanwhile, Solonga hammered away, kicking up dust and bits of mortar.

After twenty minutes, the maintenance chief pulled off the safety glasses and frowned as he walked toward them.

"What?" Matthew said.

"Only the heads are in there. Not the bodies."

****

In room 310, Benny held up a semiautomatic weapon he had found on the floor. "It's loaded, but hasn't been fired. Uhlig was afraid of something; otherwise, he wouldn't be packing heat."

"Everybody hated that guy." Matthew continued to skim through Uhlig's briefcase while Benny searched the rest of the room. A bathroom towel lay crumpled on the floor.

He didn't see anything helpful, but what he *didn't* find might be a clue. "As far as we know, Uhlig's sole client in Guadalupe was Richard Wright, and his name was also on the Desert Rose corporation papers. But there's nothing in here about the resort and that's unusual." He clutched a handful of papers. "Anyone else been in here, Benny?"

"Only me and the forensic guys and the hotel maid."

"Where is she?"

"Outside the door."

"Bring her in, please."

The petite maid's face had been branded by distress. Matthew asked her to sit.

"Don't be scared. Please tell us what happened this morning," he said.

"A guest next door complained about the water running and running in the shower. I knocked, but no one answered. I used the passkey and the place was empty, but his things were still here." She squeaked out the information.

"Nothing unusual in the room?"

"No sir, everything was in its place. Except for in there." She pointed to the bathroom.

Matthew and Benny looked in. The mirror was shattered.

"Anyone report noise coming from his room during the night? Screams? Cries for help?" Benny said.

A shake of the head.

Matthew smiled at her and they let her leave.

Benny checked his notebook. "I talked with the night manager. The last time he heard from Samuel Uhlig was at ten thirty last night. He called to complain the water wasn't hot enough. No one saw him or heard from him after that."

"So Uhlig disappears from his room. No witnesses. No noise."

"That sizes it up."

"I want some answers, dammit."

Benny focused on his face with all seriousness. "I guess this screws your theory about Richard Wright."

"What? Why?"

"His partner in the development was murdered. The killer is still on the loose."

"But so is Richard Wright."

Chapter 44

Ross Conrad waited on the front steps of the First Bank of New Mexico, checking his watch. As Matthew parked in front, the banker took on a muddy look and he didn't bother to hide it.

"Mr. Riley, I understood you were through with this part of your investigation."

"Not quite, but I have only one account to check today."

Irritation on Conrad's round face increased as he opened the glass doors, walked inside, and fired up the computer in his office. The bank closed at noon on Saturday, so it was empty by that time, and Matthew was grateful.

"I'm on the festival committee. We have lots of last-minute details to go over and I've got to prepare for our event tonight. Can't this wait, Mr. Riley?"

"No, sir, it can't."

Conrad choked back spit as if he had swallowed the sand outside Guadalupe.

"The sooner you get to work, the sooner I leave you alone."

The banker placed his fingers on the computer keys, grimacing as if someone had withdrawn all the money in his bank.

****

Johnny Valdez wheezed as he scooped pinto beans from the pot. He placed a scoop in a frypan that sizzled and then he mashed them down. Matthew sat in the kitchen of the former deputy's house on the outskirts of town. He had already removed his coat and tie. If he could, he would have stripped down to his shorts because the temperature in the small house must have been eighty degrees. A standing fan pushed a little air around the room, very little.

"Damn, Johnny, I'm going to bring you one of those air conditioners for your window or at the very least a bigger fan." He wiped the perspiration from his forehead away with his shirt sleeve.

"Well, you'll have to pay for it. My county pension is shit and Social Security don't pay nothing." Johnny put a plate of beans, green chili, and two tortillas in front of him.

"Well, cooking doesn't help in this heat." With a bit of tortilla, he dug up a mouthful of chili and refried beans. The food was good. Johnny knew how to cook.

Matthew's grandfather Paul and Johnny had been best friends for most of their lives. He trusted few people in the world. Johnny Valdez was one of them.

After Matthew's father had abandoned his mother, his grandfather and Johnny helped out in any way they could. From repairing their house to providing them produce from their gardens to deer meat in the fall from an animal they felled. Matthew told Johnny that he looked just like Henry Darrow from "The High Chaparral" TV show he'd seen in reruns. Johnny was complimented by the comparison.

For almost forty years, Johnny had served as a deputy sheriff. He had no ambition to become sheriff because he didn't want the headache. He retired fifteen years before, and age had started to reduce him to a shorter version of himself. Yet, Johnny was still energetic, funny, and astute.

Johnny also knew absolutely everything about weapons.

After his grandfather died, Matthew visited him as often as he could since Johnny's sons had moved away to

Vegas. But he wanted to stay in town and be buried next to his wife, who was just as funny as Johnny. During visits, they watched football games on TV or just sat outside drinking beer, talking, and telling jokes. Johnny knew hundreds of them, most off-color.

With a groan and harrumph, Johnny took a seat across from Matthew and started to eat from his own plate of beans and chili. "Okay, tell me why you're here," he said with a full mouth. "You haven't come for a while."

"Johnny, I'm so sorry about that. I've been busy with these murders."

"I've read about those in the newspaper. Isabel does a good job of writing."

"Yes, she does."

"Is all that stuff true? About the skinning and some nut cutting off arms and legs?"

"Unfortunately, yes, and it's even worse up close."

"Hell's bells. Then I can see why you've been too busy to hang out with a *viejito* like me." He feigned sadness.

"Knock it off, Johnny. With your veterans' group and belonging to the Moose, you've got a more active social life than I do."

He had the laugh of a grinder chewing up nails.

Reaching into his shirt pocket, Matthew withdrew the bullet that Angel had found at the development property and handed it to his friend.

"So, what can you tell me about this?"

Johnny rotated it around in his fingers. "It's not from one of the Glocks the officers carry these days. This is a large caliber. Forty-four Magnum. Only one man carries that kind of a gun. And you're right. It's new."

He shoved aside his plate.

"Anything wrong, Mateo? Don't you like the food?"

"No, it's great. I've just lost my appetite."

"So, you've heard something you didn't want to hear."

Matthew held out his hand for the bullet. "Nothing that a drink and bottle of aspirin couldn't cure."

****

The basement of the law enforcement agency smelled of mice shit and Lysol. Matthew could have tapped into the computers on the desks upstairs, but he didn't want to explain himself to anyone wondering what the hell he was up to at ten at night. At that hour, the office was still busy with police officers and deputies coming on and going off shifts, and made even busier with all the festival activities. People liked to party on well after the organized events had ended.

So, he had headed to the basement. His steps on the concrete were empty and lonesome.

He hit the lights and the fluorescents clicked on one by one over the large room. Even with the lights, the basement seemed to hold secrets in its corners. Jesus Gonzales, the courthouse janitor, forever tried to spook the female clerks with stories about the ghost of an inmate who hung himself in his cell when the jail used to be down there. How the ghost moaned and clattered at the bars with his bare feet. He spooked them so much that more than a few hated to go down there alone to look for files.

He didn't believe in ghosts, but his shoulder blades itched as if someone was watching.

One section of the basement had floor-to-roof shelves of files containing old sheriff's arrest records and reports. The commissioners, at his suggestion, voted last year for expenditures to digitize the files to get rid of the papers, and the project was half completed.

Matthew sat at a desk at the back of the basement and tapped into the law-enforcement computer. He wanted to check the log of calls into the dispatch center that served both the sheriff's office and the Guadalupe Police. He knew the date, so that would save him work. After a half an hour trying to figure out the system, he found the information he was afraid of finding. He took notes, which he slowly folded and put in his pocket.

Matthew Francisco Riley had cried few times in his life.

Once when his dog Billy got run over in front of their house. He didn't cry when his father left, but did when he saw his mother weeping in their kitchen afterwards. Both times involved losing something that he didn't know was valuable until it had vanished.

As he climbed up the stairs and out of the basement, he wept.

Chapter 45

Isabel placed her hands around his neck.

He had called her after the discovery in the basement and asked if he could come over. She said she would wait up.

They stood in the living room. "Tell me, Mateo."

"Isabel, please don't ask me anything tonight."

"I might be able to help."

"I promise you that I'll tell you everything, but not tonight."

She nodded and led him to the bedroom, undressed him, and he got into bed. They lay close. "Matthew, you don't ever have to ask to come over. This is your home."

He buried his face in her shoulder.

In the morning, they woke early and made love. He did feel home. They didn't talk about his new job, if he still had it, or their problems. He didn't want to talk.

"Get up. I'll make you eggs and bacon." She put on her robe.

"There's something I need to do. It's important."

"Not on an empty stomach."

Isabel was a great believer in breakfast.

"Matthew?"

"Hmm?"

"You're a no-nonsense attorney and I'm a tough reporter, right?"

"If you say so." He tried to pull her back to bed, but she pushed away his hands.

"Listen. I'm going to tell you something and you're going to think I've lost my mind."

"Thanks for the warning." He sat up in the bed.

"I don't believe in the *Llorona* roaming around or the boogeyman under the bed, but things are happening here that we can't explain them away."

"Come on, Isa. This is murder, plain and simple. Well, not plain and not even simple, but murder."

"But, Matthew, they are bizarre. The flaying of skin and taking of limbs. Burying heads into walls. A heart ripped out of a chest."

"And I can explain that. The real murderer has been copying the way Aztecs sacrificed their victims. I looked it up in the library. It's all there."

She slammed her first against her palm. "Shit. Why didn't I see that?"

"Because, my love, it's not obvious. Listen, I will tell you things but you can't print them in the newspaper. At least, not yet."

"Ah, man. I'm missing out on a great story."

"Isabel, please."

She smiled. "I'm kidding. I won't. I promise. But I'll be fired if my editor ever found out."

He trusted her. "All right then."

Matthew launched into his take on the investigation. How he suspected that Richard Wright had everything to gain by knocking off the victims. But he couldn't stand to tell her what he had found in the basement and at the bank. To say it out loud would make it too real.

"And it's all because of that Desert Rose development. There's just too much money at stake. Too much greed. The Aztec-inspired killings are meant to hide this very real motive."

"That makes total sense, Matthew."

He was happy someone believed him. "I just have to get my hands on evidence that will hold up in court."

"But Mateo, there's so much more going on."

"Such as?"

"Weird fucking shit." She rarely cursed.

What she heard from town residents—firsthand and second. The demon in the park. Nick Vargas's grave filled with lizards. The body of Philip Mondragon bleeding. This account came from one of his daughters, who said she had to go into counseling to deal with it. They were in a book club together.

"Don't forget the heads of all those feral hogs on Alma Chacon's lawn." She had written that up for the newspaper and took a photo after a neighbor alerted her.

"I actually saw that."

"And that's what we know about. There's probably more. I tried to sell my editor on an article about all the odd sightings and manifestations, but he declined. He called it speculative and sensational."

"You forgot the devil throwing rocks on the Elks roof during bingo."

"Oh, yeah," she said.

He had half-joked about that, but not about one more event. "The disappearance of the boy at the pool."

She sat on the side of the bed. "Matthew, have you noticed these murders and the craziness started when those two men saw that demon in the park?"

He took her hands. "Isabel, now you do sound out of your mind."

She hugged herself. "I really do."

"It all started with the resort development."

"Then why are my nerves twitching? I feel like I'm riding a flimsy boat with waves slapping the sides. I used to be the little kid who wasn't afraid of the night, but for the last few weeks I've become terrified of what could be out there.

I've never been so scared, not only for you and our son, but this town. And as much as I'm scared, I'm angry at the murders and the strangeness going on. It's like a burglar broke into our house and stole something precious."

"Someone stole your peace of mind. But I swear to God, Isabel, I'm convinced that if I can solve these murders then we might get it back."

She stood up. They heard footsteps running down the hall. Angel burst in, grinning.

"Daddy! You're home!" He bounced onto the bed with him, hugging tight.

"Yes, son." He looked at Isabel, who smiled.

"I prayed you'd come home. Now I won't have any more nightmares."

"Me, neither, Angel."

"Okay, that's eggs for three, but first." Isabel climbed into bed with them and hugged them hard.

****

Matthew had no idea why he was in a hurry. He really didn't want to get where he was going that morning. A headache dug a trench in his frontal lobe. His head hurt because of what he had to do but he had to end this.

His cell phone lit up. Dr. Whitney was on the line. He pulled over his car. He needed to hear what she had to say.

"We matched DNA from the skull tissue to hair from Uhlig's brush at the hotel room. And Mrs. Mike Rand donated some from her husband's comb." Her voice sounded beat. She was probably tired of all these murders, too.

"And?"

"It's them all right, Matthew. I broke the news to Mrs. Rand that it was indeed her husband. After his disappearance, she kind of expected it. So, you owe me."

"Yes, I do, Rosemary. Any marks on the skulls?"

"No, but there is one other thing, Matthew."

"I'm hating when you say that."

"Samuel Uhlig died a few days ago, while it's been about one week for Mike Rand."

"Yeah?"

"Their skulls were dry and brittle, like they'd been in that wall for forty years."

"Is there any goddamn scientific explanation for that? Some ingredient in the mortar of the wall? Could they have been soaked in an acid?"

"Nothing that could have caused that condition overnight. But I'll send the skulls to the state lab to determine if a chemical was responsible."

"Inexplicable." He gripped the steering wheel.

"What, Matthew?"

"One more thing that can't be explained away."

"My coroner reports are starting to read like an Edgar Allan Poe story."

"Did you tell Benny any of this, Rosemary?"

"I left a message for him."

He could hear her light up a cigarette and draw in the smoke. "I haven't told you, but you've done a fantastic job in this investigation, Doc. I'm sorry I didn't mention this sooner."

"You too, man. Even if we don't find the killer, nobody could have done better."

After he hung up, he drove on. Too much to do.

The traffic was stop and go all the way. People were coming into town for the festival. They packed the hotels or stayed with relatives, even long-distance ones.

"Amazing," he said out loud. The grisly murders apparently hadn't hampered attendance.

He headed to a residential part of town and finally stopped in front of a large house. A colonial-style beauty in the midst of a desert town. The contradiction of the architecture with the surroundings had always amused him, but not that day. He banged on the door harder than he intended.

Benny's wife Camilla opened the screen door. Despite the hot day, she wore a heavy robe. She smelled of menthol.

"Matthew, hi. Come in."

He didn't think he could look her in the face, but had to. "I need to find Benny. The office said he was headed home."

"He was here for a little bit, but left just a while ago. Let me make you coffee and I have fresh *pan dulce*."

"I don't have time, I'm sorry, Camilla. Did he say where he was going? He didn't leave word with the dispatcher." And that was against the rules. The sheriff had to be on call twenty-four seven, unless he was on vacation or too sick to raise a gun.

Shrugging, she coughed and took a sip of water. "He was planning to go out of town for a few days right after the festival is over."

"Where?"

"Benny wouldn't tell me. He just said everything would be better when he got back. All our troubles would be over."

"Over? Did he say how?"

She shook her head and clenched her hands together.

He placed a hand on her thin shoulder. "What's really wrong, Camilla?"

"Mateo, Benny's been acting strange and it scares me."

"How long has he been that way?"

"For the last six months. Haven't you noticed it? You're his best friend."

He had only noticed that Benny looked more tired than usual, and was testy and stubborn about this case. But he was the one who asked him to help with the investigation.

Camilla's neck tensed. Her skin pulled back from her face with worry. He tried not to react, but must have. She began to tremble.

"Is he in trouble, Mateo?"

"I've got to go."

He kissed her cheek and ran to his car. As he was about to drive off, he watched Camilla almost shrink to nothing and then close the screen door.

Chapter 46

The early evening air around the Guadalupe City Park eddied with smoke from grilling fajitas and taco meat sold by the many vendors around the square. The town's population grew by the hundreds as pilgrims arrived to see the statue of the Niño de Luz and pray for a miracle either public or private. And if they had a good time with the music and dancing that was okay, too. Thanks to the town's festival committee, the tourists and citizens were treated to music, dancing, and a play based on the finding of the statue, among many other events during the days of celebration. Near the now working fountain, a mariachi band played traditional Mexican tunes and kicked in a few covers of more modern music. Karaoke and a battle of the bands were scheduled later in the evening. Town residents and visitors chatted, danced, ate. Kids scrambled about laughing.

They behaved as if all was right in the world and four people hadn't been butchered. They probably felt safe because of the numerous deputies and police officers patrolling the streets and the park. In fact, there seemed to be a uniform every few yards. The law enforcement presence made him feel safe, too. But not for long.

He again tried Benny's cell phone but it went right to voicemail. He diverted and stopped at the dispatch center. Sue Barton, a lithe soul with large eyes, told him the sheriff hadn't responded to their calls, either.

"That's not like him, Matthew."

"Please try again."

"But he isn't responding."

"Just do it, but say, 'Matthew Riley wants you to meet him at six p.m. at the church. Mr. Riley has vital information that will reveal the conspiracy behind the murders. If he doesn't hear from you, he'll have to go to the state police investigators.'"

Barton wrote as he spoke.

"Go ahead then. Repeat the message to the sheriff."

She did into the microphone.

"Thank you."

She smiled. "So, you solved the case?"

"I'll let you know."

Matthew walked to the park with faint optimism of finding Benny before their meeting. That was due to the sizeable crowds in and around City Park. The music, talk, and laughing created a layer of joyful racket, but all that was muffled in his ears and mind. He only heard the gravel under his steps as he proceeded to the church.

The streetlights snapped on.

He spotted his mother and her best friend Anita Rodríguez walking toward a mass that would take place on the park lawn across from the church. He had already made his mother happy when he mentioned his reunion with Isabel.

"What about that job in Albuquerque?" she had asked.

"That wasn't up for discussion."

"I always knew you'd come to your senses."

"You knew more than me."

A temporary altar and one-hundred folded-metal chairs had been set up for the service. To the side of the altar, the baby Jesus statue in its glass case stood on a four-foot-tall pedestal. Church volunteers in yellow vests directed the people who filed past and made the sign of the cross as they did before taking a seat for the mass. Annually, his mother had taken him through the line when he was a kid, and he kissed the feet of statue. That had been stopped years before because the feet had been worn down by the devoted.

He checked his watch. Nearly six. The sun began to lower, leaving bloodshot and purple strata in the sky. The mountains in the distance were varying shades of blue. Beautiful and tranquil. Behind him, the hymns of the faithful in the park rose like mist from the desert after a rainstorm as the mass began. He should have been comforted by the singing, but he wasn't.

He'd spent his life weighing evidence and making a case, but with what he had discovered, the earth had dissolved underneath his feet. The killings. The greed. On top of that, the sensation he had entered an alien land where the fantastic ruled.

What the hell *was* going on?

Pushing open the double doors of the church, he dipped his hand in the holy water at the entrance—an automatic gesture. He took a seat in a pew toward the front. After a few minutes, the front door opened and he heard Benny's heavy cowboy boots. They were alone.

"*Hola*, Matthew. What have you been doing?" Benny's voice seemed to come from far away.

"Looking for you," he said, but choked on the words. "Everybody's looking for you. You're not answering your phone."

"I just needed to be out on patrol and didn't want to be bothered."

The excuse was feeble. His friend didn't sit but shifted about. He didn't remove his hat, which was curious since they were in a church. "This is the worst possible time for a meeting, Matthew. I got a festival to police."

"We have to talk."

Benny glanced at his watch. "Will this take long? I've really got to help out there."

"We *need* to talk. This is a good place. We won't be disturbed." He stood and walked to the front of the altar. Maybe that would elicit a confession and save them both more pain.

"Talk about what?" Benny moved toward him, his right hand in a fist.

The lights overhead flickered and went out. A strong wind blew through the building. The force was enough that Matthew had to hold onto the front wooden pew or else lose his footing. Benny held his hat on his head. The candles at the altar blew out with a whoosh.

"A summer storm," Benny shouted above the roaring gust.

They looked toward the doors. They were closed. The windows were closed. Outside, thunder rumbled. Through the stained-glass windows, lights sparked like a photographer's strobe. The storm amplified and the walls shook.

As instantly as it began, the tempest ended and the lights faded back on.

"Oh, my God." Benny's mouth and eyes reflected fright and panic.

He had never seen him scared and spun around.

A snake wound around the five-foot-tall wooden cross hanging above the altar. With a body wide as a man's waist, it must have been eighteen-feet long. Its skin wasn't slick like other snakes, but rough as gravel. The snake opened its large mouth and another snake emerged and began to consume the tail of the first one.

Matthew's heart ballooned inside his chest. "Tell me I'm not seeing this."

"You're seeing this." Benny pulled out his gun to fire.

The lights snapped off again. They shot back on and the snakes had disappeared.

"Jesus Christ," he said.

People screamed outside. Guns were being fired.

"What's going on, for fuck's sake?" Benny said.

They ran to the doors and whipped them open. Hundreds of rattlers slithered in the streets. More glided down walls of buildings or hung from the limbs in the trees at City Park and around the streetlights. Their tails flicked with a sickening vacant rattle.

"Diamondbacks." Benny pulled out his automatic weapon and began firing at the snakes crawling in the courtyard of the church. Since he was a marksman, the creatures exploded with blood and flesh. Matthew felt helpless. He had no weapon and was a terrible shot.

He called Isabel on his cell phone.

"Where are you? You and Angel safe?"

"We're fine, Matthew. We're ran into the coffee shop. Are *you* all right?"

"Yes. Stay there."

"We will. I love you."

He was tempted to go to her and his son to protect them, but couldn't. "I love you, too."

Returning inside the church, he grabbed a five-foot metal candlestick and charged out, bashing snakes as he went. He had to get to the park to check on his mother and her friend and take them to safety.

People scampered in every direction, ducking into buildings or cars. Frenzied women picked up their children and dashed around trying to find shelter and to avoid the gray and black snakes. People secure in buildings shouted and waved at others to join them. The large number of police officers and deputies already on duty for the festival shot the snakes, along with men who retrieved handguns or rifles from trucks or businesses or wherever they kept them. Others without guns killed the snakes with tire irons, brooms, chairs, or anything handy. Aside from the sounds of shouting, shots firing, and running was the shuddering of snake flesh being torn apart by bullets and bludgeoning.

Matthew spotted his mother and Anita Rodríguez holding off snakes with the metal chairs in the park. Anita hit a few on the head. He charged to them, hurdling over hissing snakes and smashing as many as he could with his shoe or the candlestick, all the while trying not to get bit. He stomped the creatures his mother and Anita were battling.

"You okay, Mama? Anita?"

"*Sí,* yes," his mother breathed out.

"You bet," Anita answered.

"Stay behind me, you two."

Killing any snake in their path, he led them back to the church, through the courtyard and up the steps. The double doors were locked. Matthew kicked at them, but swung around in case snakes were ready to strike behind them.

"Let us in, dammit," he shouted

Ron Smith, a deacon in the church, unlocked one of the doors, and peeked out. He was a white-haired soul whose face blanched with shock at the chaos.

"Open the doors, Ron!"

Smith did so reluctantly, and his mother and Anita entered. Inside were more people, most women, kids, and older people, breathing fast with panic. Young kids were crying. The older children tried to sneak a look outside at the invading snakes. More people were on their knees praying. Matthew glanced at the altar just to make sure the monstrous snakes were gone.

Had he really seen them?

Grabbing the candlestick, he hugged his mother. "You'll be safe here. I've got to go help."

She hugged him. "*Que Dios esté contigo*, my son."

Running to the front, he noticed small rubber-backed rugs near the bathrooms. He grabbed them.

"Where's rope or cord?" he shouted at Smith, who appeared ready to faint. "Come on, rope or cord."

"In the sacristy."

In the room off of the altar where the priest prepared for the mass, Smith opened a drawer holding black, white, and brown cords used for the vestments. He handed two to him.

Wrapping the rugs around his legs, Matthew secured them with the cords.

"So you won't get bit?" Smith said.

"Say a prayer."

Outside, the pandemonium continued. Snakes hung from the tree branches and slid over cars. A resourceful older man had created his own flamethrower by pouring gasoline in a weed sprayer. The man doused the snakes with the liquid and set them on fire with a match. They sizzled, and the air carried the odor of gas and meat.

He spotted Benny and three deputies shooting snakes gliding across the wide Main Avenue. He ran up to them. Benny handed Matthew a gun. "Here."

"I've never shot a gun. I'll blow off my damn foot."

"Watch it!"

A snake coiled near his leg and sprang at him with its open mouth. For less than a heartbeat, it occurred to him that Benny might not save him.

Benny blasted the snake. Bits of red and gray flesh splattered through the air, landing on his rug-covered pant legs. Suddenly, he felt ashamed for his suspicions. He shoved the gun in his pants pocket.

"Thanks."

Benny barely acknowledged him and sped off in another direction.

He headed toward the park.

A snake prepared to strike a terrified eight-year-old boy escaping up on top of the monkey bars at the playground. After thumping the snake with the candlestick, he led the crying boy back to the church, killing more snakes as he went. The kid's mother bawled with gratitude when she saw him. He knew her. She worked as a waitress at the Yucca Café a few streets over. Normally an overly friendly gal, her face held no color and she got on her knees when her son ran to her.

"Matthew, what the hell is happening?"

He was tired of the question.

"I don't know." He was also tired of answering that.

Returning to the park, he ran interference for Fathers Joe De La Cruz and Henry Cantu, who were rescuing the statue of the baby Jesus still in its glass case. They hurried toward the church, saying Hail Marys all the way. In the church courtyard, a rattler was ready bite Father De La Cruz when Matthew stepped in front. The snake bit him, but the rug protected his leg. He ripped it away by the tail and smacked its head against a wall.

The priest blessed him and they took the statue inside. The younger priest, Father Cantu, returned outside and pulled up his sleeves.

"Got something to use, Father?" Matthew asked him.

"An axe in the gardener's shed."

"That'll do."

The park still hadn't been completely cleared of people or snakes. He stopped five feet from one snake, set down the candlestick, and took aim with the gun Benny had given him. He shot and missed by a good foot.

"Dammit," he yelled. He put the gun back into his pants pocket and killed the snake with the candlestick.

Sulphur from the fired guns layered the air. Men shouted and cursed. Footsteps pounded on the asphalt. The snakes hissed and rattled. He threw his coat over a snake and killed it before it struck a teenage girl too petrified to move. He led her to a pizza parlor already crowded with people. Back outside, he cut a rattler in half. This was the stuff of nightmares. Where he smothered from fear and hopelessness.

Too damn bad he was awake.

Chapter 47

A sickly light of morning coated the town. Men threw shovelfuls of dead rattlers into the back of a city truck. Others picked up more of the thin bodies, their shovels scraping against the street.

Matthew, Benny, and Father Henry Cantu rested on a park bench facing the street. Matthew just wore shirt sleeves. Snake blood spotted his clothing. He had removed the rug armor protecting his legs and thanked God for them because they shielded him against six more bites.

The fighting of the snakes had lasted for one hour, the longest of his life. Then the snakes slithered back from where they came. He hoped it was hell. While the appearance of the rattlers was strange enough, their abrupt departure surpassed that. He watched one rattler coiling for a strike when all of a sudden, it relaxed, gyrated around, and slid away. He still killed it.

Benny's shirttails hung out and he'd lost his cowboy hat somewhere. Father Cantu yawned, his priestly collar, black shirt, and pants were dirty. His long hair had come out of its ponytail.

Benny talked on a cell phone, nodding and listening. "Thanks very much."

"What?" Matthew said.

"That was a specialist from the county extension office. He says temperatures in the desert have been unusually cold for this time of year. The snakes were probably drawn into town because they sensed heat."

"How many people were hurt?" the priest said.

"Thirty people were bitten; one died this morning. An old guy tripped and fell into a bunch of snakes."

"God rest his soul." Father Cantu crossed himself.

"With the number of snakes crawling around here last night, it could have been much worse," Matthew said.

"The hospital wants someone to drive up to Santa Fe for more antivenom. I'm gonna go myself." Benny stood up and left.

His talk would have to wait.

"Matthew, you really buying that explanation about the temperatures driving the snakes into town?" Father Cantu said.

He just rubbed his lower arm that ached from swinging that candlestick.

"Well, I think it's bullshit." The priest brushed off his dirty clothes.

He'd never heard a priest cuss before. "Then what do you think caused all this?"

Father Cantu put his hands together on his lap. "I think the town has been cursed."

"Come on, Father. You're a very educated man."

"This goes beyond anything out of a book, Matthew. It's not a phenomenon of degrees or weather."

"Then what the hell is it?"

"I believe that we've seen evil. Ever since the first murder, a growing malevolence has come to this town and county." The priest nodded with gravity.

"That your spiritual opinion?"

More scraping. More snakes.

"It's not opinion or science, Matthew. I feel it in my soul. That a darkness is upon us, one that even God might have a hard time reaching. You remember that line in the Lord's Prayer: Deliver us from evil."

"I do."

"Why mention it if it's not true?"

"I'll tell you, Father. I don't know what to believe anymore."

Father Cantu stood up and patted him on the back. "Then, there's hope for you yet, Mateo."

"Hope for what?"

"Understanding that some questions can't be answered so easily."

There was something freeing about that. But Matthew also felt cold with the realization.

"The only question left to ask is what invited the evil and how the hell do we get rid of it." The priest headed back to the church.

Matthew called Isabel.

"You coming home, baby?"

The concern in her voice made him want to cry.

"Not yet, my love. I have something to do. Just please stay put."

"Matthew, what aren't you telling me?"

He clutched his cell phone and wondered why it didn't break from the pressure. "I promise to tell you everything, but I've got to do something first."

"Then be careful. Please come when you can."

He drove to his mother's house. He was surprised he could move at all. Weariness had aged him to one hundred. "¿Mama, dónde está?"

Consuela rushed in from another room. She wiped her hands on her apron. Matthew breathed in the aroma of eggs and bacon.

"Aquí, Mateo. You all right, son? I was so worried."

They hugged. She was small in his arms.

"Come and eat. I knew you'd be hungry. Breakfast is almost done."

"I can't eat, Mama, but I've got to shower and change clothes."

"You must be tired."

"Let's go see Alma Chacon."

****

Matthew experienced a kind of light-headed foolishness sitting in Alma Chacon's living room. His mom was on one side of him on a rose-colored couch and Alma sat across from him. Religious pictures hung on the walls. Votive candles burned before a foot-tall statue of Jesus, whose ceramic arms were filled with rosaries and scapulars with pictures of saints. Just like the one at his mom's house. Yet, he also felt very sheltered in there.

A smile passed over Alma's face. "I see you've finally come to believe."

"Those snakes helped convince me." He sat back. "At least, I'm willing to listen."

"That's a start."

"I can explain most anything, but I can't explain all the fantastic things going on. The trouble is the murders and all the craziness started at the same time. And the odds of that happening are sky-high so there has to be a connection. But what?"

"It took you long enough to ask."

"Well, cops will turn to psychics on cases and I'm turning to you. My mother says you can see things that nobody else can," he spoke in Spanish. The language made the room familiar. "So, what do you see, Alma? What's happening in Guadalupe?"

She gripped her small hands together. The large veins from age seem to expand. "The old ones are alive and hungry." Her eyes were bright with hints of green in the dark brown.

"You mean Aztec gods?"

"That's one of their names. The rest are unspeakable."

"But a man is responsible for those killings."

"Is he?"

Her white eyebrows lifted with doubt. That discouraged him to no end.

"So we're talking ancient Aztec spirits? They're cutting off people's skins. Burying heads in walls. Taking arms and legs and drowning little kids."

"I believe you already know the answer, Mateo. I feel them all around us." She opened her arms wide.

"Alma, those gods and the people who served them are long dead."

"They've just been sleeping because they were forgotten."

His mother's lips moved in a silent prayer.

"Dammit." His head felt loaded down with an insight, insane as it seemed. "Mecho Hernández didn't forget them. He made sacrifices to them."

He told the women about what he had seen down in the kiva.

Alma nodded. "Ah. That explains why they're here. The old man must have revived them with the blood of those animals. He summoned them. He fed them."

He stood up and paced. "But why?"

Alma shook her head. "You're going to have to discover that."

"What do they want?" He couldn't believe he was asking about spirits.

Alma's face combined serenity and melancholy. With great emphasis and effort, she stood up. "They're bitter. They're betrayed."

"You're right about that. When the Spanish conquered the Aztec empire, they stopped the sacrifices, toppled their temples. The plentiful supply of blood dried up."

"They were in darkness, but they still had greed for life. Any life."

His mother sat back. "God help us."

Alma gently placed a tiny hand on Matthew's sleeve. "They're becoming powerful, Mateo. The more lives they take, the stronger they get, the more they want."

"That's just fucking great." Matthew switched to English.

"Mateo!" his mother said.

"I take it back. And with all due respect, Mrs. Chacon, I can't believe any of this."

"You must believe, Mateo, or they will win," Alma said.

The curtains over Alma's picture windows were open, letting in clean sunshine. She lived on a little hill overlooking the town. At night, she probably had a good view of all the lights from the houses and businesses below, as if the glows represented each soul in town. In the daylight, the town spread out before him. Composed streets and lives. Once, he could have left all this behind for a new job, but that was no longer an option.

"Then tell me what to do, Alma. How do we get rid of angry, evil spirits hundreds of years old? Who do we call? An exorcist? Speedy Gonzales?"

The women didn't laugh. He wasn't trying to be funny.

"*Perdóname,* but if I tell anyone else what you told me, we'll be put in straitjackets."

"You *can* fight them, Mateo. You must find the reason why they were called by that old man."

"Motive."

"And I'm afraid it will take much faith and sacrifice to stop them." Alma's voice was strong.

"What sacrifice?"

"The only one there can be."

He glanced at his mother, who began to cry.

"You'll know when, Mateo," Alma said.

That scared him even more than the snakes.

Chapter 48

Isabel unloaded the dishwasher. A plate shattered on the floor because she wasn't paying attention. If she'd been a cat, she would have been hanging from the ceiling with her claws.

She hoped the crash didn't wake Angel. He'd been full of questions about the snake attack.

Why were they going after people?

Why were there so many?

Have you ever seen that many snakes?

She had no good response his questions.

While they were hiding in the coffee shop during the attack, he wanted to see the snakes and pressed his nose against the glass while most others drew back.

Clink. One of the rattlers struck out at the glass.

"Angel, get back here," she had ordered.

"Whoa," he replied.

Before the snakes appeared, she and Angel stood around listening to the music in the park. He wanted to join the friends he saw running around, but she wasn't going to let him out of her sight, not with the shit taking place around town. He pouted a bit, so she bought a long churro, which they split. Thank goodness for sugar.

They stiffened on the spot when people started screaming. She thought the grass was alive, and then out came the rattlers with the diamond patterns down their long slim backs. Her only impulse was to get Angel to safety. She picked him up and carried him to the coffee house straight in her line of vision. She had no weapons and wore sandals with her summer dress, so she couldn't fight them. As she ran, she evaded anything that crawled. Near the coffee shop door, one came out of its s-shaped loop to attack, but hit her flowing dress. Angel yelled. The snake's fangs stuck in the fabric. She set down her son. Grabbing the snake's head, she tore it away, ripping the dress. She flung it out into the street where it was promptly shot by a deputy.

Inside the coffee shop, both town residents and the festival visitors watched through the windows as the snakes occupied Guadalupe. A skidding gray army with sharp teeth. They were everywhere. She carried a notebook and pen in her purse, but didn't get them out. She wasn't a reporter that night. She was a mom. She was a resident of the town. People were scared and puzzled by what was taking place outside. But in bad times, heroes rise up. One young woman comforted the terrified little kids and let them watch a movie on her phone in a corner and away from the windows. Outside, law enforcement officers shot the snakes alongside regular townsfolk with the courage and tools to kill these intruders. The shop owner passed around coffee in paper cups, although Isabel wished hers contained alcohol.

Then, three teenage boys rushed in. The one in the middle held onto his two friends. His face was warped with fright.

"Our friend got bit. What do we do?" said one of the teenagers, who was crying.

"He has to go to the ER," Isabel said. "Does anyone have a car nearby?"

"Mine is outback," said the coffee shop owner, a middle-aged guy with a man bun.

"I'll drive him," offered a young woman, who was dressed in jeans and cowboy boots.

The owner gave her the keys and she and the teenage boys left out the back. Another man wielded a large utility broom to clear snakes out of their route to the truck.

"Will he be okay?" Angel said.

"I think so," she answered and prayed it would be true. She glanced back at the window. Matthew was out there someplace fighting the snakes. She prayed for him, also.

After the invasion subsided, she carried Angel to her truck to go home. Bodies of snakes covered the road. She gripped the wheel hard so she wouldn't shake.

Safe in her kitchen, Isabel stooped to pick up the broken plate. She finished cleaning up, but couldn't seem to control her hands. They were clumsy and chilled. How nice it would be to go to sleep so that this horror was nothing more than a dream.

She heard Matthew's car and hurried to him. They hugged and kissed, and she didn't want to let him go ever.

"You okay?" he said.

"Yeah, now that you're here and safe."

"How's Angel?"

"Sleeping. He was tired, excited, and scared. He thought it was an alien invasion."

"That's my boy. Baby, I've got to try to find Benny tonight and talk with him."

"No. Stay with us, please."

"I can't." He handed her a thick manila envelope. "If anything happens to me, give this to the Attorney General's office."

"What's going to happen to you?" Her voice shuddered.

"Just in case."

She hugged him tighter. "Mateo, please."

His eyes shifted. He was doing a poor job hiding his unease.

"My mom was right, Isabel. You were right. Evil has come to town. The trouble is we invited it. Hell, we practically laid out the fucking red carpet. It's all in there. Read it and you'll understand."

She sat down at the kitchen table, opened the envelope, and read. Placing down the file, her face paled. "It can't be. Hold on, what are you going to do?"

He was dressed in jeans, T-shirt, hoodie, and tennis shoes.

"I need to go someplace. If I can find out how this all started, maybe it will end. Don't you see this can't wait?"

They kissed with a passion they both seemed to have stored up for that moment. Isabel buried her face in his shirt. She breathed in the cologne she had given him before they separated. That mixed with sweat. He had not shaven, so his beard scraped her face.

She could feel his heart against his chest.

He asked Isabel for a flashlight.

She checked the pantry. "I keep it in there."

But it wasn't there.

"That's okay. Before I go, I want to kiss Angel goodnight. I'll try not to wake him."

"Good. After tonight, it'd be impossible to get him back to sleep."

They stepped lightly down the hall. The light in his room was on.

They crept in. The room was empty, the covers of his bed on the floor. The curtains fluttered through the open window. On his desk a note written on notebook paper.

MOMMY,
I'VE GONE TO HELP DADDY. DON'T WORRY.
BE BACK SOON.
ANGEL
P.S. DON'T GET MAD.

Chapter 49

Matthew had seen most of Isabel's moods, but he never saw her hysterical. Her eyes were fire-red from crying. Her hands shook as if she stood in the middle of a blizzard. A sheen of perspiration wet her hair and face. He was doing all he could not to act the same about his son's disappearance.

"When was the last time you saw him?"

"About nine. He was so excited after we came home. I told him he could read for a while, and then I shut the door."

Matthew looked at his watch. It was ten.

Running outside, he checked the spot where Angel kept his bike. It was also gone.

Isabel called the dispatch center to report that their son was missing.

His eyes began to itch with tears, but this was no time to break down. He roughly wiped them away with the back of his hand. When his eyes cleared, Isabel stood next to him.

"You know where he went," she said.

"I know where to start looking. Go to my mom's house and stay there. I don't want to worry about you, too."

She grabbed a jacket and ran outside. He ran after her.

"Where the hell are you going, Isabel?"

She got into his car.

"Let's go get our son. After what's been going on in this town, I won't be safe anywhere."

He didn't budge. "Get out of the car."

"No."

"Isa, I can't lose you, too."

She fastened the seatbelt. "Matthew Francisco Riley, get your ass in here."

He did and they peeled out.

****

Matthew held the wheel so tight his fingers ached. The desert outside of town was black and forsaken. No water, no lights. No hope. He shook the negativity from his head. Instead, he focused on the headlights. Follow the headlights. They will lead you to Angel, he kept repeating in his head. He did not hear what Isabel was saying to him.

"What?"

"I'll bet he took the flashlight. That damn kid." She sniffed back more tears.

"He's been out there before. And you know our son, he's fearless. He thinks the answer is there and he's right."

"Why there?"

"Because that's where the whole thing started. It took me too long to figure it all out. That makes me the biggest damn fool in this whole damn county."

"My God, Angel, my baby." She cried.

He slid over his hand to hers and held it tight. "There's a reason all this madness started. That means it can be stopped." She scooted next to him trembling, although the night was hot.

Earlier, he had called Benny and said he wanted to talk with him, but he didn't pick up or call him back. No one knew where he was. With that, Matthew realized he was heading to the right place.

On the way there, he and Isabel didn't speak, both silenced by worry.

"We're here," he said at last.

He turned onto another dirt road and parked.

From the glove box he took out the gun Benny had given him. He also held a flashlight they had stopped to buy at a convenience store. Isabel retrieved a tire iron from the trunk.

His flashlight lit the sign.

FUTURE HOME OF
THE DESERT ROSE DEVELOPMENT

"We're going to walk from here," he told Isabel.

They didn't go down the road, but instead looped around. They proceeded slowly, watching out for sharp yucca plants and keeping the flashlight's beam down low. The moonlight aided them. They made their way to the back of the clearing, where headlights from two cars faced each other. In the lights stood Benny and Richard Wright. Matthew and Isabel glanced at each other. They had to get closer.

A junked car and truck stood between them and the two men. Switching off the flashlight, Matthew crouched down, sneaking up behind the car and gripping the gun. Isabel followed.

From their voices, Benny and Wright argued. He couldn't hear what they were saying.

"I don't see Angel," she whispered desperately in his ear.

He dared to peek farther out from the junker. Inside Benny's patrol cruiser, a small head bobbed up. Thanks to the headlights, he saw Angel's face.

"He's in Benny's rig."

"Thank, Christ." Isabel started for him, but he held her back.

"Wait a minute. He's safe and I need to hear this," he whispered.

She wiped tears off her face. "You and your damn evidence."

"I've got to get hear what they're talking about. Stay here."

"No."

"Shit."

They maneuvered to the back of Benny's vehicle.

"I'm amazed you wanted to meet here, Benny." Wright smoked a small cigar.

"It's time for justice," the sheriff said.

Wright laughed. "You have really gone 'round the bend."

"I'm thinking clearer at this moment than in the past six months. We have to answer for what we did."

"If I go down, then so do you. Mr. Pillar of the community. Mr. Law. We're both in this up to our fucking necks."

"You won't get an argument from me."

"I don't have time for your conscience to bite you in the ass. It's time to make money. So there was a casualty. Success isn't cheap." He checked his watch. "Mecho Hernández was a little price to pay for what we'll get in return. You and I won't ever have to worry about money again."

"I've heard what I needed to hear." Matthew stepped out from behind the patrol car, aiming the gun at Richard Wright. Dropping the tire iron, Isabel ran to the cruiser, swung open the door, and fetched Angel, kissing his face.

"Mommy!"

"Baby, are you hurt?"

"I'm okay. I came to help Daddy, but I just found Uncle Benny and that man. Can we go home? I'm really tired."

"Yes, baby. We're going home." Holding Angel, Isabel ran back beside Matthew.

"Go ahead, Benny, you were going to tell us what you've done," Matthew said.

Wright threw down his cigar. From his jacket, he took out a shiny automatic and leveled it at Benny.

Benny dared to smile. His hands didn't go for the Magnum still in its holster on his hip. "We're some crooks, ain't we, Dick? We've screwed this up from day one. Day fucking one." He looked at Matthew. "I knew you'd figure it out, Mateo. You were always smarter."

Matthew didn't think he could speak. The words were obstructed in his throat. "I saw the department log, Benny. You were out here within minutes after the neighbor found Mecho Hernández's body. What were you doing? Watching?"

"Benny, don't say a word. He's got nothing," Wright said. Each word held a threat.

"I also visited the bank. I saw your account." Matthew's voice cracked like wet ground under a heated sun.

"You've got shit, Mr. Prosecutor," Wright said.

Quick for his bulk, Benny moved to Wright and slapped the weapon from his hand. His arm went around the man's neck.

Benny began to cry. "My poor Camilla. This will kill her. One more victim, more blood on our hands."

"No," Wright squeaked through Benny's forceful grip on him.

Benny faced Matthew and grinned, but his eyes were as hollow as the nearby kiva. He released Wright, who dropped to his knees gasping and cursing. Benny kicked away his gun and his right hand went over the top of Wright's head, forcing it up.

"It happened right here."

Chapter 50

Mecho Hernández never seemed so small. Even his shadow thrown on the ground by the headlights was small. He shook his fist at Richard Wright and Deputy Jackson Rogers, who were both a head taller.

His torn white shirt was bloodied from his nose and a gash on his head, a gift from Rogers. Wright and the deputy had forced themselves into his house that night. Hernández went for a rifle near the fireplace in his living room, but Rogers got there first and took it away. He emptied the chamber of cartridges and smashed the old man on the head for good measure with the butt.

On Wright's order, the deputy forced Hernández from his house. Rogers backhanded him and dragged him in front of the headlights of the two cars parked in the clearing. Hernández cussed in Spanish and then started speaking another language.

"What the hell you saying, old man?" Rogers said with a laugh. "Is that Portuguese?"

"Who cares," Wright said.

"Fuck, I may have hit him too hard."

"I'm not selling, and don't bother me again you sons of *putas*," Hernández yelled and spit out the blood in his mouth.

"Keep on talking. Nobody can hear you," Rogers said.

Wright glanced down at his suit. "There's blood on my sleeves, you stupid old bastard." He slugged Hernández in the stomach and the man folded like laundry. "I'm tired of waiting for you to sell me this land and I'm tired of waiting for you to die. I guess you'll just have to die."

Wright held up a hand to Rogers. "You shouldn't have clocked him. How's that going to look?"

"Like he fell and hit himself before he died. A rock should make it convincing. Don't worry."

Wright nodded and Rogers grabbed Hernández by the shirt. He resisted like a wounded dying animal.

"Let me go, *cabróns.*"

"What kind of talk is that for an elderly gentleman? You should be ashamed," Rogers said.

Whipping his short arms about, Hernández hit Rogers in the face, but the deputy showed no signs he felt anything. The deputy grabbed Hernández's arms and held them behind him. From his pocket, Wright pulled out a syringe and took off a plastic top, which he placed back into his pocket. He jammed the needle into Hernández's neck.

"Let him go, Jackson. He can't hurt us. He's a dead man."

Rogers did so and Hernández fell to the ground, digging away at his heart as if to claw out the pain with his hands.

"Help me, help me," he called in Spanish.

On his hands and knees, Hernández reached out toward the car lights as if they were salvation.

"That's so pathetic," Rogers said.

Wright threw a disgusted look as the old man stood up and wobbled. Hernández again started talking in the strange language.

"I think he's speaking in tongues or something." Rogers pushed the cowboy shirt he wore into his belt.

"It won't be long." Wright checked email on his phone.

"No matter the language, it sounds like he's swearing at us."

Mecho Hernández grinned through blood-stained teeth. "I'm calling down the ancient ones and I'll say it in English so you can understand what your end will be." With effort, his arms rose toward the sky. "Take them, take them all. They are yours. Curse this town. Punish this town. Their blood is yours. Their life is yours. Hear me, your servant, your brother." He chanted again. A demand to his gods, becoming a plea and ultimately, growing faint.

He collapsed onto the dirt.

Rogers glanced up to where the sheriff sat behind the wheel of his patrol car. "Benny, what's he saying?"

Benny didn't answer or move as Mecho Hernández died in the headlights.

At last, he got out of the car and trained the barrel of his gun at Jackson Rogers and then at Richard Wright, but they laughed. Benny fired into the ground and holstered his weapon. He knew at that point his life was over.

Chapter 51

Matthew lowered his gun momentarily.

"God help me. I watched him die, but there was so much money. I needed it for Camilla." Benny's face was slick from tears. He wiped away snot with his sleeve. "I wish I could change it, but it's like the earth. Set and permanent."

"All those people, dead," said Isabel as she tightened her arms around Angel, who yawned.

"That's why you wanted me on the case. I'd never suspect you. You were, after all, my best friend." Matthew's voice fractured.

Benny dared to smile but his heart must have splintered with the confession. "Maybe I wanted to get caught, *compadre*. Yeah, we murdered Mecho, but no one else. Then again, his death started it all."

"Shut the hell up, Benny." Wright staggered up to his feet.

"They were all in on the deal. The commissioners and the mayor were paid off so that Wright and Samuel Uhlig got the land quickly and quietly. But I didn't murder any of them, I swear on Camilla's life."

Wright pushed Benny off balance, sped to the sheriff's vehicle, and pulled out a shotgun attached to a holder on the dash. Benny drew his weapon.

"Benny, drop that gun or I'll kill your best friend." Wright aimed the shotgun at Matthew's chest.

Benny dropped it with hesitating.

"Don't you see, Dick, we're responsible for everything." Benny's voice held the timbre of an altar boy who had invited the devil to dinner. "Everything that took place since we killed Mecho Hernández is our fault. He cursed us all. We invited wickedness because of our wickedness. We can't escape punishment."

"Speak for yourself," Wright said. "And I'm sick of all this shit about curses and ancient mumbo jumbo. You can repent all you want, Benny, but I'm getting the hell out of here."

"It's all over, Wright," Matthew said. "If anything happens to me, the evidence I've gathered will go the State Police. You're going down for murder."

"All you have are suspicions." He waved the shotgun about.

Matthew put his arms around his family and gripped tight. If Wright could kill once, he could kill again. "I'd say the sheriff is ready to come clean." He looked at Benny, who raised his head and nodded. "So, this is over."

"I'll say when it's over. I've got nothing to lose, and to ensure you aren't going to follow, I'm taking Isabel with me," Wright said.

"No." Matthew stood in front of her.

"Daddy, don't let him." Angel started to cry.

"I'll leave her off down the road, but that's only if you don't chase after me. Come on Isabel, or I'll shoot the boy. And I'm not taking you, Matthew." Wright gave a sick smile. "You're too much trouble. She'll be just fine."

"I'll be okay. Take care of our boy." Isabel kissed Matthew and Angel.

"I'm waiting, Isabel. And as you've heard, I don't like to wait."

"Where you going to go, Wright? You'll be hunted. And if you hurt her, I'll personally tear you apart," Matthew said.

"You're an officer of the court. You can't break the law."

"I'll start by breaking you in half."

"Isabel, let's move," Wright shouted and pointed the weapon at Benny. "And I'm not leaving you to shoot off your mouth."

Matthew dived forward, pushing Benny out of the way. He heard the bullet whiz by his head.

Isabel screamed.

"Daddy!" Angel covered his eyes and fell on his knees.

"You should have let him kill me, Mateo," Benny said.

"I couldn't."

Benny helped him up and looked at Wright. "No more, Dick."

"If you kill Benny, you'll have to kill us all because we'll be witnesses," Matthew said.

Wright's hold on the gun wavered. "Son of a bitch. Isabel, get in the goddamn car."

She took small steps. Wright opened the door of his sports car and she slid over to the passenger side. He kept the gun on her. Slipping in, Wright pressed the ignition button, but the engine and lights died the moment they had started up. He slammed on the steering wheel.

"Come on, dammit."

The lights in Benny's car also died, leaving them all under the moonlight. Isabel saw her chance, leapt out, and dashed over to Matthew.

"Get them out of here, Matthew." Benny picked up his weapon and fixed it on Wright. "You're going to get what's coming to you, Dick. We all are. Get out of the car. And if you touch that shotgun, I'll drop you I swear."

Wright obeyed.

"Matthew, I'm so sorry." Benny's voice was rough.

Before Matthew could say anything the ground rumbled under them with the force of an earthquake. Wright landed on the ground. Matthew embraced Isabel and Angel while Benny held onto the hood of his cruiser. The dirt split open and an intense red light broke out of the ground, as if lava erupted through the earth's crust. Instead, a temple of white stone rose up like a new mountain being born.

Angel whimpered with fear.

"God, Matthew." Isabel crushed his hand in hers.

"We've got to leave now!"

The rumbling stopped.

Spinning around to run away, they faced four figures shrouded in black robes, their faces covered by ragged cloth. The robes were thrown off to reveal men made of bone and decomposed flesh gray as wool spattered about their bodies. They could have been torn out of graves with eyes blackened and deep as if perdition rested there. They were dressed similar to the ancient men Matthew had seen in the library books. The Aztec warriors who captured victims for blood sacrifices to their gods. Black hair knotted on top of their heads, except for one who had a long braid. One wore a decayed skin of a spotted jaguar. Another had on an elaborate helmet shaped like a bird with shabby feathers down the back. Jade plugs expanded in their earlobes. Around their waists were cloths that probably had been colorful at one time, but were faded shredded rags. On their feet were only hints of sandals. Their powerful smell was of decay and blood. Though rotting, they moved quickly.

Two of the awful beings grabbed Richard Wright and proceeded to drag him up the narrow steps of the temple.

"Help me, Benny. Kill them." Wright began to sob and kick fiercely at his captors.

Benny scooped up his shotgun and fired into the backs of the intruders, but they didn't stop. The bullets went through them with a soft *pifft*. They continued to carry Wright up the temple.

One of them grabbed the back of Matthew's arms in a vice of bone and he dropped the gun. He yanked at his captor's arm to escape. Spoiled flesh squished between his fingers.

Another creature took the arms of Isabel and Angel who struggled violently.

"Matthew," Isabel yelled, while Angel cried.

"Benny, please," he yelled.

Benny tore over and forced himself in between Isabel and Angel and the thing that held them. They broke away. Benny pushed the creature back with one hand. With the other, he placed the muzzle of his Magnum against its head and fired. The head exploded in a spray of dried marrow and tainted flesh. The body crashed to the ground.

"Go," Matthew shouted at Isabel and Angel who sprinted toward his car.

Benny came to help him and pulled mightily at the ruined but powerful arm. He slipped free and he and Benny tackled the creature. Before Benny could shoot it, out of the dark two more decaying warriors grabbed him, his Magnum falling in the dirt. One of them pushed Matthew down so hard on his back that all the air was forced out of his lungs and he couldn't take a breath. Benny was dragged up the temple steps as if he were a child. His face was oddly complacent.

"Save your family," Benny yelled.

As his friend vanished into the darkness, Matthew saw that he didn't struggle. Benny probably welcomed whatever waited for him at the top.

"Matthew!" Isabel cried.

The remaining warrior was pulling her and Angel toward the temple. He picked up Benny's Magnum. As he attempted to put the barrel to its head, which had been effective with the other monster, the creature kicked Matthew. He fell back and down into the kiva, the weathered wooden door breaking underneath him.

With a thump and a puff of dirt and wood, he landed in darkness. Flashes dotted his eyesight.

Above the kiva, he heard Isabel screaming his name.

"Let them go you bastards!" His voice echoed.

He stood up, took a step, and plunged down on his face. He guessed his right ankle was sprained. But he had to get out of there. When he and Benny had climbed down with the metal ladder, an old wooden one lay on the ground. On his hand and knees, he searched around for it, repeating, "God, please keep them safe."

He found the wooden ladder and climbed up with effort since several rungs were missing. He had to throw himself up and over to the surface.

The temple rose before him. He couldn't tell how high it went. He heard Isabel yell. She was alive.

He picked up the tire iron she had dropped and started up the steps. He had to climb. He had to find strength. He prayed for strength. He had to save his family and Benny.

To hell with Richard Wright.

Ignoring the pain in his ankle, he ascended on hands and feet since the stone steps were narrow. One third of the way up came a *bump bump bump*. Something hit him, knocking him back to the bottom. His hoodie was wet and dark in the moonlight. Blood. He stood over the body of Benny, whose head had been cut off. His uniform had been ripped open. A two-foot-long gash centered down his chest.

Something else came toppling down the steps. Benny's head fell a few feet away.

He cried out with loss.

Removing his hoodie, he covered Benny's head. Staring up at the temple, he exhaled and started up again. He went as fast as he could but each step seemed like an eternity away from helping those he loved.

At the top, he peeped over. One creature held Isabel and Angel off to the side of a white stone structure. A great fire raged in a pit in front of it. Two of the dead men stood around the fire in a trance state, their arms up. Their putrid mouths moved but uttered no words. They seemed to be in the throes of a religious fervor. The creatures had reconstituted somewhat and began to look more like men instead of the earlier skeletal versions, except for the eyes that remained dark holes.

In front of the fire stood a rounded waist-high stone. Blood splashed the top and ran down the sides pooling at the bottom. Lines of smeared blood led to the front where they had probably drug Benny's body.

Damn them.

Two warriors held on to Richard Wright who battled them, kicking and cursing. They pulled Wright over to the stone, lifted him up and onto his back. One held down his arms and the other held his legs. From out of the stone structure emerged another man. Like the creatures holding Wright, this one's skin was almost human expect for spots of decomposition on his cheeks and torso. He was dressed finer than the others with gold pendants on his neck, jade bracelets, and more jade in his earlobes. He wore an ornate headdress and a long cape made out of once splendid feathers. This was the head priest, Matthew supposed. The head killer.

In his right hand, the priest clutched a black stone knife.

He mouthed words, but nothing came from the throat but dust. One of the creatures tore open Wright's shirt. The creature in gold held the knife over Wright, his withered lips moving faster.

Isabel held her hand over Angel's eyes. He had wet himself.

Wright shrieked as the knife ripped into him and down his chest. The golden creature cut out Wright's heart and held the still beating organ high and proud. It steamed in the cool air, the blood streaking the priest's arm like terrifying ribbons. He threw it into the fire, which burst into chutes of flame.

How can I stop this? Matthew himself asked over and over.

With a decisive swipe, one of the creatures sliced off Wright's head with a long black knife. The other then shoved the body over the temple steps and threw the head behind. They joined the two other warriors and they all swayed before the flames, arms out in prayer apparently over a successful sacrifice.

The priest rocked and then stopped. His decrepit finger pointed at Angel. The creature holding Isabel and Angel let her go but picked up the boy in one of its arms.

Angel sobbed. "Mommy! Daddy!"

Isabel kicked and clawed at the thing, trying to pull Angel away. Another creature came and held her back.

"Pray, baby. I'll pray with you. Our Father, who art in heaven."

"Give us our daily bread," Angel continued, his voice marred by fright.

Matthew charged at the creature holding Angel, hitting its free arm with the tire iron. It broke off and landed with an ugly thud. But it didn't drop his son.

The other things stopped their prayers and looked at Matthew with those dark cavities. The moment was held in time. Matthew gained clarity when he should have been terrified. How could he stop hell and revenge? He only knew of one way.

Just as Alma Chacon had said. If it didn't work, he, Isabel, and Angel would be together—forever.

"Leave my son alone. You want blood, take mine, you sons of bitches."

He jerked Angel away from them, and surprisingly, the creature didn't fight back. It just stood there as if uncertain though Matthew couldn't tell from its lack of eyes. Angel hugged his father, but he pushed him toward Isabel. The monster that had held her let her go. Angel ran toward his mother.

"Go, Isabel. I love you," he said.

"No, Matthew."

"I'll follow." He lied.

She grabbed Angel and they hurried down the steps. Matthew expected them all to be charged by the five warriors, but they didn't move. The priest held his knife up as if to strike, but slowly lowered it. They all stared at Matthew.

He tore open his T-shirt. On his chest, the medal with the engraving of the baby Jesus shone in the fire's reflection. The medal his mother gave him.

"You want a life, take mine! Here's your sacrifice! Not them. Take me. I give it to you freely, you goddamn bastards."

Matthew lay on the stone. "I *give* you my blood." He closed his eyes, expecting the knife and the end.

It did not come.

He dared to look. The great fire sputtered out. Heavy clouds rolled in. Crooked fingers of lightning slashed through the sky. The priest dropped the knife. He and the warriors glanced upward. The skin that seemed to have reconstituted on them deteriorated rapidly, as if in a time machine on max speed.

Matthew shot up from the altar stone and dashed toward the steps. He turned his head only to see if he was being followed. A blinding white from lightning struck the stone building which burst apart. The priest and his warriors disintegrated into a gray dust. He didn't wait to see anymore and hurried his escape. In the quick brightness of the lightning flashes, he saw Isabel and Angel making their way farther down. He grinned when they reached the bottom. Halfway down on his climb, the temple pulsated and began to descend back into the ground. He had to hold on or get shaken loose.

"Matthew," Isabel yelled from below.

When he could, he dove onto the dirt and then ran into the arms of his wife and son, who stood back a few yards. He picked up Angel and hugged him.

"We're okay, son. We're all okay."

The ground reverberated more and they got out of there. A good distance from the temple, they watched as it sank into nothing. Lightning flared about them, so close they could smell metal and ozone. The hair on their heads wavered straight up from the static electricity. The three of them hid their eyes from a long burst of lightning and when they opened them, the temple was gone.

All went calm.

Isabel took Matthew's hand. Angel clung to Matthew's neck. "Thank you, Mateo."

He took her face in his hands and kissed her.

"I knew you'd save us, Daddy," Angel said.

"You knew more than I did, son."

They all jumped when the lights to Benny's cruiser and Wright's sports car sparked on. The lights shone on the headless and mutilated bodies of Benny Ortega and Richard Wright in the dirt, at the base of where the temple had stood.

Matthew placed Angel in the patrol car and told him to stay there. Isabel stood behind him.

"Don't leave me, Daddy." His son hugged him tight and wouldn't let go.

"Angel, we'll only be a minute. You're safe and no one will hurt you, son." He gently pulled away his son's arms. "Lay down, now. We're going to say goodbye to your godfather."

He and Isabel stood over Benny's body.

"He tried to save you from those monsters, Matthew."

He nodded and kneeled down to touch Benny's hand. They found a blanket in the patrol car and covered his body. A cool rain began to fall.

Battered and worn out, Matthew, Isabel and Angel headed back to town in his car. Angel was asleep ten minutes into the drive. The sheets of rain refreshed the air.

The rain had stopped by the time they reached Guadalupe. Festival-goers who sought refuge in a large tent that had been set up in the park began to reappear and wipe water off of tables and chairs. Musicians played a soft Spanish ballad. People laughed and danced to the music in wet shoes.

"Apparently not even a rattlesnake invasion could discourage these people," Isabel said as they drove by the park. "You have to love them for that."

"They're probably just celebrating that they're alive," Matthew said.

He stopped the car to watch. Isabel cuddled against him while their son slept in the back. They both smiled at the lovely scene of the park, lit up with strings of lights on the trees.

"It's so beautiful. I can't believe you ever wanted to leave this town," she said.

He leaned in and looked at the people and lights, and then at Isabel, so beautiful and vibrant, and their boy Angel, who laughed out loud in his sleep.

"Me, neither."

Chapter 52

Public records are meant to be clean and clear, or so Matthew had learned in law school. But the accounts of what had happened in Guadalupe were just going to have to be cloudy and wrong. He and Isabel agreed not to say anything about that night when the moon was resonant. No one would have believed them anyway. A temple rising out of the plains. Rotting ancient Aztec warriors. Sacrifices. Then all of it collapsing into dirt. Hell, he still had trouble with what had taken place and he had lived through it—barely.

But there had been two more deaths and they had to be accounted for.

Because a county sheriff had been murdered, the New Mexico State Police took over the investigation. That was protocol—no law agency should investigate one of its own when something criminal occurred. As usual, Guadalupe Police Chief George Wilson let his second-in-command, Lt. Manuel Alvarado work with the State Police. Wilson also announced he was retiring earlier than planned.

"I can't take this shit anymore, Matthew," he told him at the courthouse one day.

"I don't blame you one bit, George."

The state investigators set up in a conference room at the Law Enforcement Agency. They were led by Beau Thompson, who stood six-feet tall if he was a day. He wore a crew cut with confidence and had the voice of a drill sergeant that would terrify other drill sergeants. Sitting across the conference table from him, Matthew was a tad terrified also, until Thompson expressed condolences about Benny. He wasn't faking his sincerity.

"I heard you guys were tight. Brothers from another mother," Thompson said.

"We were. There'll be no one like him."

"Understood."

Then Thompson started in.

For once, Matthew was the person who sat in the proverbial hot seat. He should have been nervous, but he wasn't. There had been justice. The killers were killed. The conspirators, including his best friend, had been eliminated. An odd kind of judgment, but still justice.

The detective studied the autopsy reports on the bodies of Benny and Richard Wright. They revealed that most probably an obsidian knife was the murder weapon, given the shards left on them. Similar shards were found in the wounds of three of the five other victims. He didn't have much to say on the buried skulls of Samuel Uhlig and Mike Rand.

Matthew would help him along.

"Sheriff Ortega believed that a cult or crazy person was imitating Aztec ritual killing," he said.

"That makes sense because it looks to me like the same loony tune killed all these people," he told Matthew.

"I can't disagree, Lt. Thompson."

Dr. Rosemary Whitney was in the room in case the state detectives had any questions. She crossed her arms. "Matthew, I thought you were convinced the murders had something to do with the Desert Rose development. You were even talking about Richard Wright as a person of interest, namely that he was bumping off his business partners."

The state detective studied him. "That so, Mr. Riley?"

He had expected this. He had polished his new version of the events until it was brass.

"Rosemary, Lt. Thompson, that was true, mostly because Benny and I didn't have any other substantial leads. In other words, no good suspects. I was trying to make a case to fit the facts, but that line of investigation didn't go anywhere. I couldn't uncover any solid evidence to link Wright with any of those killings." He disclosed how he had checked the bank statements in following that line of inquiry and found large deposits in the victims' accounts. "Again, I couldn't come up with any proof of a plot or Wright's involvement. I was proved very wrong because Wright was also murdered."

He couldn't tell if the State Police detective believed him. His face was emotionless.

"But Benny, I mean Sheriff Ortega, he didn't go along with my theory. He believed the murders were the work of a psychotic killer or killers unknown who were obsessed with Aztec sacrifices," Matthew said.

"So, what's your conclusion, Mr. Riley?" Thompson said.

Matthew sat up and stared the detective in the face. "I believe the killer has left this jurisdiction." That was absolutely damn true. Those monsters had all gone back to hades or wherever they sprang from and he hoped to God they'd never have cause to return.

"You were the one who found the bodies, Mr. Riley."

"Yes. That night, I went out to the development site searching for the sheriff. I wanted to discuss the murder investigation and thought he might have gone there."

"At night?" the detective said.

"He wasn't answering his phone or dispatch. I was also a bit frustrated by our whole lack of progress. I guess I wanted to talk and maybe go have a beer. I saw the lights of their cars and that's when I discovered the bodies of Sheriff Ortega and Richard Wright. It was horrible."

"I saw the photos. It *was* horrible."

"How'd you hurt your ankle?" Thompson was smart.

"I panicked when I saw them and stepped in a hole. I felt pretty stupid."

After dropping off Isabel and Angel that night, Matthew headed to the Law Enforcement Agency to tell them about the two bodies. Returning there was worse. The floodlights set up by the deputies made the scene surreal as a waking nightmare. Luckily, the rain had washed away any sign that Isabel and Angel had been there.

He also told the acting sheriff that he wanted to inform Camilla Ortega about Benny's death. With Isabel at his side, he did later that morning. Benny's wife came apart and they called a doctor to help her. She was admitted to the hospital and hadn't emerged since.

The cost of betrayal had been great.

Matthew did all he could not to involve Isabel and Angel in the state investigation. For one thing, he'd have to explain why they were out there when he found the bodies of Benny and Wright. Mostly, he didn't want cops asking Angel questions in order to distance their son from the horror of that night.

"It was a nightmare, but the kind you have when you're awake," Isabel had explained to Angel the day after.

"That's right, Angel. And nightmares are best forgotten, most especially that one," Matthew added.

"Good. It was really scary then, but in the morning, it didn't seem like anything real, not like now."

"And please, you can't ever talk about what happened with anyone. It might hurt people if you did, like Benny's wife Camilla," he said.

"I'm not going to tell anybody. I don't want no one to find out I peed in my pants that night." Angel crossed his heart. "I'm not even telling my best friend. It's nobody's business but ours."

"It does belong to our family and we'll deal with it." He hugged him.

"If you're going to remember anything, remember, Angel, that you were a brave kid who wanted to help his father." Isabel caressed both of them.

He and Isabel watched their son carefully over the next weeks for signs of trauma, but they saw nothing. Isabel called it a miracle and Matthew didn't debate that. Angel also told them there were no more bad dreams. That was a bonus.

"Mr. Riley?" the detective said.

"I'm fine. It's been an emotional few weeks."

Dr. Whitney said she had an appointment. Before she left, she gave Matthew's shoulder a comforting squeeze. She appeared happy to accept his explanation. Most probably because she was sick of examining mutilated bodies that defied the laws of forensics.

"Mr. Riley, why do you believe the murderer has fled your jurisdiction?" the state detective said.

"We haven't had an incident in three weeks. And that's very good news."

After another week, the State Police investigators ruled that the murders were the work of assailant or assailants unknown. After news of the decision was printed in the newspaper and reported on television, Matthew swore he heard the whole town take a collective sigh of relief. Not only because there were no more killings but because the odd visions, specters, and just plain weird stuff had stopped also, according to Isabel and his mother who knew most everything going on around town. People walked with livelier steps down the sidewalks. They ambled about the park with ease and drove with windows down, music loud and thumping. He believed they were, indeed, celebrating life, and the fact they were still around to enjoy it all.

For good measure, he sent Alma Chacon two dozen red roses.

Returning to her job at the newspaper, Isabel found it difficult to say nothing about what happened that night.

"It was a hell of a story. Too bad I can't tell it," she said one night while they were in bed.

"You can always write a book. A horror novel. I'll bet it would be a bestseller."

She waved her hands about. "No, I don't want to relive it."

Except for going to work, he and Isabel hadn't been apart since then. He asked his mom to move in with them, but she loved her house. He saw her every day, mowed the lawn on Saturday, and they all had Sunday dinner together.

When the investigation was completed, Benny and Wright were buried at the Guadalupe Cemetery. Wright's funeral had been sparsely attended. He certainly didn't go, and apparently many other people felt the same way about the businessman.

Benny's funeral services, however, were the largest seen in the county. His wife Camilla had been too ill to attend and it fell to Matthew to make the arrangements. Camilla did ask him to speak at the funeral mass. He had already burned anything showing his friend had been part of the conspiracy that invited hell to town. He'd spare Camilla and the town that. After all, Benny's attempts to protect him, Isabel, and Angel that night amounted to some redemption for his crime. The rest would be between Benny and God.

At the mass, Matthew kept his eulogy short. He decided to hold onto the years of friendship.

"Benny Ortega and I grew up together and I'll cherish those days with him until I pass on. He loved his wife Camilla and this town. He was a simple man and one who protected those he loved." His voice tightened. "He was my best friend. He saved my life and that of my family. That is the best you can say for any man."

****

Like every fall, the aspens burned a fiery red on the mountains. Matthew smiled at the scenery He was also happy that he won a case against a man who swindled a grocery store out of $8,000. He could take reward in that win.

He had decided to stay put as county prosecutor and the state AG office took the news better than he hoped. Even if they hadn't, he didn't much care. The AG himself even called and said if he ever changed his mind, he'd be a welcome addition to the staff. He wouldn't change his mind, he told them.

He didn't miss ambition.

On a whim, Matthew drove to Mecho Hernández's land. The Desert Rose Resort development sign was gone. He quivered a bit thinking how his world had sidled up against another and far more hazardous one, but the beauty of the property dispelled those feelings. Nothing bad could conquer when there was so much loveliness. He hoped so anyway.

A rancher and his family from California ended up buying the land and built a huge house on the south end of the property. The pueblo had been bulldozed and the kiva filled in. The rancher was going to serve his stock all organic feed.

Matthew drove on and wondered sometimes if he hadn't dreamt the whole thing. Maybe one day it would be just that.

When he pulled into the driveway, Isabel and Angel were kicking around a soccer ball in the front yard. His son said he liked that sport better than baseball. They both waved with love when they saw him.

Getting out of the car, he loosened his tie and sat on the porch.

"Home," he breathed out. "Home."

Acknowledgments

Thanks to Carmelina Hart, Santa Fe County Communications Coordinator. I am also grateful for the helpful information on the websites of the U.S. Department of Justice, Michigan State University Extension, New Mexico Fish and Game, State of New Mexico, Wound Care Centers, Very Well Health, Mythopedia, and the always useful Wikipedia. Thanks to my good friend and great writer Bonnie Dodge for her wonderful help and to my husband for his wonderful understanding and support.

About the Author

Patricia Marcantonio grew up in southern Colorado and is the granddaughter of Mexican immigrants. She is the author of the Felicity Carrol mystery series. Arte Público Press, the largest US publisher of contemporary literature by US Hispanic authors, published her courtroom drama *Verdict in the Desert*. Her children's book *Red Ridin' in the Hood and Other Cuentos* earned an Anne Izard Storyteller's Choice Award and was named an Americas Award for Children's and Young Adult Literature Commended Title and one of the Wilde Awards Best Collections to Share. She received an Alexa Rose Foundation Grant to direct her original play. As a reporter, she also covered crime and courts for many years, has won several awards for her journalism and was named a Newspaper Association of America New Media Fellow.

She's always been inspired by Mexican folk and ghost tales she heard growing up.